BREATHLESS

Jason and Azazel, Book One
V. J. Chambers

Punk Rawk Books

BREATHLESS
© 2009 by V. J. Chambers
www.vjchambers.com

Punk Rawk Books

ISBN: 978-0-9841206-1-1

Printed in the United States of America

10 9 8 7 6 5 4 3 2 1

Breathless
Jason and Azazel, Book One
by V. J. Chambers

Part One

"Re-examine all you have been told at school or church or in any book, dismiss whatever insults your own soul; and your very flesh shall be a great poem."
-Walt Whitman, Preface to *Leaves of Grass*

Chapter One

To: Hallam Wakefield (hwakefi@risingsun.org)
From: Alfred Norwich (anorwic@risingsun.org)
Subject: Re: New England
Hallam,

Clearly, Jason has left the region where he was sighted last. You must pursue him south, where our Intel has determined he is heading.

Keep me in the loop regarding any new developments in this situation.

Yours in pursuit of the Purpose,
Alfred

It was a typical Friday night in Bramford, West Virginia, and I was spending it in a typical way, making out with my boyfriend Toby in his Ford pick-up truck. As usual, I was trying to fondle his crotch. He was pushing my hands out of the way.

Yes, that's right. While the situation was typical for Toby and me, we were the reverse of the standard American teenage couple. I wanted us to have sex. Toby wanted to wait so that it could be special.

Seriously. In all other ways, he appeared to be a normal, red-blooded teenage boy. He played football for Bramford High. He was addicted to video games. He and his friends even went to great lengths to snag cheap beer in order to fuel parties they held when their parents went out of town. Most guys Toby's age would die to date a girl who wanted to go all the way. Not Toby.

"Azazel," Toby sighed, grabbing my wrist and forcing it away from his pants' zipper. "Not tonight, okay?"

It was an old argument. I was getting sick of it. Toby and I had been dating since freshman year. We were seniors now, both of us seventeen. Everyone else was doing it. Sometimes, I felt like we were the oldest virgins in our school. No. In the world.

I sat back in the seat, gazing out of the windshield at the shadowy trees surrounding the truck in the darkness. We were parked somewhere off a dirt road in the middle of the woods. I crossed my arms over my chest. "What's wrong with me?" I asked the trees, not looking at Toby.

"Azazel, please," said Toby.

I turned on him. "Am I ugly? Aren't you attracted to me?"

"You know I think you're beautiful," he said.

"Then what is it?" I asked. Why wouldn't any teenage guy in his right mind jump at the chance to have sex with his girlfriend?

"I just want it to happen when it's ... you know, right."

"I *don't* know," I said, sulking.

"And I don't want it to be in this truck," he said.

"Right," I muttered. "You want music and candles and rose petals and champagne."

8

"Don't make fun of me," said Toby. He shook his head and looked out the window, looking pissed.

Toby was hot. He had blonde hair and blue eyes, and his shoulders were huge and muscled, because he lifted a lot of weights. He was a nice guy, too. He volunteered at the animal shelter in town. He was polite to my parents and respectful to authority figures. He made good grades at school. In most respects, he was the perfect boyfriend.

"When is it going to be right?" I asked. I felt like I was always asking this. I didn't know why I bothered anymore. I guess I just kept thinking that if I got beyond his zipper, I might be able to get him so turned on that he wouldn't be able to stop himself. Not that I really knew how to get a guy turned on. It was supposed to be easy. I was just supposed to be willing, and he was supposed to jump my bones.

"I don't know. But we'll know when it is. Can't we just kiss?" Toby asked, looking frustrated.

"I don't feel like kissing you anymore," I said.

"God," said Toby.

"It's just you're always rejecting me," I said. "After a while, it tends to wear on a girl's self-esteem."

"Look," said Toby, "you can't just try to make me have sex with you all the time. I'm the guy. It's my job to set this stuff up. You're ... you're just rushing things."

I glowered at him. Sometimes, he was just so damned annoying. "I love you, Toby," I said. "I know that. And I want to lose my virginity to you. I want to be with you. I want to be as close to you as I can possibly get. And I want it all the time."

"I love you too," said Toby, leaning across the truck to kiss me again.

His kiss was sweet and soft, and he stroked my cheek with the back of his fingers. I let myself get lost in his kisses. Let my hands roam over his back, barely caressing the hard muscle of him. His body was gorgeous. Every time I saw him, I felt a little stirring between my legs, as if something there was waking up. Seeing Toby, being with him, made me feel like I was slave to this strange desire. I stroked his back, my hands going a little lower to cup the curve of his ass.

Toby pulled my hand off.

"You've got to be kidding!" I exclaimed.

"Please," he said. "Let's just kiss."

"Screw you," I said, pushing him away. "Are you gay?"

He glared at me. "You want me to take you home?"

Ooh. Maybe saying that was hitting below the belt. "What time is it?" I asked.

Toby looked at his watch. "Ten-thirty," he told me. "We've still got a few hours before your curfew."

"You wanna go get a milkshake or something?" I asked. The McDonald's drive-thru was open late. Sometimes kids in town got food and then sat on the picnic tables behind the restaurant. I thought that some of our friends might be there. Somebody might even have beer. Not that I really liked beer. It tasted awful.

"Well," said Toby.

But he never finished, because we both suddenly heard a thrashing sound, as if something were running through the woods.

Our heads both snapped towards the sound.

"Probably a deer," I said, craning my neck to see.

Toby turned the key in the ignition. Flipped on his headlights.

But instead of a deer, what we saw was a boy — a man — a guy — racing into the clearing we were parked in. He ran like something was chasing him. His dark hair was plastered to his forehead with sweat. His clothes were dirty and torn.

"Jesus Christ," I said, flinging open the door to the truck.

"Azazel, wait," said Toby.

But I was already out of the truck, hurrying to intercept the stranger. I rushed to him, throwing my arms out to stop him.

He couldn't stop in time. He collided with me.

Up close, I could smell him. He smelled like sweat and earth and fear. His eyes were deep and dark. His breath came in gasps.

"Are you okay?" I asked.

The guy shot a glance over his shoulder, still breathing hard. "Get me out of here," he said.

I grabbed his hand. Pulled him towards the truck.

Toby had gotten out too and was making his way towards us.

"Toby, let's go," I said, pushing the boy into the truck ahead of me and squeezing in beside him. I slammed the door shut.

Toby got back in the car too. He looked at me and at the guy, his eyes full of questions.

The guy's eyes never left the woods, as if he expected someone or something to burst out at any second. "Go," said the guy. "Drive! Just drive."

Toby put the car in reverse. His tires squealed as he pulled out and back onto the road.

*   *   *

My name is Azazel Pandora Jones. My parents named me after a Jewish demon and the girl in Greek mythology who was responsible for bringing evil into the world. Azazel himself was sort of the Jewish Prometheus. Instead of bringing fire to the people, however, he led the rebellious Nephilim before the flood and taught the people the art of warfare. Like Prometheus, he was chained to a rock somewhere for eternity as punishment. Unlike Prometheus, no eagles ate out his guts every day. My mother said she thought the name was pretty. But my parents were both sort of second-generation hippies, and they probably thought the names were significant. My parents didn't believe in evil.

Really. When I was a little girl, instead of being told that hoarding my toys was bad, my parents sat down with me and said, "Now, Azazel, if you don't share your toys, your friends won't want to play with you."

If I replied, "I don't want to play with them anyway," then my parents would shrug apologetically at my friends and my friends' parents, and say, "She doesn't want to share."

Once, when I was in elementary school, I dug my fingernails into the forearm of a boy who was picking on me. I got punished at school, but when I got home, my parents asked me, "Did he stop bothering you after you did that?"

"Yes," I said.

"You might try asking him to stop in the future before you resort to violence."

And that was it. My parents viewed the world in terms of actions and consequences. There were productive consequences. There were nonproductive ones. They didn't believe any action was wrong. They evaluated it in terms of its consequences. The most productive consequences were the ones which made the world better for as many people as possible.

That all being said, I don't want you to get the idea that my parents were neglectful or anything like that. To the contrary, everyone in town considered my parents swell people. My parents were foster parents. I was their only biological child, but I had three adopted brothers (two of whom were older than me and didn't live at home anymore), and there were always at least two or three other kids temporarily placed at our house. My parents often gave a home to adolescent boys. The more troubled, the better.

Adolescent foster boys often didn't find permanent living situations, and my parents wanted to make a difference. Often, these guys came to us when they were sixteen and stayed with us until they outgrew the system.

While my parents weren't rich enough to send all of their foster kids to college, they did the best they could to help all of them out in some way, shape, or form, even if that meant being a character witness in their grand theft auto trials. Hey—my parents gave these guys a loving home. That didn't mean that they saved them from whatever path they were already on.

My home was always filled with people. There was rarely anything in the refrigerator. Teenage boys ate. A lot. I had to deal with the fact that usually there were at least four guys crowded around the television, watching sports or playing video games. The toilet seat was very rarely left down. But overall, my home was a warm, happy place. It was a place where people felt like they belonged.

And so I didn't think twice before I told Toby that we should take the stranger to my parents' house. He kind of fit their profile, if you know what I mean.

Sitting in the truck with him, wedged between Toby and me, I wondered who he was. Even though we'd driven away from the woods, had put miles between us and the site where we'd picked him up, he kept looking over his shoulder out the back of the truck, as if he expected something to be following us.

Toby seemed a little annoyed. "You want me to take you home then?" he asked me. "Leave you there with him?"

Did Toby still think I wanted to go the McDonald's drive-thru? After something this exciting had happened? I just said, "Yeah."

I looked at the guy again. He looked like he was about our age. Maybe a little older or younger. It was difficult to tell. He had dark hair and dark eyes. His face was dirty, and he had few days' growth of stubble on his chin. He looked desperate and frightened and harrowed. I was intrigued.

"Are you okay?" I asked him.

His breathing was starting to slow. He looked at me. "Yeah," he said breathlessly. "Yeah. Um, thanks. Thanks for getting me out of there." He looked at Toby, including him in his statement.

"Was someone chasing you?" I asked.

"Yeah," he said. He rubbed his face and looked behind us again. He swallowed. His Adam's apple bobbed.

"Was it the police?" I asked. "Are you in some kind of trouble?" I sounded like my dad. He was always asking things like that of the foster kids we took in. My dad was also a high school history teacher, and he coached football. He spent a lot of time talking to teenage boys.

"Not the police," said the guy.

"So who?" I asked.

The guy shook his head. "Doesn't matter," he said.

We were quiet. Toby leaned forward and switched on the radio. Music filled the truck, loud. I reached over and turned the music down, annoyed with Toby. Wasn't he curious about this guy?

"What's your name?" I asked him.

"Jason," he said.

"I'm Azazel," I said. "And this is Toby."

"Nice to meet you," said Jason. "Both of you. And thank you. Again." He stole another glance behind us. "Look, you two can just drop me off along the main road."

"No," I said. "I'm taking you back to my house. My parents are foster parents, and they take in a lot of teenage boys. It'll be safe there, and you can, you know, get some food and get cleaned up and—"

"No," he said. "I can't. It won't be safe."

"I swear, it will. Even if you're on the run from the police, my parents will work with you. They're not gonna just turn you in."

"I'm not running from the police," said Jason. "And I didn't mean safe for me. I meant it won't be safe for your family."

"Where do you want to me drop you off?" asked Toby. He was pulling his truck onto Route 50, which was as much the main road as anything is in Bramford.

"You're not dropping him off!" I said. Why was Toby being like this? To Jason, "You're coming back to my house."

"Azazel," said Toby, "he doesn't want to go there."

"We can't just leave him on the side of the road," I said to Toby.

"I'll be fine," said Jason.

"He says he'll be fine," said Toby.

"Who's after you?" I asked Jason. "Are they dangerous?"

"The less you know about that, the better," Jason said. To Toby, "Anywhere along here is fine."

"Toby," I said, "we aren't dropping him off. We're

taking him back to my place. What if something horrible happens to him, and we could have stopped it?"

Toby sighed. "She's right," he said to Jason. "I can't just drop you off. We should take you to the Jones' house." Finally, he was acting like a rational person.

"That's a bad idea," said Jason.

"Well you're not talking me out of it," I said. "I'm pretty stubborn."

Jason looked at me and laughed. It was a short laugh, and it almost sounded as if he were out of practice. Like he didn't laugh very often. "You are, huh?" he asked.

"She is," said Toby.

Jason looked away from me. "Just for a while," he said finally. "I can't stay too long."

* * *

My mother was in her nightgown and robe in the kitchen when we got home. My brother, Chance, and the two foster kids who were living with us at the time (Cameron and Nick) were in the family room playing *Diablo* . My dad wasn't home. He played poker with his friends on Friday nights. My mom and the guys all dropped whatever they were doing when I brought Jason into the house.

My mom went into mothering mode. She stuck Jason in the bathroom with fresh towels and a change of clothes. While Jason was showering, she heated up some frozen pizza. She shooed the guys and me into Chance's bedroom to put new sheets on the extra bed. Chance was always complaining because I was the only one in the house who got her own bedroom. He always had to share. Our house had four bedrooms. At times, we had as many as three guys in one bedroom, and at Christmas, the house became a crowded madhouse. My older brothers came home. Many of my parents' previous foster children came home. There were guys sleeping everywhere. On the couches. On air mattresses. On the floors in bedrooms. And the bathrooms were a mess. They were covered with shaving cream and hair gel and bottles of cologne. Guys had just as many grooming products as girls these days.

I was used to the frenetic atmosphere of my house. After we made up a bed for Jason, and the other guys donated various articles of clothing to him, which we piled next to his bed, we all went back to the living room. Toby had stuck around for a little bit, helping my mother in the kitchen to make hot chocolate and set the dining room table. He joined us too.

The guys couldn't shut up. Chance made Toby and I retell the story of how we picked up Jason at least four times. Nick was convinced that Jason had escaped from prison. Cameron thought he was a drug dealer and had sold someone bad stuff.

"He says he's not on the run from the police," said Cameron.

"He's lying," said Chance. "Nobody runs like that unless they're on the run from the police."

"Oh, like you'd know," said Nick, shoving Chance playfully. My parents adopted Chance when he was five.

He'd lived a pretty normal life, unlike Nick, who had rattled around in the foster system for years. Nick was fifteen, like Chance.

"Whatever," said Chance. "Like you've ever run from the police."

"I have," volunteered Cameron.

"Yeah, but you did it in a car," I pointed out.

"I think he's running from the authorities," said Toby. "I think that Jason guy is bad news."

I glared at him. "Yeah, you wanted to leave him on the side of the road."

"He wanted to be left on the side of the road," said Toby.

"Because the police are after him," said Nick. "That's the only reason he wouldn't want to come back here. If he was running from some guy who bought drugs from him, he wouldn't want us to turn him in."

"I don't think he's a drug dealer," I said.

"Why not?" asked Nick.

"If he dealt drugs around here, why wouldn't we know him? Why wouldn't he go to our school?" I said.

"He doesn't need to go to school, because he makes bank selling drugs," said Cameron.

"No way," I said. "Something bad was after him. He was terrified."

"It was the police," said Toby. "I should just call my dad and ask if there's an APB out on this guy." Toby's dad was the local sheriff.

"Don't you dare," I said to Toby. "I promised him he'd

be safe here."

"And for all you know, you're protecting a criminal," said Toby.

"Oh," said Chance pointedly, " *hi* , Jason."

Jason was standing in the doorway to the living room, wearing a pair of Chance's pants — they were too short — and a t-shirt. His hair was still wet from the shower. He'd shaved. He looked better now that he wasn't dirty, but he still looked flighty, like he might run at any second. His eyes darted around the room, like he was checking for the exit if he needed it.

Toby looked embarrassed. "Hey," he said. "I didn't mean ..."

I bounded up from the couch. "My mom's making pizza," I said. "You hungry?" I took Jason's arm and led him into the dining room.

I gestured to a seat at the table. It had been set with paper plates and napkins. There was a steaming pot of hot chocolate in the center of the table and a cluster of mugs.

Jason stared at the table. "Look, I should go," he said. "I really shouldn't — "

"Sit down," I interrupted him.

He hesitated for another second, but then he sat down.

I smiled at him. "Everything's gonna be fine. You'll see. You want some hot chocolate?"

"Okay," said Jason.

I poured two mugs full of hot chocolate and handed one to Jason. I took the other one and sat down across the table from him.

"So, um, Toby is your boyfriend?" asked Jason.

"Yeah," I said.

"And he thinks I'm a criminal?"

I rolled my eyes. "He'll come around. Don't worry about it."

"I-I'm not," said Jason. "You know. A criminal." His eyes nervously searched the room again. Did he think something was going to jump out and get him at any second?

"It's okay," I said. "It's safe here."

Jason put down his hot chocolate. "No," he said. "It's not."

At that moment, my mother swept into the room, carrying a pizza. Using her amazing mothering skills, she slid the pot holder off her hand and set the pizza on top of it in one fluid movement, all without burning herself. "Jason," she said. "You're out of the shower."

He nodded.

My mother surveyed him. "Chance's clothes are a little too small for you, but he's the biggest of the boys we've got in the house. We'll have to see if Noah left anything in the closet. I think Noah's about your size." Noah was one of my adopted brothers.

"This is really fine," said Jason. "Thank you."

"Oh, please," said my mother. "Anyone who found you would have done the same thing." She turned to me. "Zaza, there's another pizza on the counter. Can you bring it into

21

the dining room for me?"

I nodded and ducked into the kitchen, listening as my mother called, "Boys! Pizza!"

By the time I got back into the dining room with the second pizza, the first one had already been divvied up between the boys at the table. I set the second pizza down amid scrabbling amongst the guys for hot chocolate. Mom and I each took a piece of pizza from the second pie in a civilized fashion.

I sat down and looked across the table at Jason. There were two pieces of pizza on his plate, but he was just staring at them.

"Don't you like pizza?" I asked him.

He gazed around the table, watching the other guys shove pizza into their mouths and tease each other. "I've just never ..." he trailed off. "I love pizza." And he smiled. Like the time he laughed, it looked kind of like he wasn't used to smiling. It was a tentative smile. It flashed across his face for a second, lighting him up. Then it was gone. And he dug into the pizza.

My dad came home around then, and my mom took him into the living room to explain the situation. Toby decided to leave. He had his own curfew to make, and he said eating the pizza had made him tired. So finally, all the pizza was gone, and we sat around the table: my parents, Chance, the guys, Jason, and me.

"So, Jason," said my dad, "are you in some kind of trouble?"

Everyone at the table gazed at Jason expectantly.

Jason looked at my dad. "I tried to tell Azazel that I don't think it's safe for your family if I'm here. She insisted I come back here anyway."

"Why don't you think it's safe?" asked my dad.

"The people who are after me are ... They can be dangerous. I don't want to lead them here."

"Who's after you?" asked my dad.

"It's someone you sold bad drugs to, isn't it?" asked Cameron.

"Cameron," warned my dad.

"Sorry," said Cameron. Then, as if he couldn't help himself, "Do you sell drugs, though? I mean, Nick and I have a bet."

"That isn't very polite, Cameron," said my mother. "What kind of consequences do you think a comment like that is going to have?"

"Probably unproductive," Cameron sighed.

"Probably," said my mother.

"It's okay," said Jason. "I don't sell drugs." He took a deep breath. "I don't want to give you too many details. That could put you in further danger. But the people who are chasing me, they're fanatics. They believe what they believe entirely. They're ready to die for it. They're ready to kill for it. And they think I'm in the way."

Chapter Two

michaela666 (12:02:43 AM): got your message. what's the alert?

morningstar68 (12:02:46 AM): He's arrived. as predicted.

michaela666 (12:03:02 AM): is he contained?

morningstar68 (12:03:30 AM): for the moment.

michaela666 (12:04:14 AM): good. your job is to keep him there, then. what about the vessel? is she ready to perform her part of the ritual?

morningstar68 (12:05:04): I had hoped to give her a bit more time. but she can be ready. soon. what's our next move?

michaela666 (12:05:54): for now? We wait. don't let him out of your sight. and prepare the vessel.

My mother furrowed her brow in concern. "Like terrorists?" she asked Jason.

Jason shook his head. "Like Freemasons," he said. "But with guns."

"Freemasons?" I asked. I'd read up on this stuff. I thought it was very interesting. I'd read my copy of *The Da Vinci Code* so many times it was falling apart. "Why do they want you?" I asked, wide-eyed.

"They're crazy," he said. He looked at my father again. "Like I said, I don't want to put your family in danger."

"We should go to the authorities," said my dad.

"No," said Jason. "Trust me. The police can't do anything about this. They wouldn't stand a chance."

"You can't expect us just to let you go back out there," said my mother.

"Where are your parents?" asked my dad.

"Dead," said Jason. "I guess. I never knew them. The people who are chasing me killed the man who raised me. That's when I started running. It was, I don't know, maybe four months ago."

"And you've been on the run ever since?" asked my mother. "That's horrible. Jason, you have to stay with us."

She turned to my dad. "Daniel, we can't let him leave."

My dad considered. "Listen, son, if you are in trouble with the law, you can tell us. We can help."

"They are actually pretty good about that stuff," said Nick.

"I'm not in trouble with the law," said Jason. "I swear."

I believed him.

"Why are these people after you?" asked my father.

"They think I'm something I'm not," said Jason. "It's complicated. It's not important."

"I just don't know," said my dad. "I can't really believe that there are—"

"Dad," I interrupted, "do I have to go and get a dollar bill and point out all the Masonic imagery on it again?"

"No, Zaza, that's okay," said my dad. He considered. "Well, Jason, you're not going anywhere tonight. You'll sleep here. Tomorrow, we'll talk more. We can get this sorted out."

* * *

When I woke up on Saturday, my father and Jason were on a drive together, discussing Jason's situation. I asked my mother if she'd talked to Dad. Would Jason be staying? I wanted him to stay. I didn't know much about him, but I felt protective of him, probably because I was the one who'd found him. My mother said that after Dad and Jason talked, it was just a matter of getting everything legally settled. There would be papers to sign and things like that.

I helped my mother clean the dishes after the boys' breakfast. They had demolished a box of frozen waffles. I skipped breakfast. I usually did. Besides, it was already eleven o'clock. I'd slept so late that it was going to be time for lunch soon anyway.

Chance and the guys were out somewhere, probably eating up all the food at one of their friend's houses. I basked in the idea of having the television to myself, and settled down to watch something girly. Twenty minutes into something on E! about fashion, Jason and my dad came back.

My dad and my mom talked in the kitchen. Jason came into the living room and glanced around like he usually did, checking every corner for near danger.

"You want to sit down?" I asked.

He shrugged. Then he sat down on the other couch. He glanced at the television, then back at me.

"We can watch something else," I said.

"This is fine," he said. He looked back at the television. But he didn't relax. He sat up straight on the couch. It looked like he might jump up and make a run for it any minute. He was like a scared rabbit or something. I wondered what had happened to him.

We watched TV without speaking for a while. The E! show ended. I walked over to Jason and gave him the remote control. "You can pick something to watch if you want," I said.

He looked at the remote like it was an artifact from ancient Egypt or something. "It's okay," he said. He set the remote down on the couch next to him.

I felt awkward. I sat down next to him. "Are you going to stay?" I asked.

"I'd like to," said Jason. "Your dad is nice. So's your mom."

"I told you," I said.

"Yeah," he said. "Your dad wants to check on some things. If it's legal. If it can be done, he wants me to stay."

"But what about the people after you?" I asked.

Jason laughed his short laugh again. "Uh, I think your dad thinks I'm crazy."

"Crazy?"

"I think he thinks I imagined it." Jason picked up the remote control. Stared at it. "Maybe ... Maybe I did."

"What?"

"Maybe nobody was chasing me last night," said Jason.

"But you were running like Freddy Krueger was after you," I said.

Jason nodded. "I know." He aimed the remote control at the TV and started flipping through the channels. "I've been running for a long time. Last night, it was dark. Maybe there wasn't anybody there. Or maybe it was an animal or something. I'd really like to stay here."

Huh. Jason had seemed so sure of himself last night. Maybe my dad was right. Maybe he *had* made the whole thing up. Lots of the guys who stayed here told impossible stories. Apparently, it was a defense mechanism. My mom had a degree in psychology, but she didn't practice anymore. Instead she stayed home to take care of us kids. And she worked as a self-employed medical transcriptionist to help out with bills. Her psychology background helped her deal with the foster kids. It was also why I knew about defense mechanisms.

I didn't know what I believed about Jason. Whatever had happened to him, last night he'd believed that something was chasing him. I did know that I wanted him to stay. Finding Jason was pretty much the most exciting thing that had happened to me, well, ever. Plus, I was interested in these people who were chasing him. People that he described like Freemasons with guns. What did that mean?

"What do you want to watch?" Jason asked me.

I hadn't even been paying attention to the channels he was flipping through. "Um, you pick," I said.

"There's so many," he said. He looked a little

overwhelmed. "It's been a long time since I watched TV." Jason flicked the channel up, paused, stared at the screen and then repeated the process. His dark hair was a little long in the front. It kept falling in his eyes, so he kept reaching up to push it out of the way. He had a look on his face of deep concentration, as if he wanted to make sure he got this right. He was the most interesting boy I'd ever seen. He was quiet, which was so different than the guys I knew, both the ones who came to us for foster care and the guys I went to school with. There was something very serious about him. Something mature. I couldn't get enough of it. He was like someone from a foreign country. I wanted to lock him in a room and study him.

"Am I doing this wrong?" Jason asked.

I realized I'd been staring at him. I was embarrassed. I blushed. "No, you're fine," I said. I forced myself to look at the television screen.

Jason was flipping through the ESPN channels, barely stopping on any of them.

"You don't like sports?" I asked.

"I, uh, don't know," he said. "I guess I've never really watched them."

How strange. Had he been living in a bubble or something? Maybe he had amnesia.

We were back around to E! Jason stopping flipping through the channels. He looked at me, sheer terror on his face. "I don't ... I mean, I ..."

"It's okay," I said.

"Can you pick something to watch?" he asked.

I nodded. "Sure." I reached for the remote from Jason, when Toby walked into the living room.

"Toby," I said. "What are you doing here?" I bounced over to him and threw my arms around his neck. He encircled my waist with one arm, and we kissed quickly.

"I'm here with my dad," he said.

I backed away, angry. "Toby!" I said. "You said you wouldn't say anything to him."

"Your dad called him," said Toby. "I just came along for the ride."

"Oh," I said. I looked at Jason. "Did my dad tell you he was going to do that?"

"He said he wanted to see if my background checks out," said Jason. "He wanted to know where I was born and stuff like that."

I hoped that wasn't dangerous for Jason. "And that's okay?" I asked Jason.

He shrugged. "I don't know. I hope so." He was staring intently at the show on E!

It was good that Jason seemed a little more laid back this morning. Last night, he'd been so intense. But I hoped everything was okay. I didn't want anything bad to happen to Jason. I didn't want the people who were chasing him to find him.

"Well," I said. "Cool, then, I guess. Um, I'm going to get some iced tea. Either of you guys want?"

"Totally," said Toby.

I looked at Jason.

"Um, if it's not too much trouble," he said.

"No big," I told him.

I scampered out of the living room, through the dining room towards the kitchen. My parents and Toby's dad, Sheriff Damon, were in the kitchen talking. Instead of entering, I flattened myself against the wall, so that I could hear them talk, but they couldn't see me.

"... didn't find anything," Sheriff Damon was saying.

"So, he's lying?" asked my mom.

Were they talking about Jason? They had to be talking about Jason.

"Actually, it doesn't prove anything," said my dad. "The story he told me is impossible to verify. He was born in a home in Shiloh, Georgia. He said the Shiloh in Harris County, but I think there are three Shilohs in Georgia."

"I checked 'em all. No birth records for a Jason Wodden," said Sheriff Damon.

He didn't have birth records? What did that mean? Who was Jason?

"Yeah, but if he's telling the truth, he doesn't have a birth certificate," said my dad.

"Well, what else did you find, Jim?" asked my mother.

"I didn't find *anything* ," Sheriff Damon repeated. "It's like this kid doesn't exist. No social security number. No medical records. No fingerprints. No priors. He doesn't have a driver's license or own a car."

Like he didn't exist. Weird. Like he'd popped into

existence in the woods outside of Toby's truck. Jason was definitely strange. He was interesting, but he was strange.

"And the mother?"

"Marianne Wodden?" asked Sheriff Damon. "Yeah, I found a death certificate. She died in '91, right after the kid says he was born."

"So that checks out," said my dad.

"Yeah, kind of," said the sheriff.

"Kind of?" asked my mother.

"Well, the kid said she died in childbirth, right?" asked the sheriff.

"Yeah," said my dad.

"Marianne Wodden was shot to death by her husband. Then he committed suicide. There's no record of a baby."

"But had she given birth?" asked my mother.

"I don't know," said Sheriff Damon.

So, Jason's mother had been murdered? I couldn't believe this. Jason was getting more and more interesting with every passing moment.

"What about the people that Jason claims raised him? The man who he says they killed?" my father asked.

"Yeah, there's no record of an Anton Welsh, either," said Sheriff Damon.

"Are these people like a cult or something?" my mother asked.

My dad sighed. "He won't talk about them. So we don't have a lot to go on. But I think we all know what they are."

"You think this is *him* , then?" asked Sheriff Damon.

What were they talking about? How did they all know what the people who raised Jason were? And why had Sheriff Damon placed such an emphasis on the word "him?" I was so engrossed in the conversation, I didn't see Toby approaching.

"Azazel," he called.

"Shh!" I said.

But it was too late.

My mother called from the kitchen, "Zaza, you out there?"

I glared at Toby, but entered the kitchen. "Hey, Mom," I said. "I was just getting some iced tea for Toby and Jason."

"Oh, that's sweet, honey," said my mom. "But why don't you go back to the living room? I'll get it."

I left the kitchen, fuming. When I caught up to Toby, I said to him in a pointed whisper, "Why did you *do* that? I was listening to them."

"You were eavesdropping on them, you mean," he whispered back.

"Well, how else am I supposed to find anything out?"

"Maybe you don't need to know."

But we were back at the living room at that point. Toby had changed the channel to ESPN, and there was a cheerleading competition on. Jason was gaping at the TV, his mouth slightly open. Great. Toby was already corrupting him.

"Ugh," I groaned. "Do we have to watch this?"

"You're jealous of cheerleaders on TV?" Toby asked,

settling down on the couch.

I plopped down next to him. "Why wouldn't I be? You're clearly attracted to them, and it's doubtful you're even attracted to your own girlfriend."

"I'm not even going to respond to that," said Toby. But he picked up the remote and started changing the channels. "There's a party at the Nelson farm tonight," he said to me. "You wanna go?"

"I don't know," I said. "Those things never get good until after my curfew."

"So sneak out," said Toby. "It'll be fun."

* * *

My house was dark and quiet as I tiptoed through the kitchen towards the front door. I didn't sneak out of my house much. My parents were pretty cool and let me stay out late on weekends—until one o'clock. Still, I was seventeen years old, and a lot of the parties my friends threw went on much later than that. I didn't always want to party until dawn, but sometimes I did. The parties at the Nelson farm were infamous.

Nelson was an old family in Bramford. Their farm covered acres and acres of land, and they owned fields that weren't being used for anything. Fields far from any houses. The Nelson kids, who always threw the parties, were twin guys. Derek was on the football team with Toby. He was a nice guy. Eric was on the wrestling team. He was an absolute jerk. They always managed to get several kegs, and they would set up on one of the abandoned fields. Half of

34

Bramford High would show up, pulling their cars onto the field, creating a circle of shining headlights. People would blast music on their car stereos. People would dance.

Once, at a Nelson farm party in the summer, my best friend Lilith and I got roped into a wet t-shirt contest. We were both kind of drunk. Generally, I found that sort of thing pretty sexist and stupid, but at the time it seemed like a good idea. Lilith won. She was much better endowed than I was. Plus, Lilith was no virgin. Not like me. Lilith hadn't been a virgin since the tenth grade. In fact, Lilith lost her virginity at a Nelson farm party. To some guy named Jack, who had moved away last year. Lilith was a lot crazier than I was. I would have liked to be a little crazy, but it was like everybody had somehow decided for me that I was supposed to be this goody two-shoes. Even if I wanted to do something crazy, someone was always there to stop me. Like Toby not having sex with me or cutting me off after five beers. "I don't want you to get sick," he would say. Maybe I was insane not to be grateful for such a considerate boyfriend, but just once, I wanted to do something completely outrageous without anyone "looking out for my best interests."

Other people did all kinds of crazy things at Nelson farm parties. Like drugs. And chicken contests in their cars. And beer pong. And, for God's sake, pre-marital damned sex. Which I might never, never have.

Tonight, I was going to the Nelson farm party. I took careful steps towards the front door. Several times already, the floor had creaked so loud I was sure my parents were going to wake up and ask what exactly I thought I was doing. But so far, I was safe.

I placed my hand on the doorknob and turned — slowly, slowly. The doorknob's turning didn't make any noise. But as I eased the front door open, the door moaned on its hinges. To me, the sound was deafening. I paused, holding my breath, waiting for the sound of my parents wandering downstairs to investigate the noise. But no one came.

I slid out the front door, carefully closing it behind me, and started across the lawn. Toby was going to pick me up in his truck at the end of my driveway, which twisted up around a hill so that it was out of sight of the house. Once I crossed the lawn and got on the driveway, I only had a few feet to go before I was out of sight and home free. I tried not to make noise as I hurried. It didn't take long until I was on the driveway.

The gravel crunched under my feet, but I was pretty sure that I was too far away from the house for anyone to hear. Still, I tried to tread as quietly as possible. Then I noticed something.

I could still hear the sound of gravel under feet.

But it wasn't coming from my feet.

It was a different rhythm than my footsteps. There was someone else walking on the driveway!

Damn it! I knew someone had heard me. I whirled, looking behind me. I could still see my house, still and dark in the night. There was no one there.

But I could still hear the footsteps.

Were they ahead of me?

I stepped forward, then thought about what Jason had said. He'd said that his staying with us would make it dangerous for our family. Were the people after Jason walking down my driveway? Were they coming for Jason? For us?

For a brief moment, I was ready to run back to my house and crawl into my bed. Tendrils of fear had knotted themselves around my spine, and I wanted to hide under my pillows.

Then I shook myself. I was going to a party, damn it. I was not going to let anything get in the way of that. I stepped forward again, squaring my shoulders. If I had to meet these crazy people that were after Jason, then so be it. If they were as dangerous as Jason said, I wouldn't be safe in my bed anyway.

As I walked, I could still hear the footsteps. They sounded close. My heart started to speed up. I rounded the bend in my driveway, and my hands were shaking.

Ahead of me, I could see a shadowy figure walking away from me.

Chapter Three

To: Alfred Norwich (anorwic@risingsun.org)
From: Hallam Wakefield (hwakefi@risingsun.org)
Subject: South is no go
Alfred,

Sorry, no can do. I just got a lead that someone matching Jason's description has been sighted in upstate New York. I've got to go check it out. I don't think Jason is going south, no matter what Intel says. He knows better than that. He was born in the south. He was raised in the south. He knows we'll look for him there.

I'll let you know how this lead pans out. Oh, and tell Richard that West Virginia is a dead end. There's nothing there but woods and rednecks. Jason wouldn't have anywhere to hide.

Yours in pursuit of the Purpose,
Hallam

The figure was a guy. He wore pants that were a little bit too short for him—

It was Jason.

Apparently, I wasn't the only one sneaking out of my house tonight.

I ran to catch up with Jason. He heard me approaching and stopped.

"Azazel," he said.

"What are you doing?" I asked.

He looked away from me. I could hardly make out his features in the scant light, but he seemed even more desperate than before. "I wanted to believe that I could stay here," he said. "All I've ever wanted ..."

"You're not leaving, are you?"

"I have to," he said. "I can't put you and your family in danger."

I didn't know what to say. Moments before, I'd been frightened out of my wits of the people chasing Jason. Was he right? Was he a danger to us? To me?

Well, it didn't matter, did it? Because, if there were danger, I couldn't let Jason go running back into it, could I? No, I'd found him. I'd rescued him once. I couldn't let anything bad happen to him.

"I'm not letting you go," I said.

"I didn't think anyone heard me leave," he said. "I can't believe you followed me."

"I didn't," I said. "I'm sneaking out to go to a party."

"Oh," he said, stunned.

I guess parties weren't something Jason thought about very much. Well. Maybe we should change that.

"You should come with me," I said. "It'll be fun."

"To a ... party?" he said. It was like he had trouble saying the word.

"Yeah," I said. "You know, parties? They're all the rage these days. Kids sneak out, drink beer, get away from their parents. Have fun. It's what all normal teenagers are just dying to do."

"Normal," Jason repeated. Then he grinned at me. It was a brief grin again. It barely touched his eyes. "Okay," he said.

"Great," I said, excited now. "Come on, Toby's picking me up at the top of the driveway."

"Wait," said Jason. "Toby? I don't know if —"

But he was interrupted because Toby's truck pulled up at the top of the driveway. I grabbed Jason and dragged him up to the truck. Toby had leaned across to open the door for me. When he saw Jason, he looked less than happy.

"Oh," he said. "You brought Jason."

I didn't know what was wrong with Toby. He was being totally rude. Jason needed people to take him under their wings. He had nowhere to go, and he seemed to have lived a sheltered, dangerous life. We owed him some fun.

I stood aside from the door. "Get in," I told Jason.

"Uh," said Jason, "maybe you want to sit next to your boyfriend?"

Oh. I guess that did make sense. "Don't run off while I'm getting into the truck," I warned Jason.

He smiled again.

I liked it when he smiled.

I climbed into the truck, and Jason got in after me, pulling the door shut after him. Toby took off.

It was quiet.

We drove for miles and miles without speaking. I kept trying to think of something to say, but I couldn't. I wanted to ask Jason about his dead mother and the possibility of his being raised by a cult, but that seemed rude, so I kept my mouth shut.

Toby was silent. It had been his idea to go to this party in the first place. I couldn't figure out why he was in such a bad mood.

Finally, I said, "I'm excited about the party. Lilith said it's going to be absolutely nuts."

"Oh, well, that's great," said Toby sarcastically.

Wrong thing to say. Toby and Lilith didn't get along. Back in middle school, eons ago, they got along fine. Lilith even had a crush on Toby during our seventh grade year. But after I started dating Toby, they got in some huge fight about something, and now they hated each other's guts. It was awkward, considering Lilith was my best friend, but at least I didn't have to worry about them hooking up behind my back. They couldn't stand each other.

"Who's Lilith?" said Jason.

"My best friend," I said. Lilith was dying to meet Jason. I'd told her all about him on the phone. She'd be excited he was at the party.

"I don't want you to drink too much," said Toby.

"I won't," I said. "I never do. You never give me a chance."

"I'm just looking out for you," said Toby. "You know that. I care about you."

"I know," I said.

"And if anyone finds out Jason's here, I'm going to deny

bringing him," said Toby.

"Okay," I said.

"Sure," said Jason. "I don't want to get you in trouble." Which was pretty decent of Jason, I thought. After all, I had talked him into coming to this party in the first place.

But Toby just rolled his eyes. "Don't worry about me," he said. "Just watch yourself, Jason."

I looked sidelong at Toby. Did he hate Jason for some reason? I was going to have to have a talk with him. Toby needed to learn some manners. Poor Jason didn't know anyone except us, and Toby was being a total dick.

We arrived at the Nelson farm not too long after that. Toby pulled his car up onto the field and into the circle of cars. Lots of people were already there. It was after one in the morning. The party was just starting to rage.

I hopped out of the truck behind Jason, my excitement buzzing inside my head like a swarm of bumblebees. I couldn't wait, couldn't wait. Lilith saw me across the car circle. She waved and sprinted over to meet me. We hugged.

Lilith was tall, with long red hair. She had, as I already mentioned, huge boobs and a tiny waist. I so envied her figure.

"Oh my God, I thought you'd never get here," she said. She turned to Toby. "Hi Toby," she said, grinning at him.

Toby glared at her. "Don't get her drunk," he said.

Lilith flipped him off.

"I'll catch up with you later," Toby said to me, leaning down to give me a kiss.

"Bye," I told him.

"I don't understand why you guys can't just get along," I said to Lilith.

"Because your boyfriend is a dumbfuck," she said.

"Lilith," I sighed. "Never mind. Look who I brought."

Lilith's eyes fell on Jason. They widened. "Well, hello," she said, clearly liking what she saw. "And who might you be?"

"Uh ..." Jason was intimidated by Lilith. Or maybe he was intimidated by the circle of brilliant headlights in the middle of a cornfield. Or the blaring, bass-heavy music. Or maybe he was just shy. I didn't know him very well. "I'm Jason."

Lilith's jaw dropped. "This is Jason? Geez, Zaza, you didn't tell me he was hot."

Jason looked at me, the same terror on his face as I'd seen when he couldn't find a channel on the TV.

"It's okay," I said. "She's less scary than she seems."

Jason tried to smile, but he still looked pretty freaked out.

"How is it scary for me to think you're utterly gorgeous?" Lilith asked Jason. She was a little drunk already.

"I'm not scared," said Jason. He was totally scared. "Um. Thanks. I guess."

Lilith brushed Jason's nose with her forefinger. "You are *precious* !" she said.

"Lilith, don't," I said. Was it me, or was everyone just

being completely weird to Jason?

"Oh my God!" Lilith exclaimed. "You guys are beerless! Let's hit the keg." She linked arms with me and started leading me away.

I looked over my shoulder to make sure Jason was coming. He trailed behind us, looking lost. I felt bad. Maybe I shouldn't have made him come to this party.

"Fuck me, Zaza," Lilith whispered to me, "he is *beautiful* . I want to do him. Can I do him?"

"No!" I said. For some reason, Lilith's overstated attraction to Jason was bugging me. Sometimes, I thought Lilith was a nympho. And with a nympho for a best friend, was it any wonder I wanted to have sex with Toby? All she talked about was sex. I just wanted to be able to relate for God's sake.

Lilith rolled her eyes. "Fine," she said. "You're too protective of your foster kids, you know that?"

"You just want to have sex with every boy in sight," I said.

"Not *every* boy," she said. She dropped my arm and reached back to yank Jason up between us. "It's okay," she told him. "Azazel has proclaimed you off limits. I promise to be good."

Jason laughed disbelievingly.

"Did I mention this was my best friend Lilith?" I asked him. I was a little embarrassed.

"I gathered," he said.

We'd reached the keg. Lilith pumped, and I poured us

two very foamy plastic cups of beer. I handed one to Jason and took the other.

He held up his cup, studying it. "So ..." he said. "Beer, huh?"

"Beer," I said.

"I've never actually ..." he said. Jason trailed off a lot.

"No way," said Lilith. "You're a beer virgin?"

"Leave him alone!" I scolded her. The way things were going, Jason really was going to run away. But it wasn't going to be because he was worried about anybody's safety. It was going to be because he wanted to get far, far away from all my crazy, rude friends.

I clinked plastic cups with Jason. "Cheers," I said. And we both drank. I made a face. I didn't like the taste of beer. To my amusement and delight, Jason made one too.

"It doesn't taste very good, does it?" I asked.

"Alcohol rarely does," he said.

So, he'd drunk alcohol? Just not beer? I wanted to ask, but I wasn't sure how to phrase it without sounding like I was accusing him of lying or something.

"I've mostly drunk wine," he told me, as if he could see the questions on my face.

"Oh," I said. "Do you like wine?"

"Not really," he said, laughing. He took another drink of his beer and surveyed the party.

Several girls were dancing in the middle of the circle, the headlights reflecting off their hair and curves. They twisted and writhed to the beat of the music, thrusting their hips in gyrating circles. Kids stood in groups, clutching their cups of beer — laughing and talking. Someone had brought his dog and was attempting to get him drunk by offering him beer. The dog was lapping it up. The guys surrounding the dog were jeering.

"So," said Jason, "this is a keg party?"

I nodded. "Yeah." It seemed so stupid. So tame. I didn't know why I'd brought him here. Someone like Jason probably had more sophisticated tastes. He seemed so old. Like he'd seen the entire world.

"I like it," he said, surprising me. He took a long swig of beer.

"Well, that's good," said Lilith. "Cause we're all gonna get fucked up."

"Not me," I muttered. "Toby doesn't want me to get plastered."

"Fuck Toby," said Lilith. She turned to Jason. "Don't you think her boyfriend is an utter jackass?"

Jason laughed another surprised laugh. "Um. I ..."

"Lilith!" I said.

"It's okay," said Jason. He looked at Lilith, raising his eyebrows. "I don't know him real well. But I don't think Azazel needs someone to treat her like a kid. I think she can take care of herself."

"Thanks," I said. I thought Jason was pretty cool. I had to get him to stay. I just had to.

I looked back out over the party and was stunned to see another familiar face. Cameron!

I didn't say anything to Lilith or Jason. I just marched over to Cameron and took him by the arm. Then I jerked him over to where I was standing with Lilith and Jason. How was this possible? Had everyone in my entire house snuck out tonight?

"What are you doing here?" I demanded.

"Partying," said Cameron.

"If my parents found out you were here—" I started.

"If they found out you were here," he interrupted, "you'd be in deep crap too."

I narrowed my eyes. "Cameron, you can't be here."

"I'm here," he said. "Deal with it." He recognized Jason. "Hey, Jason, man! Good to see you."

"Hi Cameron," said Jason.

"Come meet some people," said Cameron to Jason.

"You can't just—"

Cameron silenced me with a look. Damn it. He had me. I'd have to keep his secret if he wanted me to keep his. I wondered how often Cameron snuck out. Cameron used to have a big problem with drinking before he came to live with us. He was my age, and he'd already been through AA. I did not think a keg party was a good place for a reformed alcoholic. But I guess he didn't have a beer in his hand, so that was saying something. I was the one who was drinking. Not Cameron.

Cameron led Jason off to meet some of his friends. I was left with Lilith.

Lilith came out to parties like this more than I did. "Do

you see Cameron out a lot?" I asked her.

She shrugged. "I can't keep track of all your parents' foster urchins," she said.

"Does he drink?" I asked.

"Maybe," she said. Clearly, Lilith didn't want to talk about Cameron. "So, why'd you bring Jason?"

"He was trying to run away. I stopped him."

"Good!" said Lilith. "He can't leave."

"I know. He's like the most exciting thing that's ever happened in Bramford," I said.

Lilith took a drink of her beer, raising her eyebrows. "That's more true than you know."

What did that mean? "Anyway," I said, "I want him to have a good time, so he won't try to leave again. So, lay off him, okay, Lil? Sometimes you're a little much to take."

"Don't worry," said Lilith. "I'll leave him alone. I have to. I'm not allowed not to."

"What do you mean?" Lilith was sounding cryptic and weird. Maybe she was drunker than I thought.

"I mean, you said I'm not allowed," she said.

But I didn't think that was what she meant. "He's really interesting, don't you think?"

"Fucking gorgeous is what he is," said Lilith.

"Yeah," I said. "I guess." I hadn't really considered whether or not Jason was attractive. I'd been too busy trying to figure out who he was. Plus, I was in love with Toby. It wasn't like I was scoping out other guys.

"Speaking of gorgeous," said Lilith, "Did you see Eric

Nelson tonight without his shirt on? That boy is like a golden god."

I laughed. "But he's such a jerk."

"Who cares?" said Lilith. "As long as he's not talking, I could spend like an eternity with him."

"Is Eric your latest conquest then?" I teased. Lilith didn't really date boys. She sort of steamrolled them. But she might have met her match in Eric Nelson. He was pretty much a dick. He used girls like toilet paper.

"Maybe," said Lilith. "But, you know, it wouldn't be much of a challenge to bang Eric. He'd fuck anything in a skirt. If I go after Eric, I have to make him fall in love with me."

I laughed. "Good luck! I don't think that word is in Eric's vocabulary. And besides, since when was it in yours?"

Lilith shrugged dramatically. "I'm getting older," she said. "I'm a senior now. I'm developing mature feelings."

"Oh whatever," I said.

"Seriously," she said. "Besides, Eric would look so good in my prom pictures. He's beautiful. And those things will end up on my grandmother's refrigerator for like a thousand years. I want to be able to look at them when I'm old and fat with seven babies and say, 'I was beautiful in high school, and I had a beautiful boyfriend.'"

"Since when are you planning on having seven babies?" I asked. But I was thinking about my own grandmother — the one who was still alive. She had disowned my mother. She didn't speak to our family. I'd never known her. Where would my prom pictures go? When I moved out, my mom was sure to turn my bedroom into a haven for two or three foster kids.

"Maybe not seven," said Lilith, "but I'll definitely have kids. Everyone ends up doing it, even if they say they won't." She held up an empty beer cup. "I need more beer," she announced. "You?"

I didn't, but I chugged the rest of mine and followed her back to the keg.

"I know you dream about birthing Toby's blonde brats," she said.

"I don't," I said. "I don't want kids." Lilith was leaping pretty far into the future, wasn't she? Just because Toby was my high school boyfriend didn't mean we'd start ... breeding. If it worked out that way, I guess it wouldn't be so bad, but —

My thoughts were interrupted by a loud yell behind us. "Fight!"

Great. I rolled my eyes. Lilith and I turned to watch as nearly everyone in the party rushed towards the struggling figures of two guys, illuminated from behind by the headlights. We moved forward too, carried by the tide of bodies.

Why did guys have to resort to violence all the time? Civilization might have been created by a male-dominated society, but it sometimes boggled my mind to figure out how. I groaned, wondering if this meant the party was going to get broken up. I'd just gotten here!

Next to me, I heard two girls talking.

"Who is that guy?" one asked.

"I don't know. One of the Jones' foster kids, I think."

Oh God! Cameron! I knew it had been a bad idea for him to be here.

Spurred on by the thought of dragging a beaten, bloody Cameron into the house, I pushed through the bodies that had formed a tight circle around the fighting guys. I shoved people out of the way. Ducked under their elbows. Finally, I cleared the mass of bodies, and I could see.

But it wasn't Cameron.

It was Jason.

Jason was fighting with Eric Nelson.

There wasn't much to see. Limbs flailed, occasionally making contact. They grasped at each other, one grabbing the other in what looked like a bear hug. Then the other would slip from his grasp and grab the other guy in a similar hold. I could hardly tell who was who. They moved so quickly. I yelled, but it didn't matter. Everyone was yelling.

It seemed to go on an agonizingly long time. I didn't understand why no one was breaking this up. Didn't fights usually get broken up in just a few seconds? This one seemed to be dragging on and on.

Eric leaned over and drove himself into Jason's midsection, head first. His arms wrapped around Jason's waist. Jason went down, but he held onto Eric's arms and Eric went down with him, collapsing on top of Jason.

Eric was struggling to extricate himself, but somehow Jason flipped Eric over, turning the tables, so that now he was on top of Eric.

Pinning Eric, Jason let loose on him, raining punches onto Eric's face.

I could see now that Jason's face was bleeding, but so was Eric's now.

Blood spattered the grass. Jason's fist connected with Eric's nose, and there was a sickening crunching sound.

Now, suddenly, Toby rushed forward, pulling Jason off Eric and throwing him on the ground.

"Break it up!" Toby said, and several other football team members, who echoed his words, soon flanked him.

I ran up to Jason. He was half sitting, half reclining on the grass. He rubbed his mouth with the back of his hand. I collapsed on my knees next to Jason.

"Are you okay?" I asked. "What happened?"

Jason just shook his head, too out-of-breath to speak.

I glared up at Toby. "What were you thinking? How did you let this go on so long?"

Toby looked at me darkly. "Oh, of course," he said. "You're worried about *him* . What about Eric? I think your precious Jason broke his nose."

"What happened?" I asked Jason again.

Cameron appeared behind Jason. "It wasn't his fault," he said. "It was me."

"You?" I said. "It was Eric." I had no problem believing Eric had started this fiasco.

Cameron smirked. "Well, yeah. But Eric was ragging on me. You know, typical orphan stuff."

The guys at school picked on the foster guys sometimes. Eric tended to lead the pack. Like I said, he was a jerk.

"So Jason attacked him?" Toby said. He was holding Eric's chin in his hand, surveying the damage to Eric's ruined face.

"No," said Cameron. "No, I told him to shove it, and he said we should make him. Me and Jason. I told Jason to ignore him, but Eric came over and pushed me. Jason told Eric to get lost. Eric pushed Jason. And then, well, you saw what happened."

"Is that what happened Jason?" I asked him.

He'd caught his breath enough to nod and say, "Pretty much."

"Sure," sneered Toby. "Of course he'd say that. It makes him look innocent and pure like the driven snow."

"Why would Jason pick a fight?" I asked Toby. "He's new here. He wouldn't want to make trouble."

Toby dropped Eric's chin and stood up straight. "What do we even know about Jason anyway?"

I stood up to face him. "Well, we know enough about Eric to know he's a dick, don't we?"

"A bleeding dick with a broken nose," said Toby.

"So, you're on Eric's side?" I wanted to know. Toby and Eric got along okay, but they were not exactly close friends.

"So, you're on Jason's?"

"Why are you so pissed?"

Toby didn't answer for a second. He looked down at his hand, which he balled into a fist and then released. "Maybe I'm just not crazy about watching my girlfriend kneeling over some other guy, okay?"

"What?"

"You rushed over to him, didn't you?" Toby said. "'Oh, poor Jason,'" he mocked me.

What? Jason was hurt. Why was Toby being like this? I hadn't done anything wrong. I'd just wanted to make sure Jason was okay. That was all. Why was Toby bent out of shape about it? I looked up at him. I felt hurt. I didn't deserve this. "Go to hell," I said softly.

I turned away from Toby and offered Jason my hand to help him to his feet.

"Are you okay?" I asked him again.

"I'm fine," said Jason. He looked at my hand, but didn't take it. Instead, he pushed himself to his feet. "I'm sorry about this. I shouldn't have fought that guy."

"You were defending yourself," I said. "You were defending Cameron."

Jason shot a glance over my shoulder. "Maybe you should talk to Toby," he said.

I shook my head. "I don't have anything to say to him." I looked at Jason. "Come on. We'll find another ride home."

Chapter Four

morningstar68 (02:33:05): it can't happen any earlier than samhain.

michaela666 (02:33:44): that's weeks away. he's got too much time between now and then.

morningstar68: (02:34:14): There's no way to prepare the vessel adequately before then. even this is rushing things.

michaela666 (02:34:58): are you sure? time is of the essence in this, as I'm sure I don't have to tell you.

morningstar68: (02:35:08): you don't. but I have to say, I'm not excited about this turn of events. are we sure we have to use her? couldn't someone else be the vessel?

michaela666 (02:35:48): you've know this was her destiny since she before she even existed. I saw her in the vision, when I saw him.

morningstar68: (02:36:24): I know. I know. but it can't happen before samhain. can that work?

michaela666 (02:37:01): I guess it will have to. it's the best we can do.

Jason, Cameron, and I sat at the dining room table, facing my parents. Considering Eric's nose was broken, he'd had to go to the emergency room. And because of that, everyone had found out about the party at the Nelson farm, including my parents. They were less than happy about the fact that all three of us had snuck out.

I'd expected them both to be livid. I'd expected them to yell and possibly throw things. However, they just seemed very sad and disappointed. This was kind of worse than their anger. It made me feel guilty and ashamed. Plus, I was worried about Jason. If they punished Jason, he might just leave and never come back.

Because I didn't want to look at my parents, I looked at Cameron and Jason instead. They were on either side of me. Cameron was inspecting his fingernails, looking about as guilty as I felt. Jason however, held my parents' gaze, his face blank. He didn't look worried or guilty. Then, of course, he didn't know my parents. They were pretty good at making you feel the way they wanted you to feel. They didn't tell you how to feel or that you were wrong. Instead, they just laid out all the possible consequences of your actions. I hated that. It made me feel so ... responsible.

I just wished they'd get it over with already. All this sitting in silence was getting to me. I knew my parents weren't talking because they wanted me to contemplate what I'd done wrong. It was working. I felt wretched.

Finally, I couldn't stand it anymore. "I was the one who made Jason come to the party," I blurted out.

My mother and father just looked at me.

"He wouldn't have even been there if it wasn't for me," I said. "I totally talked him into it."

Seeming to follow my lead, Cameron spoke up. "I'm the reason that Jason got in the fight with Eric. I kind of picked a fight with him. It's not Jason's fault."

"None of this is Jason's fault," I said.

Jason looked down the table at us, raising his eyebrows. "Well," he said, looking at my parents, "I did consent to go to the party. And I am the one who broke Eric's nose. So, I guess some it is my fault."

What was Jason's problem? Cameron and I were trying to take the fall for him. Couldn't he see that?

"I'll understand if you guys don't want me to stay here anymore," said Jason. "That might be the best thing for everyone."

"Jason," said my mother, "let's not get drastic."

"Of course we want you to stay," said my father. "Believe me, this isn't the first time one of our boys has gotten in a fight."

"Right," said Cameron. "And this one didn't even involve knives."

Aaron, a boy who'd lived with us a year ago, had gotten in a knife fight at school once. He'd gotten expelled. My parents fought to keep him, but the state took him away anyhow. He still kept in touch sometimes. We all visited him in jail last Christmas. Apparently, he got in a bad bar fight (amazing, since he wasn't even eighteen, let alone twenty-one) and the other guy didn't survive. Aaron was serving time for manslaughter. Poor Aaron. If my parents had been able to keep him, maybe ...

"Thanks for the perspective, Cameron," said my father.

"Listen," said my mother, "you all know—well,

Cameron and Azazel know — that we want to encourage you to make your own decisions. We're not here to impose a rigid order on your lives. These are your lives, and it's your job to make them into whatever you want them to be. However, we do try to provide boundaries for you."

Oh, God. Not this speech. Please not this speech.

My mother continued, "We feel that these boundaries can help guide you. We feel that they can open you up to options that you might not consider otherwise. While it's a perfectly valid choice to live in the moment, and to live for fun, we feel that there are other valid choices, and we feel that since you're very young, you might not think of those choices."

"And," said my father, picking up where my mother left off, "once you've made a series of certain kinds of choices, it can be difficult to decide to make different ones. You can rack up all kinds of nonproductive consequences that get in the way of a productive life."

My head was swimming. Why couldn't they just be like normal parents and say that what we'd done was wrong and now we were going to get punished? It all amounted to the same thing anyway. This was just psychobabble. It was rationalization.

I stole a glance at Jason. His forehead was wrinkled as if he was trying very hard to concentrate, or if he was very, very confused. I didn't blame him. My parents' reasoning was complicated.

"I feel," I said, "that we've all seen what kind of

nonproductive consequences happen when we sneak out. Jason got punched. I got in a fight with Toby. And we all had to ride home with Lilith, and her car is very small. To that end, I don't think we need any more punishment. We've all learned our lesson."

"We're not going to punish you," said my mother.

What?

"All three of you are seventeen years old," said my father. "You are young adults. You're practically old enough to make your own decisions legally."

"We'd created the curfew as a boundary for you," said my mother. "We knew it was only a matter of time until you tested that boundary."

"Now that you have," said my dad, "it proves to us that you've outgrown it."

What?

"Um," said Jason. "I didn't have a curfew. And I was the one who broke someone's nose."

"And we want to talk to you about that," said my father. "But first, we want to let you all three know that we are going to allow you to make your own decisions about when you come home at night."

"Bear in mind," said my mother, "that those decisions will affect all manner of things. Your performance in school for instance. Your ability to get your chores done at home. Your relationships. These are all things you'll need to weigh as you make your choices."

Yuck. Leave it to my mom to make a privilege sound like

a burden.

"Now," said my father, "Cameron and Jason, I want to talk to you about this fight with Eric."

Cameron and Jason looked at each other. They didn't look too excited about this chat. Jason was catching on to the way my parents worked. They made you feel so adult. The guilt was almost too much to take. When you were around them, you just wanted to do better. They totally sucked.

"Why did you choose to engage in an altercation with Eric, Cameron?" my dad asked.

"Alter-what?" asked Cameron.

"Argument," I said.

"Why didn't you just say argument, then?" Cameron wanted to know.

Neither of my parents answered.

Cameron sighed. "He was pissing me off. He said that he was sick of seeing all those motherfucking Jones orphans at his party. Then he said, 'Oh, wait. I forgot. They don't have mothers.'"

"And that comment was designed to make you react, wasn't it Cameron?" my mother asked.

"Yeah, I know. He was just trying to get under my skin," said Cameron.

"If he made you angry, he had power over you," my mother said.

"I know!" said Cameron. "And I tried to do what you said. I told him to shove it and shut up, and I started to walk away."

Jason spoke up. "I thought that guy needed to be taught a lesson."

"Oh?" said my dad.

"Yeah. People shouldn't say things like that."

"And if they do, they should have their noses broken?" my father asked.

"Well, something like that." Jason shrugged. "Weren't you just talking about consequences, Mr. Jones? Eric said some awful stuff. The consequence was that I beat him up."

Huh. Jason kind of had a point.

My father considered what Jason had said. "I don't agree with what Eric said either," he said. "But let me ask you this, Jason. What if it hadn't gone your way? What if Eric had broken your nose? Then what consequence would he have received?"

"Well, that wouldn't have happened," said Jason. "I wouldn't have gotten in the fight if I didn't know I could win."

Really?

"How could you have known that?" my father asked. "Eric's a lot bigger than you. He's a strong boy. He works on his parents' farm. He's on the wrestling team at school."

"He was drunk," said Jason. "I could tell that his reaction time was pretty screwed up and that he could hardly stand straight."

"So you got into a calculated fight with Eric because you were sure you could beat him?" my father asked.

Oh. My father was backpedaling. When he started

rephrasing people's statements, I knew it was so he had some time to think about what they'd said, so he could formulate a response. In addition, sometimes restating someone's argument caused them to start arguing with themselves or backing down.

Not Jason. "Yeah," he said. "I wasn't angry with him. It's pointless to get angry with people. They're the way they are. There are two options. You either accept what they're doing. Or you make them stop doing it."

Wow. My mother said something like that. But the end part was different. My mother didn't believe in making people stop doing whatever they were doing. She believed in asking them to change.

For maybe the first time ever, both my parents were speechless.

Finally, my mom said, "Jason, what gives you the right to determine whether someone else's actions are right or wrong? What gives you the right to decide that someone else shouldn't say or do what he's doing?"

Jason furrowed his brow. " I don't decide," he said. "Some things are right. Some things are wrong." He shrugged. "What Eric said to Cameron was just wrong. It was cruel. It was ignorant. And it was juvenile. He deserved what happened to him."

"And punching him in the nose? That wasn't wrong?" asked my mom.

"Punching him in the nose for no reason would have been wrong," said Jason. "But what I did ... I guess I could have let it go. In the end, it probably won't make him stop saying that kind of stuff. But I guarantee he won't say anything like that in front of me again."

Jason looked so sure of himself. So certain. So convicted. I'd never seen a boy our age who knew so clearly what he thought. I was impressed.

And my parents weren't saying anything. They exchanged a look. This whole conversation had not gone the way they wanted it to. It was probably because Jason had said that some things were right and some things were wrong. I think I explained before that my parents didn't believe in evil. By extension, they didn't believe in right and wrong either. Jason was opposed to everything they believed. It was weird, because I'd always known there were people like that. But I'd never met someone who had as much conviction as Jason. And he could defend his beliefs too. Jason was pretty cool.

I wondered if this meant that my parents would reinstate our curfew now. After all, it seemed like they'd kind of lost an argument.

I waited for one of them to say something.

Finally, my mother did. "Jason," she said quietly, "how do you know what's right and wrong?"

Ooh. She went there. Right to the heart of things. I always thought this was the place where the opposite argument kind of fell apart, so I waited for Jason's answer.

He hesitated. "Um, I guess I'm not totally sure," he said. "I know I was taught right and wrong, but the people who taught me ... Well, when I got older, I decided that some of the things that they said were right were actually wrong. And vice versa. But, I mean, if my only concept of right and wrong had come from them, then how did I evaluate their beliefs using their concepts? So, I guess I think that right and wrong must be sort of ... like ideas that people just ... know, somehow. Like ... like Plato or something."

Plato? What was he talking about?

My father looked surprised too. "You've read Plato?"

"I think it's the 'Allegory of the Cave,'" said Jason. "You know that essay?"

"Of course," said my mother, who also seemed shocked.

"Well, so there's a world of ideas, right? And right and wrong are in the world of ideas. But we mess them up, because we live in the cave, and we can only see shadows of the world of ideas. I mean, something like that anyway."

Both of my parents stared at Jason, slack-jawed. They didn't say anything.

"I'm glad we all talked about this incident," my mother said abruptly. "I feel like it was very productive. Don't you, Daniel?"

"Sure," said my dad.

And we were dismissed. The score? Jason-1. My parents-0.

* * *

On Monday, we went to school. I usually caught a ride with Toby, but I was still pissed at him, so I rode the bus with the guys. Even though I had my driver's license, I didn't have a car. My parents were great, but they didn't have the money for another car. Not when they had to feed five teenagers. I didn't really mind. I liked riding with Toby. However, that Monday morning, waiting at the bus stop, I felt kind of stupid. Here I was, a senior in high school, riding the damned bus. My dad worked at the high school too, but we couldn't all fit in his car. Plus, my dad always got to school about an hour before class started so that he could make copies and get ready. Nobody wanted to get up that early.

Overall, it was good, because I would have felt bad about making Jason fend for himself on the first day. Sure the guys would have looked out for him, but all of them except Chance were strangers in Bramford. The town looked on them as outsiders. And Chance was only fifteen, so he was a lowly sophomore. He wouldn't have been much help.

I took Jason to the office first thing. My dad had set it up with the school so that Jason could get a schedule. They were used to it, since my family was always getting new foster kids. I sat with Jason in Mrs. Clem's office. Mrs. Clem was the Dean of Students, and she set up all the schedules. I liked Mrs. Clem, but when we arrived, it was obvious she'd already heard about what Jason had done to Eric over the weekend. Bramford was notoriously protective of its own. Jason didn't belong in Bramford and had already damaged a member of one its oldest families. That wasn't good in the minds of most of Bramford's inhabitants.

Mrs. Clem seemed a little cold. She pursed her lips.

"Are we going to get your transcripts, Jason?" she asked.

"I don't have any," he said.

Mrs. Clem raised her eyebrows in disbelief.

"I was kind of home schooled before," he said.

"But he reads Plato," I said, feeling like I should defend him in some way.

Mrs. Clem didn't react to that. She just poured over her computer screen, lost in thought. Finally, she began punching keys. "Normally, with no transcript, I'd put you in General Education classes," she said to Jason. "But most of them are overcrowded, and it occurs to me that since you seem to be a little ... volatile, it might be better to keep you away from ... overexcitement."

She was referring to Jason's fight. She was so prejudiced! She'd never even met Jason, and she'd already judged him.

"So, I'm going to try you out in Honors classes," she said.

Really? Maybe I was the one who was judging Mrs. Clem. That was pretty decent of her.

She printed out Jason's schedule and handed it to him.

"Cool," I said, looking over his shoulder at it. "You've got three classes with me!"

Bramford was on a semester block schedule, which meant we only had four classes a day. I was going to be seeing a lot of Jason. Of course, it also meant that Jason was going to be seeing a lot of Toby. Toby and I had the exact same schedule.

Ugh. And we sat next to each other in every class. I

66

didn't want to see Toby. I was still angry with him. But I was going to have to. In exactly five minutes, I noted as the opening bell rang.

I smiled at Jason. "I'll show you around," I said. "We've got the same first period."

Jason, Toby, and I began the day in Ms. Campbell's Advanced Placement English class. It was downstairs, directly under the main office. Jason followed me as I navigated the crowded halls and staircase. As we approached the door, I wished as hard as I could that Toby wouldn't be there.

No such luck. He was sitting in his normal desk. Ms. Campbell was shuffling through some papers at her podium, not monitoring the hall like she was supposed to. She claimed she always forgot to do it, but once or twice the principal had ducked his head in the classroom and asked her to come into the hall. She'd said sweetly, "Sure. One sec!" And then she'd never gone into the hall.

Ms. Campbell was kind of a rebel, I thought. I liked her. She'd let us read *Lysistrata* , which was a pretty racy ancient Greek play about a group of women who withheld sex from the men so they would stop fighting a war. It had penis jokes! I couldn't believe we'd been allowed to read it in class.

I took Jason up to Ms. Campbell.

She looked up. "Hi, Azazel," she said. "What's up?"

"You've got a new student," I said. "Jason Wodden."

Ms. Campbell looked at him. "The kid who beat up Eric Nelson?"

God. Had everybody heard about this?

Ms. Campbell leaned forward conspiratorially. "Nice going," she whispered. She straightened back up and went back to her papers. "Of course," she said, "if you tell anyone I said that, I will deny it."

Ms. Campbell was cool.

"So, I guess I need to get you a textbook and a syllabus," she said to Jason. "You can sit—"

"Actually," I said. "I was hoping I could move my seat for today."

"Really?" said Ms. Campbell. "You and Toby—trouble in paradise?"

I didn't say anything.

"Sure, it's fine," she said. "Any open seat then. Both of you."

Toby turned around in his seat and saw me. I looked away, ushering Jason and me to some desks in the back of the room. Jason and I sat down. Ms. Campbell's classroom was long and thin. The desks faced a whiteboard, but there were only three long rows. Toby and I usually sat in the front. There were several sets of seats between Toby and me now. Purposefully, I didn't look at him.

Ms. Campbell dropped off a textbook and syllabus at Jason's desk. Jason began flipping through it. It was *Perrine's Literature: Structure, Sound, and Sense* . I busied myself with beginning our journal prompt, which we had to do each day in class. As I got out my notebook, I pointed it out on the board to Jason. "We have to write a paragraph about whatever the question is every day," I told him.

Jason nodded.

Today's question was, "What is the purpose of rules?" Ms. Campbell always asked weird things.

"Azazel," said Jason.

"Yeah?" I said.

"Toby's staring at us," he said.

"I don't care," I said. I didn't have anything to say to Toby. I was still mad at him.

"I think maybe you should talk to him," said Jason.

"No way."

"It's just you sitting with me like this ... He might think ..." Jason trailed off again.

His trailing off was maddening!

"He might think what?" I demanded.

Jason shook his head. "Nothing. Never mind."

"No! Tell me."

But the tardy bell rang, and Ms. Campbell said, "Okay, guys, get to work on your journals. No talking."

English class went by pretty quickly, as it usually did. There were some avid conversations going on from other students in the class, about the short story we'd read, "A Rose for Emily." I didn't join in. I usually didn't. I just liked to listen to what everyone else said. I watched Jason soak it all in. He hadn't read the story, but I could tell if he had, he'd throw in his two cents.

Second block was the one class Jason and I didn't have together. He had biology. Toby and I had French. Mrs.

Zimmerman, the French teacher, would not let me change seats, so I had to sit next to Toby.

I settled into my seat, sulking, and vowing not to speak to him.

"Azazel," said Toby, "we have to talk."

We most certainly did not. In fact, we weren't going to talk if I had anything to say about it. I buried my face in my French book and tried to ignore him.

"Listen, I'm sorry," he said. "I was rude to you for no reason at the party."

Damned right he was. But just because he was correctly describing his behavior didn't mean I was going to forgive him. He'd really hurt my feelings. He'd *mocked* me. In front of everyone. In that second, I'd had this flash that maybe Toby really saw me as ridiculous.

"Please look at me," he said.

I didn't.

Thankfully, class started right about then, and I had other things to pay attention to besides Toby.

After French, Jason rejoined us for history. That was my dad's class. It was weird having my dad for a teacher, but it was either do that or not take Honors History, which just wasn't an option. My dad didn't have a seating chart in his classroom. My dad didn't actually have rules in his classroom. He solved problems by classroom quorums, where we all sat in a circle and talked about how we felt the class was going. This worked fine in Honors classes, but I knew that some of the General kids took advantage of my dad. He didn't see it that way though. He thought it was important that the students had the ability to make their own decisions and to discover the consequences.

I was glad that there wasn't a seating chart. I usually did sit in the same seat by Toby, but I sat somewhere else today, and I waved Jason over to me when he came into the classroom.

"How was biology?" I asked him.

Jason sat down, noting that Toby and I weren't sitting together. "You haven't made up with Toby, yet, huh?"

"No," I said. Maybe I wasn't going to make up with Toby at all.

"Biology was okay," said Jason. "I've done most of the stuff in there. Should be a breeze."

"So, were you really home schooled?"

"Kind of," said Jason and that was all. He never elaborated on anything! I was dying of curiosity. How was I going to get Jason to trust me with his secrets?

After history, we went to lunch. Usually, I sat with Toby. We ate at a table with a bunch of football players and their girlfriends. After I ate, I usually went into the gym to find Lilith. Lilith never ate lunch.

Today, however, for some reason, she was in the lunch line. She saw Jason and I and motioned for us to come stand with her.

"We'll be cutting the line," I called to her.

She rolled her eyes, but she left her spot in the line to come back and stand with us. "There," she said. "Happy?"

I made a face at her. "What's up?" I said. "How come you're eating lunch?"

"I'm pregnant," she said. "Baby needs nutrition."

"Shut up!" I said, whacking her with my purse. "You are not!"

"No," she said. "I'm not." She smiled at Jason. "And how are you?"

"Uh ... good," said Jason.

Every time Jason said something to Lilith, he started out with "uh" or "um." I wondered if Jason was attracted to Lilith. I considered the prospect of Jason and Lilith dating. For some reason, I didn't like the idea of it at all.

"You still pissed at Toby?" she asked me.

"Of course," I said. How could she ask me this? Last night, when I'd talked to her on the phone, I'd explained exactly how I felt about the situation in excruciating detail. We'd dissected everything he'd said, trying to figure out his motives.

"Maybe you should give the guy a break," said Lilith.

My jaw dropped. What was Lilith saying? "You hate Toby," I said.

"Yeah," she said. "I do. He's a total idiot. But, I don't know, the two of you are like the teen dream couple. You're good together, you know."

"Obviously, we're not if he makes fun of me in front of everyone at that party," I said. "Plus, he treats me like I'm twelve or something. He's so overprotective. And he won't have sex with me."

Jason cleared his throat.

Lilith and I both looked at him.

"The line moved forward," he said.

We shuffled forward in the lunch line.

"What do you think, Jason?" I asked.

"About?" he asked. He looked a little embarrassed. I realized I'd been talking about my sex life (or lack thereof) in front of him. Maybe that made him uncomfortable.

"Toby," I said. "You don't think I should forgive him, do you?"

Jason didn't say anything.

"You're gonna forgive him," said Lilith. "You guys never fight for long. You might as well just get it over with."

"Do you want to break up with him?" Jason asked me.

I thought about it. Did I? I was in love with Toby. I was mad at him right now, but did I want him out of my life forever? "Let's talk about something else," I said. "Like why are you really eating lunch, Lilith?"

Lilith rolled her eyes. "I'm hiding from Eric Nelson. He was a total jackass to me in the gym because I gave you guys a ride home."

I smiled. "I thought you were going to make Eric fall in love with you."

"Not in this lifetime," she said.

* * *

That evening, Toby called me four times. I wouldn't take any of his calls. I still didn't know what I wanted to do. Before, I hadn't thought of my anger in terms of ending our relationship. I'd just known that I was angry and hurt and that I didn't want to talk to Toby. But after Jason had asked me if I wanted to break up with Toby, I realized I wasn't sure. Was there something really, really wrong with my relationship with Toby? Maybe I only dated him because it was comfortable. We'd been dating since we were fourteen. The thought of not having Toby in my life seemed foreign and strange. But I couldn't just keep dating him because I was used to it.

Could I?

The fifth time he called, I was in my bedroom working on my history homework. My mother knocked on my door, phone in hand. "It's Toby again," she said to me.

"I told you. I don't want to talk to him," I said.

My mother put the phone to her ear. "Let me talk to her, Toby."

Oh, great. Not another heart to heart with mom. I loved my mom, but she had this annoying habit of making me examine all my actions and realize how silly I was being. I didn't want that. I wanted to wallow in my anger towards Toby.

My mom came into my room and sat down on my bed. She set the phone down next to her.

Sighing, I closed my history book. "Mom, I just don't want to talk to him."

"Sweetie, I think he's sorry," she said. "He sounds pitiful on the phone. He misses you."

"Well, good," I said. "I hope he does. And he can just go

right on missing me."

"Is that what you want?" my mom asked. "He's not going to miss you forever, you know."

"Geez, I didn't break up with him or anything. We're just having a fight." Why was everyone making this into such a big deal? And why was everyone, even Lilith, on Toby's side? *He'd* made fun of *me* !

"So you don't want to break up with him?"

"I don't know!"

My mom took my hand. "Zaza, have I ever told you about the time I almost broke up with your father?"

"No," I said.

"It was when we were dating in college," she said. "We got in a big fight one night about something silly. Funny, I can't even remember what it was anymore. But I was so angry with him. I didn't talk to him for weeks."

"What happened?"

"He started seeing someone else."

"Really?"

My mother nodded. "I was devastated. I saw them together at a restaurant one night, and I realized that no matter how angry I was with your father, I couldn't bear the thought of not being with him. So, I called him and told him that."

"And he dumped the other girl?"

Mom laughed. "Actually, it turned out that he wasn't even dating her. She was just a friend. I'd leapt to conclusions."

I laughed too.

"But the important thing, sweetie, was that I realized I didn't want to lose your dad. I couldn't face life without him."

"Right," I said. My mom wanted me to think about life without Toby. But I'd been doing that. Still. I wondered how I'd feel if I saw Toby with another girl. I didn't think I'd like that very much at all. Toby was mine. Even if sometimes he was a big jerk, he was my jerk. "Give me the phone."

My mom smiled and handed it to me.

I dialed Toby's number.

"Azazel?" he said, sounding very happy to hear from me.

"Hey," I said.

"Can we talk?"

"Yeah."

"Face to face," he said. "I'll pick you up?"

"Okay," I said.

Toby showed up in ten minutes. I climbed into his truck. It felt natural. It was the way things were supposed to be. We went back to Toby's house. Neither of his parents was home, so we had the place to ourselves. Still, we went to hang out in Toby's room, like usual. Some habits were hard to break.

I perched on Toby's bed. He sat in his desk chair.

"I'm so, so sorry," he said.

"Look, Toby—" I started. I was going to tell him about what my mother had said to me and about my epiphany about us.

But he interrupted me. "No," he said. "Let me say this." He took a deep breath. "I was an ass. I was jealous."

"Jealous?" I said. What could he have been jealous of?

"Yeah. I mean, Jason shows up, and suddenly, he's all you talk about. And he's always around. And you're always with him. I couldn't handle it."

"You were jealous of Jason?" I asked. How could he think that? I mean, sure I thought Jason was interesting. But I didn't think of him like that. The idea was so ridiculous that I started laughing.

Toby looked worried. "Why are you laughing?" he asked.

I tried to stop. "Jason?" I said between giggles. "Really? Jason?"

"So that's funny?" said Toby. He looked confused.

My laughter started to subside. "Yes, it's funny. I don't have any feelings for Jason!"

"You sat beside him in every class today."

"Because he's new, and he doesn't know what's going on!"

"So, you're not going to start dating him or something?"

"Don't be silly," I said. "I love you, Toby. We've been through so much together. I could never just leave you like that. Besides, Jason is weird. He's strange and mysterious and nobody knows anything about him. And he's really strong, and he beats people up, and he never talks, and he doesn't know what he wants to watch on television."

77

"And those are bad things?"

"Not bad, exactly, just weird," I said. It was true. I found Jason intriguing, but that was as far as it went. Toby was my boyfriend.

Toby looked relieved. "Okay," he said. "Good."

"Good," I said.

"So, we're cool, then?" he asked.

I nodded. "We're cool."

He grinned. He got up from his desk chair and came over to the bed to sit next to me. I burrowed into his chest, and he put his arm around me.

"I thought I was losing you," he said.

"You can't get rid of me that easily," I said.

And he kissed me.

Toby was a very good kisser. And I loved how kissing him felt so familiar and safe. This was the boy I'd been kissing for years and years. Kissing Toby was like coming home. It felt like wrapping up in a worn, warm blanket. One that I'd had since I was a kid.

He pulled me close, and I lost myself in his strong arms.

We lay back on Toby's bed, wriggling around so that we could rest our heads on the pillows. Our lips met again and again. Our tongues darted in and out of each other's mouths. And we held onto each other so tightly. During times like this, I sometimes felt like Toby and I were becoming part of each other. Like we were one entity, and we were melding into each other. It was such a lovely feeling. It was what I imagined sex with Toby would be like.

The two of us joined together, completing each other.

Toby's hands started to shift on my body. He traced the curve of my spine, my waist. I moved my hands too, caressing his arms, his chest. Toby rolled over, and suddenly, he was on top of me. His hips pinned mine to the bed. He kissed me. I wrapped my legs around his. He propped himself up so that he could look at me. I gazed into his blue, blue eyes. He was so beautiful. I reached up to touch his chin, his jaw. He stroked my cheek, my neck. His fingers went lower, tracing the outline of my clavicle. They eased inside the collar of my shirt. My breath caught in my throat. His hands barely skimmed the surface of my skin. I had goose bumps. And he was inches, inches from my breast, which no one had ever touched before. I held my breath as his hand got closer and closer, inching over my skin—

And then he sat up.

He wasn't touching me at all. He buried his face in his hands.

"Toby?" I asked in a small voice. What had just happened?

"We can't," he said, and his voice sounded agonized.

"We can," I said.

"No," he said. "No, no. We're not allowed."

Not allowed? Someone else had something like that. Who was it?

"It's okay," I said, sitting up and touching his shoulder. "We're not in the truck. It's nice here. That was ... that was

79

special." And it had been. It had been like something out of a romantic movie. And now it was all ruined.

Toby appeared to get hold of himself. He looked up at me, dropping his hands. "I mean, I can't," he said. "Not now. This isn't how I want it."

God! Wasn't anything good enough for Toby? "How do you want it?" I asked.

He sighed. "I'm sorry, Azazel. But it's got to be perfect."

I didn't buy it. He'd leaped off of me. Like he'd realized what he was doing, and he found me disgusting. I wasn't sure that Toby was even attracted to me. It had seemed like he was, but then ... And on top of all of it, now I felt a strange sort of warmth between my legs. It demanded some sort of satisfaction, which it wasn't going to get, and I felt a brand of frustration I'd never felt in my life. I folded my arms over my chest, wanting to cry.

"Let's go somewhere," said Toby.

I looked up at him. "Okay," I said. But I didn't feel very excited about it.

Chapter Five

To: Richard Durham (rdurham@risingsun.org)
From: Hallam Wakefield (hwakefi@risingsun.org)
Subject: Re: West Virginia
Richard,

No, I'm not in West Virginia. I'm in upstate New York. I emailed Alfred and told him this. I don't know why Intel hasn't seen me in New York. Answer me this: why are we wasting Intel confirming my whereabouts?

If we're going to find Jason, we have to work together, not against each other. I've told you exactly what I think about Georgia. There's no way Jason is there. I don't know why you insist on staying there. Why don't you go west?

Yours in the Purpose,
Hallam

Everything had gone back to normal. Sort of. Toby was picking me up for school again. I was sitting next to him in class. We were going out on dates and making out, but not going any further than that. The only thing that was different was Jason. He lived in my house. He was in three of my classes. He was around—a lot. My parents had submitted some paperwork to keep Jason as foster parents, but it was taking a long time to go through, because Jason wasn't in any of the foster systems. There was a long search going on. Everyone was trying to pin down Jason's birth records. It seemed impossible that a boy could have lived seventeen years and never left any evidence of his existence. But that seemed to be what Jason had done.

About his past, he was close-mouthed. He didn't like to talk about it. I could tell. But he protested at the thought of staying less and less. And he almost never talked about being a danger to our family anymore. My mom thought this was a good sign. I knew from eavesdropping on conversations she and my dad had. They often talked in their bedroom at night, after everyone had gone to bed. I would leave my room and stand in the dark hallway in my nightgown, my ear pressed against their door. I wanted to catch any bit of information about Jason I could.

But they didn't seem to know anything. And they rarely spoke about anything interesting. Generally, they talked about how their days had gone. They talked about Chance. They talked about the other foster kids. They never seemed to talk about me. They were planning something around Halloween. Probably a party or something. My parents liked to throw alternative, safe parties for teens where there wasn't any alcohol or drugs. The parties were utterly lame, and I almost always had to show. I hated that. I kind of hoped they didn't throw a party at Halloween. I wanted to do something cool with Toby that night.

Jason wasn't volunteering any information about himself. My parents didn't know any. I was left with only one means of gathering data. Observation. I watched Jason. I saw how easily he fit into our Honors classes. He was very bright. He made insightful comments about whatever we were reading. He got in arguments with my father in history class. I could tell that my father found Jason's intelligence bothersome. In gym class, he also seemed to do well. He was strong and fit.

But even though Jason fit in academically, he seemed socially awkward. He sat alone at lunch. I wanted to sit with him, but after Toby had confessed he'd felt jealous of Jason, I didn't think I should. I didn't want to upset Toby again. Jason was friendly whenever people talked to him but distant. He rarely smiled, and when he did, it was his brief smile. The one that lit up his face for a second then disappeared into his brooding eyes. There was something about Jason that screamed untouchable. And I realized that I desperately wanted to penetrate the wall he'd built around himself and find out what was behind it.

I didn't have much luck. I couldn't spend much time with Jason. At school, I hung with Toby. Toby didn't seem to want to have anything to do with Jason, and I didn't know why. After school, I had homework. My parents gave me chores that never seemed to overlap with Jason's. I barely even saw him at dinner, because Toby was asking me out a lot, and we ate together most of the time. When I did have free time, Lilith called me on the phone, and we had to talk for hours, because that was what we did. In some ways, it was almost like the whole world was conspiring to keep me away from Jason. But I watched him. I watched him a lot.

One Sunday morning, I woke up earlier than usual. Everyone else was asleep, and so I padded downstairs in my pajamas to watch television in blissful silence. I was surprised to find Jason in the living room, watching a televangelist giving a sermon. He didn't look up when I came into the room, as if he hadn't heard me.

"Hi," I said.

He jumped.

"Sorry," I said.

"It's okay," he said.

I sat down on the couch. Stared at the screen. The man was preaching about the end of the world. "The bible tells us," he said, "that before the coming of the Antichrist, there will be many earthquakes. Now, I want to show you something." Behind him, a map appeared on a screen. As he spoke, spots on the map began to light up. "In February 1991, an earthquake hit Afghanistan and Pakistan. In April 1991, there was an earthquake in Georgia. Also in April, an earthquake struck Panama and Costa Rica. In June of 1991, there was an earthquake in southern California.

"The Gulf War ended in 1991," he continued. "The Warsaw Pact dissolved. The Dead Sea scrolls became public. Brothers and sisters, the Antichrist was born in 1991. He is living among us! The end times are here."

Jason *was* weird. Why was he watching this? "Are you religious?" I asked Jason.

He looked at me. "Do you want me to change this?"

"I don't care," I said. I wanted him to change it.

Jason changed the channel to MTV. "I guess I'm not," he said.

"Not what?"

"Religious," he said. "Your family isn't, are they? No one in this town is."

"People in town are," I said.

"Like who?"

"Well, no one I know," I admitted. "But I know people are."

"There aren't any churches in Bramford," said Jason.

"Sure there are," I said. But then I thought about it. There weren't.

"No," said Jason. "There aren't. I looked. I even checked the internet. Closest church is like 20 miles away."

"Really?" I said. Huh. Why had I never noticed this before? I guess I didn't think about churches much. Or religion. "How come you were looking for churches?" I asked.

He gazed at the TV screen. "Sanctuary," he breathed.

"What?"

He turned to me. "No reason," he said, smiling his quick smile. "Just curious, I guess."

I didn't believe him.

* * *

Toby and I were sitting on one of the picnic tables outside McDonald's with several of our friends. It was dark outside. The wind was a little chilly, and I huddled in my sweatshirt as I sipped flat beer out of a travel mug. It was Wednesday night, and it was late, but I was taking advantage of my lack of curfew.

Sherry Astor stood up. She shivered. "I'm cold," she announced.

"Me too," I murmured.

"Let's walk," she said.

I got up and so did Eve Newcomb. We walked behind the McDonalds, away from the tables. There was an empty parking lot behind us, and we walked in circles, hunching our shoulders to try to stay warm.

"God," said Eve, "I'm so sick of hanging out outside McDonald's."

"Me too," said Sherry. "This town is so boring. I wish there was something to do."

I nodded my agreement. Having no curfew wasn't as exciting as it was cracked up to be. Bramford was not the most happening place on earth. I couldn't wait until I'd graduated, and Toby and I were in college at WVU. There'd be all kinds of things to do then.

"Darius asked me if I wanted to hang out at his place," said Eve. Darius was Eve's boyfriend.

"But you picked here?" I asked.

Eve sighed. "Whenever we go to Darius' place, all he wants to do is have sex."

Sherry groaned in sympathy. "I know what you mean. It's all Tom wants to do too."

I didn't say anything. I had nothing to say. I couldn't

relate.

"God," said Eve, "it's like there's all this pressure, and they want you to let them do it forever, and finally you just can't handle anymore, so you give in, thinking that will be the end of it. But it never ends. It's like all that's on their minds."

"Well," said Sherry, "I wouldn't mind if we could do it at Tom's house. You're lucky that Darius' mom is never home. Tom always wants to get it on in the back seat of his car, in like broad daylight. Which is just ... weird."

"Yeah," agreed Eve. "That is weird."

"So, what's the big deal?" asked Sherry. "How come you're not at Darius' place, getting busy? Does Darius just suck in bed or something?"

Eve considered. "No ... yes. I don't know. I've never had sex with anyone besides Darius. How would I know if he sucks?"

"Well," said Sherry as if it were obvious, "do you like it?"

"Sex?"

"Yeah," said Sherry.

"Sure," said Eve. "I mean, I guess so."

"You guess so?" said Sherry. "He's definitely bad in bed. Don't you think so, Azazel?"

I shrugged. "I guess I wouldn't know," I said.

They both stopped short and looked at me.

"You mean you and Toby aren't doing it?" Sherry asked me.

I sighed. "No."

"You're a virgin?!" said Eve, her mouth open.

"Oh my God," said Sherry. "How come you're not doing it?"

"I don't know," I said. "Toby doesn't want to."

"Oh whatever," said Eve. "All guys want to."

"Toby doesn't," I said. "Or, I don't know. Maybe something's wrong with me."

The girls looked at each other and then back at me. "Like what?" asked Sherry.

"I don't know," I said. "But he hardly touches me, so there's got to be something."

"Yeah," said Eve. "Weird."

The conversation turned to other things, and I went home soon after that. Toby kissed me chastely when he dropped me off, and inwardly, I fumed. The look those girls had given me still was stuck in my head. It was like I was a leper or something. I hated feeling so weird. Why didn't Toby want to be with me? Why?

I didn't sleep well that night. I couldn't stop thinking about what might be wrong with me. I couldn't help but think that Toby was just being nice to spare my feelings, but there was something about me that was different than everyone else. I wished he'd just tell me what it was. How was I supposed to fix it if I didn't know?

The next morning at school, when Toby and I walked into the hallway, I suddenly felt all eyes on me. And everyone started whispering to each other. My heart dropped into my stomach. It was obvious that everyone was talking about us. What were they saying?

I made my way to English class. I tried to ignore the stares and whispers. What could I have done? Why was everyone talking about me? I looked at Toby, but Toby seemed oblivious. On my way to class, I looked everywhere for Lilith, knowing she'd give it to me straight. But I didn't see her anywhere.

Even in class, the stares and whispers continued. I tried to concentrate on writing my journal prompt. The question today was, "Is it wise to subvert popular culture?"

We were reading *1984* . Annoyingly, the hero and heroine of the book were rebelling against a fascist government by having sex. Everyone on earth had sex, it seemed. Everyone except me. And now I was apparently a circus freak, because everyone was talking about me.

I scribbled something ridiculous for my journal prompt. I couldn't concentrate on it. I hissed to Toby, "Everyone's staring at us."

Toby looked around as if he hadn't noticed. "No, they're not," he whispered back.

"Toby, Azazel," said Ms. Campbell, "please don't talk."

I could feel the gaze of everyone in the class on me as I wrote. I couldn't concentrate as we discussed the journal. I could hear that Jason was saying something. As always, Ms. Campbell thought it was brilliant. I prayed that she would not call on me. I couldn't concentrate on anything.

Luckily, she decided to move the class along before she

got to me. "Well," said Ms. Campbell, "as you guys probably guessed, I want to discuss this journal in terms of *1984* ." She picked up her copy of the novel and leaned forward on her podium. "Winston says that sex is a rebellion. Desire, Winston thinks, is 'thoughtcrime.'"

No one said anything.

"Oh come on, guys," Ms. Campbell. "I know you're all teenagers, and it's weird to talk about sex, but you're seniors. This an AP class. What are your thoughts on that?"

Eve Newcomb tentatively raised her hand. "I guess he's right?" she asked. Eve had a way of answering every question with a question. "The Party doesn't want him to have sex with Julia? And when he does, he starts rebelling against everything?"

"Okay," said Ms. Campbell. "But is sex itself a rebellion? Or is it only a rebellion if society tells us that we shouldn't have sex?"

Jason raised his hand. "Obviously, you can't rebel against something by doing what it tells you to do," he said. "So it's got to be because society says so."

Ms. Campbell considered. "Everybody agree with Jason?" she asked.

Lisa Huron spoke up. Lisa was one of those know-it-all girls who seemed to like to argue with Jason just because he was Jason. She hated that Ms. Campbell seemed to think Jason was so brilliant. "I think sex is rebellion in general," she said. "It's Freudian. I mean it's the way the ego symbolically eradicates the shadow of the father figure. By symbolically copulating with a mother figure stand in."

Ms. Campbell nodded. "Well, no one's gonna deny that Freud was a brilliant man, Lisa. But let's all keep in mind that he did do a lot of cocaine."

Everyone laughed.

"What I'm getting at," said Ms. Campbell, "is that I'm again trying to see if we can find parallels between our society and the society Orwell predicted in *1984*."

According to Ms. Campbell, Orwell had predicted text messages. They were newspeak. Ms. Campbell was cool, but sometimes she just dug a little too deep.

"He was wrong about this," said Lisa, "because in our society, we aren't forbidden to have sex."

"No," said Jason, "but maybe it's just backwards. I mean, if you live in a society where you're sexually repressed, then having sex is an act of rebellion. But if you live in a society where sex is condoned and encouraged, then the opposite would be true."

"So not having sex would be an act of rebellion?" asked Ms. Campbell.

Half of the class snickered. I looked around. They were staring at me. Suddenly, I knew what this was all about. I should never have confided in Eve and Sherry. Those girls had big mouths. Everyone was laughing at me because Toby and I weren't having sex. I wanted the earth to open up and swallow me whole.

Ms. Campbell furrowed her brow. "Why is that funny?" she asked.

"I don't think it's funny at all," said Jason. "Actually, if someone did that in a permissive society like ours, I think it would be brave."

He was looking right at me. Jason was taking up for me. That was cool of him. I caught his eyes for a moment, trying to communicate that I was grateful.

"Am I hearing you right?" asked Ms. Campbell. "Jason, you're saying that in today's society, abstinence is a form of rebellion?"

"Kind of," said Jason.

Later on, in French class, I intercepted a note that was making its rounds across the class. It said, "Azazel Jones has a deformed pussy." I crumpled it up and stared straight ahead. This was awful.

I barely made it to lunch, and when I did, I exploded to Toby in the lunch line, "I can't take this!"

Toby seemed confused. "Take what? Why are you upset?"

I showed him the note.

He uncrumpled it. "This is kind of messed up," he said, finally sounding a little concerned.

"Kind of?" I said. "I happen to mention to Sherry and Eve last night that we aren't having sex, and now I'm *deformed* ?!"

We took our trays off the rack and proceeded into the kitchen.

Toby looked confused as he slid his tray along in front of the cafeteria workers. "How are those things even related?"

He looked across at one of the cooks. "No jello, okay?"

"They said that there was no way you wouldn't want to have sex with me unless something was wrong with me," I told him. "And now everyone thinks something's wrong with me."

"Jesus," said Toby. "I can't believe those girls." He shook his head, looking angry for a second. Then he stopped. "Why'd you tell them that anyway?"

"They were talking about having sex with their boyfriends," I said. "They asked me a question. I couldn't relate, what was I supposed to say?"

"Say it's private," said Toby. "Say it's none of their business."

"Is that what you say?" I demanded. We emerged from the kitchen, carrying our lunch trays.

We started across the cafeteria to our regular table. Several of the girls spotted us as we approached. They huddled together, speaking in voices too low to hear. Then they burst into laughter.

I stopped. "I can't eat at that table," I said.

"Oh geez, you don't even know if they were talking about you," said Toby.

"I do know," I said. "I'm not even hungry anyway."

I dumped my tray in the trashcan and tore out of the cafeteria and through the halls. There was a little alcove behind the gym that I knew about. Maybe nobody would see me if I just went there and cried.

There was no one in the alcove. I leaned against the wall.

Rested my head against it. This had to be the worst day of my entire life. Why was everyone being so awful? When I'd thought that I was the oldest virgin on earth, I'd been exaggerating. Surely there were other girls in school who hadn't had sex. Surely I wasn't the only girl. And I couldn't be the only person who thought it was okay to be a virgin, could I? I slid down the wall and covered my face with my hands.

Someone rounded the corner, calling my name. I expected it to be Toby. I expected that he would have followed me. But it wasn't. It was Jason.

"Hey," I said, feeling dangerously close to tears.

"Hey," he said. "I, um, saw you run out of the cafeteria. I'm sorry everybody's being so awful."

"It's not your fault," I said. Jason was being nice to me, and that didn't do anything to stop the impending flood of tears. They started to leak out of my eyes. I brushed them away angrily. "It's just stupid," I said. "I hate it. I feel like everyone else has done it and that they're right. Something is wrong with me."

Jason sat down next to me. "Well, not everyone else has done it," he said.

"I know, but it just seems ..." Then I realized he was admitting something to me. "Oh," I said.

He smiled at me. "I've never even had a girlfriend," he said.

"Really?" I said. "But you're so ..."

"Weird," he said.

"No, you're not," I said. But hadn't I said about him, thought that about him, too many times to count? "That wasn't what I was going to say. You're ... smart and brave and strong and you're ... you know, very attractive."

Jason laughed. "Right," he said sarcastically. "Sure."

"I'm serious," I said.

"Stop. I came here to cheer *you* up, not the other way around."

I smiled. "Well, whatever you did, it kind of worked." I wasn't crying anymore.

"Cool," he said.

We were quiet for a couple minutes.

"You know, Azazel," he said, "I don't know if I ever really told you how grateful I am that you found me when you did. And that you took me back to your house and ... This ... all of this, the school, your parents, everything. It's so great. I always wanted to have a life like this. And it's because of you."

"What?" I said. "I just did what—"

"Who's back there?" interrupted a voice.

A teacher? Weren't we allowed back here at lunch?

But it was Adam Neels and Joe Anthony, the two worst troublemakers in our school. They practically lived in ISS. They stood in front of us, with their greasy hair and camouflaged jackets and pimply faces, and I could just tell this wasn't going to be good. How was I supposed to know this was their spot?

Jason and I both stood up.

"Oh," said Adam. "It's Azazel Jones with one of the foster fucks."

"We're going," I said.

"No, it's cool," said Joe. "You two can stay."

"Hey Azazel," said Adam. "I hear that you don't have a cunt, and that's why your dumbass boyfriend can't figure out how to fuck you."

"No," said Joe, "that's not what I heard. I heard she's actually a dude. Her mom just makes her dress up in girl clothes."

Jason folded his arms over his chest. "Don't talk to her like that," he said calmly.

"What are you gonna do about it?" asked Joe, advancing on Jason.

Joe was at least a head taller than Jason, and much wider. Standing next to Jason, Joe looked like an overgrown oaf.

"Yeah," said Adam, coming closer to me. "You packing a dick in those jeans, Azazel? Why don't you let us see?"

Adam took another step forward, and his face was right in my face, and his hands were on my waist. I flattened myself against the wall, terrified. What was he going to do? Should I scream?

"Don't touch her," said Jason's voice, still quiet and calm.

Adam whipped his head around to face Jason. "Her?" he mocked. "You sure that she's a her?"

It happened so fast. Jason drove his fist into Adam's face.

Adam yelled and backed away, his hand going to his lip, which was gushing blood. Joe lumbered for Jason, but Jason nimbly ducked under Joe's outstretched arms. Behind Joe now, he gripped the back of Joe's neck and slammed Joe's forehead into the wall. Then Jason reached out, took my hand, and pulled me away from the alcove.

"Let's get out of here," he said.

We hurried out into the crowded gym. I looked behind us, expecting Adam and Joe to be hot in pursuit. But they weren't there. I stared at Jason, stunned.

It had been so matter of fact. So precise. He hadn't thought. He'd just acted. He'd quickly and neatly dispatched both of the boys. Jason hadn't even broken a sweat.

"Are you okay?" he asked me.

"Fine," I said, dazed. I couldn't believe he'd just done that.

"People are jerks," he muttered.

* * *

Apparently, Joe and Adam were so embarrassed that they'd been bested by one guy half their size that they didn't tell anyone about the incident. Unsure of why, I didn't say anything either. Not even to Toby. Especially not to Toby. I wasn't sure why I didn't say anything to Toby. It just seemed like it wouldn't be a good idea. He'd probably feel guilty for not being there to protect me. And it was weird that he hadn't come after me in the first place, wasn't it?

It took a week, but the rumors about my gender and deformed genitals eventually died down at school. People were starting to focus on Homecoming, which was only a week away. The dance happened to coincide with Halloween, and the girls that Toby and I ate with were buzzing with theme ideas. They wanted the Homecoming Dance to be a costume ball. It sounded okay, as far as I was concerned. I didn't know what I was going to dress up as. There was one clear silver lining in the whole set up. If there was a Homecoming Dance on Halloween, my parents couldn't force me to attend one of their lame parties.

Actually, I hadn't heard any talk about a party from my parents. Apparently, a party hadn't been their big plan for Halloween. Or, if it had, it was no longer on the table.

The big news at home was that the state was going to let us keep Jason. He was officially registered in their system now, and there was no chance of the arm of the law swooping down and sending him to a shelter or something. I hadn't really thought that would happen. Jason wouldn't stay in a shelter. There was just no way. He would just run off.

I still knew next to nothing about Jason. I'd started waking up early on Sundays, trying to catch him alone again. But he was never awake anymore, and there wasn't anything good on TV on Sunday morning. Sometimes, I formulated theories about Jason. He'd said he was running from a group of people who were like Freemasons with guns. I wondered if they were the Illuminati. The Illuminati was a secret society that controlled everything on earth. They had ties to numerous world governments. They pulled hidden strings.

But that didn't make sense. Why would the Illuminati be looking for Jason? I considered the facts. Jason was very, very smart. He was educated. Someone had taken pains to make sure Jason was well read. That sounded like something the Illuminati might do, but again ... why Jason? Jason also was skilled in hand-to-hand combat. He had excellent control over his emotions. I'd never seen him angry. None of that fit with the Illuminati.

Sometimes, I thought Jason was a robot, a secret prototype that the government had created to be a killing machine or something. I speculated that Jason maybe didn't know he was a robot. That was why he'd been told this story about his mother, who was dead, and all of that. He thought he was human, but actually he was a machine.

I didn't think that was really true.

But it bothered me. Who was this boy who lived in my house? Why couldn't I crack his secrets? And why didn't anyone else seem as concerned as I was with figuring out who he was and where he came from?

Jason had blended into my family. He ate like the rest of the Jones boys. He played video games with them, even participated in their good-natured teasing. He did his chores. He was respectful to my parents. To my knowledge, he hadn't gone out to any parties or been drinking since the incident at the Nelson farm. But even though he seemed like a regular kid—albeit an obedient, responsible one—there was something about him that just seemed, well, different.

He was quiet a lot. He was separate. Even when he was laughing, he didn't seem ... happy. He seemed haunted. I thought that something very bad had happened to Jason at some point in his life. I wanted to know what it was, but at the same time, if it had damaged Jason so deeply, maybe I didn't.

Halloween and the dance loomed. Lilith was excited about it, even though she didn't have a date. "I'll go solo if no one asks," she said. "Then I won't be stuck dancing with the same stupid boy all night." She wanted to find a costume, and she invited me to go shopping with her.

Since Bramford was in the middle of nowhere, we had drive forty-five minutes to Cumberland, Maryland to do any decent shopping. Lilith was excited on the way up, chattering about her various costume options.

"I'm thinking," she said, "slutty nurse, or maybe slutty cheerleader, or maybe just slut."

I laughed. "Lilith, you know there's a dress code for this dance."

She sighed. "I know. And it drives me nuts. Halloween is the one night of the year where you can get away with wearing next to nothing, and this dance is just raining on my parade."

I had no idea what I was going to dress up as. I'd tried to get some ideas from Toby. I thought it might be kind of cute if we had matching costumes. But Toby had decided to dress up as Michael Myers, and I was so not dressing up as a helpless victim. So that idea was out.

"I know exactly what you should dress up as," said Lilith. "The Virgin Mary."

"Lilith!" I exclaimed. "That's so mean. Why would you say that?"

"Oh, it's a joke! It'll show all those bitches at school that you don't care what they say about you. It would be hilarious."

"No way," I said. "But maybe a Vestal virgin."

Lilith laughed. "Really?"

I thought about it. "Vestal virgins are way sexier than the Virgin Mary," I said.

Lilith allowed me that.

Our first stop was the Goodwill store, in order to find cheap pieces that would make up the bulk of our costumes. We'd spend more money on accessories. All of this was Lilith's scheming. I didn't think about things like this. I hit the racks, looking for something that looked kind of like a toga. I didn't even know what Vestal virgins looked like. I figured it didn't matter. No one else would know what they looked like either. After all, they hadn't been around for over a thousand years.

Lilith combed the store on her own. We met up twenty minutes later at the dressing rooms with our arms full of clothes. I had about four different options. Lilith maybe had ten. I finished before she did. I'd found a dress that I thought would work pretty well. It was white and gathered at an empire waist. It draped in several different layers. It didn't look exactly like a toga, but it was close enough. While I was evaluating each new dress that Lilith tried on, I talked to Lilith. And before I knew it, the whole story about Jason beating up Adam and Joe just came pouring out.

I hadn't meant to tell Lilith about it. Not because I usually kept things from her. It was just that the story was embarrassing. I didn't like to think about the things that Adam and Joe had said. I didn't like to think about the look in Adam's eyes when he was close to me or his hands on my waist. Or about what might have happened if Jason wasn't there. But it felt weird keeping something like that from my best friend. I told Lilith everything.

When I got to the part about Jason punching Adam, Lilith threw open the door to the dressing room, half-dressed. "You are fucking kidding me!" she exclaimed.

Everyone in the entire Goodwill seemed to hear her. They looked up from the children's clothing section. From the furniture section. From the cashier's desk.

"Sorry," said Lilith. She smiled in embarrassment. To me, quieter, she said, "So, how come nobody heard about this?"

"Well, I guess no one said anything."

Lilith ducked back in the dressing room. When she emerged, she was back in her own clothes. "I'm gonna go with the first thing I tried on," she said.

Hmm. It wasn't like Lilith to decide so quickly. She hung up the other clothes she didn't want on the rack to be restocked. Then she took my hands. "Look, Zaza," she said, "I don't think it's a good idea for you to spend too much time with Jason."

She seemed so serious. When was Lilith ever this serious? I took my hands out of hers. "I don't spend much time with him," I said.

"Okay," she said. "But, you know, maybe you shouldn't get too attached."

"Attached?" Lilith was just acting weirder and weirder. I felt like I hardly knew my best friend. "What do you mean?"

"It just seems like you like him a lot, that's all," she said, surveying the dress she was about to purchase. It seemed like she was purposefully not looking at me.

"He's interesting," I said. "That's all."

"Well, he just might not be around forever, you know?"

"What do you mean?"

She dropped the dress to her side, heaving a huge sigh. "Oh, God, Zaza, I can't really talk about it, but you just have to trust me."

"Why can't you talk about it?"

"I'm not allowed," she said.

That was it! Lilith had said that before. She'd said she wasn't allowed to get it on with Jason. And then Toby had said he wasn't allowed to have sex with me. And now Lilith wasn't allowed to talk about something? What was going on here? "Who says you're not allowed?" I asked.

"God, I need to shut up," Lilith muttered.

"No, you need to explain yourself," I said. "You really, really do."

Lilith held up her dress again. She held it up against

herself and looked in the mirror. "Trust me, okay? I know what I'm talking about."

"Well, I don't know what you're talking about," I said. I was getting frustrated. Were both Lilith and Toby being told what to do by the same authority? What was it? Or was I grasping at straws? Trying to put something together when there was nothing there at all?

Lilith looked at me. "Everything's gonna be better after Halloween, okay? This thing with Toby, everybody making fun of you, all of it. After Halloween, you'll see. None of it will matter."

"Why? What's going to happen at Halloween?"

"I can't," said Lilith. "I told you too much already. Just believe me." She looked around the store. "And don't tell anybody I said this to you."

And that was all. And try as I might, I couldn't force Lilith to even acknowledge she'd said what she'd said, let alone elaborate on it.

Chapter Six

michaela666 (10:24:05): this is getting out of control. he's got too high of a profile. people are going to notice if he disappears.

morningstar68 (10:24:43): we're trying to keep as much of a lid on it as we can. you of all people should understand this is a delicate matter we're dealing with. not all of the coven is even behind it.

michaela666 (10:25:12): screw the coven then. this has to be done. With or without their support. now I know I can count on you, can't I?

morningstar68 (10:26:30): I told you. samhain. it'll be done.

michaela666 (10:26:54): You're sure it can't be sooner?

morningstar68 (10:27:01): it's going to be next to impossible to pull off as it is.

Toby and I were parked in his truck again. It was getting colder outside. Almost too cold to make out in cars. We hadn't done much kissing since everyone at school had made fun of me. We'd barely talked about it. I didn't know what to say. It wasn't Toby's fault, but I still wished he'd been a little more sympathetic. He hadn't seemed to care that everyone in school had made so much fun of me. I hadn't pushed the issue, however. I couldn't be mad at Toby all the time. He was Toby, after all. I loved him. I couldn't expect him to be perfect.

So, I was glad to have some time alone with him in the car, even if we weren't kissing right now or talking. Instead we were sitting in awkward silence, neither sure of what to say or do.

Lately, I'd been wondering why Toby and I were dating at all. I couldn't figure out what it was we had in common. Sure our parents had been friends since we'd been kids. When we were younger, we'd played together. We'd always gone to same schools. But Toby played football. He'd always hung out with the jocks and cheerleaders. I was kind of a nerd. And I didn't have any close friends besides Lilith. While I'd never been unpopular, I kind of was beginning to think that most of the people who hung out with me only did because I was Toby's girlfriend.

I couldn't even figure out why we'd started dating. My last year in middle school, eighth grade, Toby and I had barely spoken. When we crossed each other in the halls, we didn't even smile at each other. And that summer, I hadn't seen much of him. Even when our parents got together, Toby hadn't been there. So it was weird that right after Halloween my freshman year, Toby had started calling me. At the time, I'd never even thought about Toby in that way. But he'd been so persistent. Like he was convinced we were destined to be together. I hadn't had the energy to fight him. I hadn't even felt like I should. And now here we were, four years later. Still together. But what had we talked about for four years? Did Toby even know who my favorite author was? Did we even like to watch the same kinds of television shows? Did I even know him?

Especially after what Lilith had said to me in the Goodwill, I worried that I didn't know Toby. I worried that he was keeping something from me. So, I couldn't help it. I had to ask him. I knew I shouldn't. I knew that it wouldn't get me anywhere. But he was my boyfriend, and I loved him, and I couldn't bear the thought that he was keeping secrets from me.

"Toby?" I said.

"Yeah?" He sounded relieved that I was starting to talk. The silence between us had been palpable.

"What did you mean, that time we were making out and you said you weren't allowed to have sex with me?"

He looked away sharply. "I don't know what you're talking about," he said.

"In your room. After the fight we had. A couple of weeks ago."

He shook his head. "I didn't say that."

"But you did. You did." I paused, then plowed on. "Toby, who's telling you that you aren't allowed to do things with me?"

"Look, you're crazy. It's not like that. I told you already, we'll have sex when it's the right time. I don't feel like having this argument with you again."

"That's not even what this is about," I said. It wasn't. I was just trying to figure out what his cryptic statement had meant. What Lilith's statement had meant. What were they hiding? Were they connected?

Toby started the car. "If you're gonna be like this, I'm just taking you home."

"But ..." I was surprised by the violence of his response. There was no reason for him to get upset. "I don't want to have the argument about sex either," I said. "I just want to know why you said that."

"I didn't say that. You heard me wrong."

"I know you said it," I said. "I remember. I remember distinctly."

"You heard me wrong," he insisted. He was backing up his truck.

"Toby, why won't you talk to me about this?" I asked.

"There's nothing to talk about," he said.

And he drove me home. And dropped me off. And it was eight o'clock in the evening. I wandered down the driveway to my house, noting that both my parents' cars were gone. It was Monday. Sometimes they went to dinner at the Tompkins' house on Mondays. I let myself in the front door. "Hello?" I called out.

No one answered.

They might have taken the guys to the Tompkins' house. Leroy Tompkins was about their age. He had a Gamecube or something. Video games excited my foster brothers.

I turned on the light in the kitchen. The dishes were still in the sink, unwashed. Chance and Cameron had left a baseball bat, mitt and ball on the counter. They'd been hitting fly balls in the yard that afternoon. Yeah, no one was home. My mother wouldn't have allowed the boys to leave their sports' equipment around if she hadn't been planning on going out. I opened the refrigerator door. I wasn't really hungry, but I was kind of bored. There was some salsa on the refrigerator door. I got it out, poured some in a bowl, and found some chips in the cabinet. Idly, I took my food into the dining room and sat down at the table. I dipped a chip into the salsa and took a bite. The chip crunched as I chewed. What the hell was wrong with Toby? I shook my head and thrust another chip into the salsa.

"Azazel," said a voice.

I started.

It was Jason. "Hey," he said. "I thought you were out with Toby."

"I was," I said. "Until he got pissed at me and dropped me off."

"Sorry," said Jason.

I gestured to the salsa. "You want some?"

Jason sat down next to me and got a chip. Dipping it in the salsa, he asked, "You and Toby had a fight?"

"Whatever," I said. "I feel like all we do is fight." And it didn't used to be like this. Did it? Had our relationship always been so ... cold? Why had I ever fallen in love with him?

Jason pushed his chip into his mouth and chewed. He shrugged. "Dump him," he said.

I laughed. "Like I could do that," I said.

"It would be easy," said Jason. "Just send him a text

message: 'Sorry. I'm not in love with you anymore. Have a nice life.'"

I rolled my eyes. "You're joking." Besides, I didn't even have a cell phone. My parents couldn't afford to give all of us kids one, so no one got one.

"Sort of," he said. "You don't seem happy when you're around him, Azazel."

"Don't I?" I asked.

"Well, sometimes you do. But not most of the time. Most of the time, he just seems to upset you."

Jason was kind of right, wasn't he? I munched on a chip thoughtfully. Lately, every time I'd been upset, Toby had had something to do with it. But could I break up with Toby? I still remembered the story my mother had told me about her and my dad. I didn't want Toby to move on. I did care about him. I couldn't break up with him. "I can't break up with him," I said to Jason. "I love him."

Jason nodded. "Guess that's a good reason not to break up, then," he said. He scooped up some more salsa with a chip. "I'm sure you'll figure out how to handle it. Maybe you two are just ... I don't know, growing as people or something."

I laughed a little at the cliché. But maybe he was right. For someone who claimed never to have been in a relationship, Jason seemed to have some insight into relationships.

"You're a good guy, Jason," I said. "So, how come you've never had a girlfriend?"

Jason didn't answer for a minute. He looked a little surprised at the change of topic. "Well, for one thing, I guess I was just never really around girls."

"Because you were home schooled," I said.

"Yeah, kind of," he said.

"So you mostly just saw your family?" I asked, even though I knew both of Jason's parents were dead.

"Not my family, exactly. A man named Anton raised me. He was kind of like a father to me. And a teacher."

Jason was opening up. Neat. Curious, I pressed my advantage. "So he's the one who taught you all the stuff you know?"

"Yeah."

"So, why'd you run away from him?"

"I didn't. He died."

Oh. "I'm sorry," I said. Damn it, that was right! Jason had said something about that before. Why was I such an idiot? He'd probably just clam up now.

But Jason kept talking. "Anton knew a lot of things, and he taught me all about them. But he really didn't know much about ... women. Or relationships or any of that."

I didn't know what to say. "I'm sorry," I said again.

"After he died, that's when I took off," said Jason. "And once I was on the run, I couldn't hang out with girls either."

"Is that why you ran? Because of Anton?"

"I can't talk about it," said Jason.

Damn it.

But then he continued. "I watched him die. He died in

my arms."

Oh my God. That was horrible. I couldn't say I was sorry again, so I didn't speak.

Jason had a faraway look in his eyes. "They thought they could contain me after that, but they forgot that they trained me, and I know all their secrets."

"Who?" I asked. I couldn't help it.

Jason took a chip out of the bag and stared at it. He took a deep breath. I waited, anxious to know something, anything, more about him.

And there was a knock on the front door.

Augh. I couldn't believe we'd been interrupted just when Jason was on the brink of revealing something. Besides, who could be knocking on the door after eight o'clock on a Monday? "I wonder who that is," I said.

"It's probably Toby," said Jason.

"At the front door?" I said. Toby knew we almost always used the door in the kitchen. Why would he come to the front door?

Jason looked alarmed. "Doesn't anyone you know use the front door?"

"Not really," I said. "Maybe it's a salesman."

"At this time of night?" Jason said. "Maybe we should just get out of here."

The knock came again, a little more insistent.

"And go where?" I asked. "Why?"

Jason swallowed. His eyes darted around the room, looking for danger or an exit or whatever it was he looked for when he was scared. I hadn't seen him do that in a while.

"You're paranoid," I told him. "I'll get rid of whoever it is." I got up and started for the living room.

"Azazel, wait!" said Jason. "You don't know who that could be."

But I was already crossing the living room to the front door. I swung it open. On the other side was a young man. He looked to be somewhere in his early twenties. His hair was short cropped against his head. He wore an expensive-looking jacket. His smile was warm and unassuming.

"Hello?" I said.

"Sorry to bother you this late," he said, smiling. He had a British accent.

"Can I help you?" I asked, feeling suspicious of the man.

The man shrugged. "Well, maybe. I hope so." He rubbed his hands together briskly. "It's a little bit cold out here. Would you mind if I came in for a moment?"

"Uh ..." I didn't want him to come in. "I'm here alone," I said.

"Really?" he said. "I thought I heard voices."

"It was the television," I said.

"Don't hear it now," he said. His voice sounded friendly, but there was something about this line of questioning. Something threatening.

"I switched it off." My suspiciousness about this man was growing.

"Well," he said. "I promise to be a gentleman." He held up his hands. "I'll keep both of these where you can see them at all times." He grinned at me again.

I didn't answer, but he pushed past me and into the house.

"What do you think you're doing?" I demanded. He was inside my house! How was I supposed to get him out?

"This will only take a moment," he said. I wanted to wipe that smug smile off his face.

"I think I want you to leave my house," I said.

"I just want to ask you a question," he said. He was looking around me at the living room.

"I didn't ask you to come in," I said. I was starting to feel scared. What if he didn't leave?

The man took several steps into the room. I tried to step in front of him, to block him. For some reason, I didn't want him going into the dining room where he might see Jason.

"Please leave," I said.

"I've lost my brother, you see," he said. "He's run away. I'm looking for him. I miss him very much."

"I haven't seen any British boys in this town ever," I said. "Now, please get out of my house." He wasn't leaving. He wasn't listening to me at all.

The man walked around me and into the dining room.

"I'm calling the police if you don't leave right now!" I nearly screamed, running after him.

But Jason wasn't in the dining room. My bag of chips and bowl of salsa sat at the table, all alone.

The man looked around. His shoulders slumped. "I'm sorry," he said to me. "I shouldn't have barged into your house. I just thought I heard ..." He trailed off. "I guess I was mistaken."

"You *shouldn't* have barged in," I said. "And you need to leave."

"Okay, I will," he said. "Just ... I have a picture, with my number? Might I leave it? If you see him, you could call me? I really do just want to help him."

"Get out," I said.

He took a picture out of his jacket pocket anyway and handed it to me. "And by the way, he's not British," he said. "He's my half-brother. He was raised in the States."

I took the picture and ushered him towards the door.

"I'm sorry," he said again. "I'm really sorry."

I pushed him out and slammed the door after him. I locked it. And the deadbolt. And then I slumped against the door in relief. My heart was pounding away in my chest. I had been so scared.

Jason ducked out of the dining room, brandishing the baseball bat from the kitchen like a weapon. "He's gone?" he asked.

I nodded.

"This is bad," said Jason. "This is very, very bad."

I looked down at the picture the man had given me. It was of Jason. He was a little younger. His hair was shorter. And he was smiling. His smile was radiant and free as if he didn't have a care in the world. I'd never seen Jason smile like that. But it was definitely Jason in the picture.

"Do you know that man?" I asked.

Jason clutched the bat, looking furious. He was shaking, all over. I'd never seen him so out of control.

"Jason? Is he your brother?"

"I don't have any brothers," Jason bit out. He stalked to the window in the living room. Pulled the curtain back a little and peered outside. "Fuck," he said.

"Jason, who was that man?"

He lowered the bat. Rubbed his face with one hand. "He was a very dangerous man," he said. "A very, very dangerous ..." He stopped and looked at me. "Call your parents. They need to come home *right now* ."

Terrified, I did what he said. Within ten minutes, my mom and dad, both looking very worried, were standing inside the kitchen with the two of us.

My mother gathered me into her arms. "Azazel, what happened?" she asked, her voice high pitched. "I've never heard you sound so scared. Sweetie, what happened?"

Jason was pacing the floor, his face a mask of anger. He didn't look like a seventeen-year-old boy. He looked like a commanding officer in the army. "Someone showed up here," he said. "Just like I was afraid someone would. I can't believe I was so stupid. I can't believe I thought I could just live here like I was normal and that nothing would happen."

"Jason, slow down," said my father.

Jason stopped pacing and pointed a finger at my father. "You have to keep all the doors locked all the time," he ordered. "And you can't let Azazel out of your sight. Or your wife. Or the other guys. You have to keep them here, and you can't let anyone in."

"Wait a second," shouted my dad. I was stunned. I'd never heard my father yell before. My parents weren't exactly yelling kind of parents.

My mother released me and went to my father, touching his arm. "Daniel," she said.

He shrugged her off.

Jason lowered his hand. He took a shuddering breath. I could tell he was trying to pull himself together.

"Now," said my dad, "you're going to start at the beginning, and you're going to tell me what happened."

Jason didn't say anything.

I moved forward and handed my dad the picture the man had given me. "A man came here looking for Jason," I said. "He pushed his way into the house, and I was afraid he wouldn't leave. Jason said he's dangerous."

My dad studied the picture. "Did this man threaten you, Zaza?"

"No," I said. "He was polite."

"Did you know the man, Jason?" my dad asked.

Jason didn't say anything.

"Jason," said my father sharply.

Jason nodded. "I know him."

"Who is he?" asked my dad.

"That's not important," said Jason.

"You're telling me to lock up my family, and you say it's not important for me to know who he is? I think it's important," said my dad.

"Just trust me," said Jason. "I've seen what this man can do."

" *What* can he do?" my father asked. His voice was steadily rising again. I didn't think I'd ever seen my dad this angry.

"I—" Jason broke off. He hung his head. Stared at the tile floor of the kitchen. Quietly, "I don't want to talk about it."

My mother put her hand on my father's arm again. "Daniel," she said, "maybe we should all just calm down. Now, I know it's a little early, but we're all excited. Maybe we should go to bed. We can talk about this tomorrow after we've had some time to think."

"Jodi, I need to know who this man is," said my dad. "I don't think we should just sleep on it."

"You can't keep pushing Jason," said my mom. "Look at him. He's very upset."

"I'm fine," said Jason. He looked up at us, and his face was a carefully controlled mask. He looked calm, collected. "I think sleeping on it might be a good idea, though."

Really? Jason had been so angry. Why didn't he want to talk more? I didn't think he'd convinced my dad of the danger he seemed to think we were in. I'd expected him to push and push until he got his way. Why was he just giving up?

"See?" said my mom. "Let's just all calm down."

My father took a sharp breath. "Fine," he said. "But first thing tomorrow morning, before school, we're getting this straightened out."

Jason nodded. "Mr. Jones, I'm so sorry I brought this on your family. You've all been wonderful to me. I never meant for anything like this to happen. I promise we'll talk about it tomorrow."

But the next morning, Jason was gone.

Chapter Seven

Nobody knew where Jason was.

Sheriff Damon was in our dining room, talking to my parents. I had just missed the bus to school, and I hadn't heard from Toby since last night. I had no idea if he was going to pick me up or not. I didn't even know if I was going to make it school. My mom had sent the guys out the door this morning. She'd even fed them a balanced breakfast. I had stayed behind in case the sheriff wanted to ask me some questions. Right now, I was in the living room. I could hear my parents talking to Sheriff Damon. I didn't know if I was supposed to be listening to them or not.

"A few other people in town say they spoke to a British man with a picture of Jason," said Sheriff Damon. "They probably sent him here."

It all made sense now. Why Jason had given up so easily when he was talking to my dad last night. Jason had been planning on leaving. He wouldn't stay here if he knew he was endangering us. I knew that much about him. I just wished I understood why he was running and what kind of danger he was in.

"Do we have any idea who this man is?" asked my mom.

No sound.

"None?" asked my mother, sounding desperate. Maybe Sheriff Damon had shaken his head.

"I'm sorry, Jodi," said the sheriff. "I know how important this boy is. To all of us."

Important? Weird way to put it.

"For all we know, then," said my dad, "this man got into the house last night and took Jason away."

Oh. I hadn't even considered that. I was sure that Jason had run away. But my dad was right. Jason could have been captured. Taken against his will. I gaped in horror at the thought of it.

"It's possible," said Sheriff Damon. "But let's not sell Jason short. You didn't see the number he did on the Nelson boy. I don't think anyone could have gotten Jason out of here without waking you all up."

He was right. Jason would have put up a fight. And Jason could fight. I knew that. I'd seen it first hand.

"Then we think he ran away," said my mother.

"Yes," said Sheriff Damon.

"Oh no," said my mom.

But Jason could take care of himself, couldn't he? He wouldn't end up hurt or ... worse. Would he? I couldn't stand this. I was suddenly very angry with Jason for leaving like this. Didn't he know how worried we'd all be? Didn't he think anyone else cared about him?

"Don't worry," said Sheriff Damon. "Finding Jason is my first priority. I've got all three of the deputies out there, and we're alerting the entire community by the radio and the internet to be on the look out for him."

"But Jim," said my mom, "this county is so big. He could slip out."

"We can't let him do that," said my dad. "We can't let him escape."

Escape? That was another strange way of putting things. Or maybe I was just distraught. I hoped that we could find Jason, but my mom was right. Jason could get away so easily. We didn't even know when he left or what kind of head start he had on us.

"We'll find him," said Sheriff Damon. "I'm doing everything in my power."

I wandered into the dining room. "I hope you do find him," I said. "I'm so worried."

"Azazel!" said my mother. "Have you been out there the whole time?"

"Yeah," I said.

"You missed the bus," she said.

"You told me to stay to talk to Sheriff Damon," I said.

"Oh," she said. "Right. Well, I guess I'll have to take you to school. Or is Toby coming?" But she didn't ask me that. She asked the sheriff.

"Aren't you going to school, Dad?" I asked.

He shook his head. "I'm taking the day off to help search for Jason."

"I want to help!" I said. "Please?"

"No," said my dad. "You need to go to school. And maybe you've been spending too much time with Jason, anyway." He turned to the sheriff. "Get Toby here."

"Don't worry," said Sheriff Damon. "He's on his way."

So Toby and I weren't fighting anymore? I was so confused. I couldn't even remember why we'd been fighting last night. But I wasn't sure if I wanted to see Toby. For some reason, I didn't think he'd like it that I was so concerned about Jason. Maybe I should—

But right then, Toby appeared at the kitchen door, dangling his truck keys.

"Azazel!" he exclaimed. He threw open the door and ran to me, gathering me in his arms.

Wow. This was weird. Wasn't Toby mad at me for some reason?

"I can't believe I dropped you off here, and that man almost got to you!" he said, covering my face with kisses. "If anything had happened to you, I never would have forgiven myself."

Me? "I'm fine," I said. It was Jason who wasn't fine. But I didn't say that out loud.

I pushed out of Toby's arms. I gave my parents a pleading look. "I don't think I can concentrate on school today," I said. "Please let me help look for Jason."

Toby pulled me back. "No way. That's way too dangerous. I'm not letting you out my sight."

"My thoughts exactly," said my dad.

So I went to school. Toby fawned over me the whole way there. I tried to respond to Toby. He seemed genuinely concerned about me. And I was grateful, especially since Toby had seemed distant lately. But I couldn't appreciate it since I was so worried. I tried to pay attention in class, but I was too distracted. I kept thinking about Jason wandering around in the woods somewhere, running from the man who'd been in my house last night.

In my imagination, Jason looked exactly like he had the first night I'd seen him, desperate and terrified, running for his life. The man didn't seem polite or civil anymore at all. In my mind, his face was twisted into an evil sneer, and he was gaining on Jason.

Try as I might, I couldn't help but picture him catching Jason. I imagined all kinds of unspeakable horrors that he imposed on the boy. Gunshots riddling Jason's body. The man stabbing Jason over and over like in a horror movie. Jason tied up and bloody. The man beating him or burning him or cutting him. It was horrible.

Ms. Campbell asked me to read my journal prompt in first block. I hadn't even written one. I just shook my head, muttering that I couldn't. In French, we had twenty minutes at the end of class to work on a translation. I tried to complete it, but the words kept swimming in front of my eyes, changing places with each other, sinking into the page. In history, my father's substitute put on a movie. Unfortunately, it was a documentary about the Holocaust. Watching those people be tortured and killed on the screen only fueled my macabre fantasies. I almost left the room three times, and towards the end of class, I broke down in tears.

The bell rang, and I just sat in my desk with my head down, my shoulders shaking as I sobbed.

Toby touched my back. "Was it that bad?" he asked. "Did that man scare you that bad?"

I lifted my tearstained face. "No, it's not me," I said. "I'm worried about Jason. I can't imagine what's happening to him right now."

Toby pulled his hand back like I'd burned him. "Oh," he said.

I didn't say anything else. But I didn't understand why Toby wasn't worried about Jason. Sure, he didn't seem to like him very much, but Jason was a human being. Surely Toby had to respect that much at least. Even if he didn't like Jason, he couldn't wish him pain, could he?

I mopped at my face and got up. We went to lunch. Lilith met me in the lunch line. She and Toby stared each other down. I knew Lilith wished Toby would leave me with her, and I also knew that Toby wasn't going to go anywhere without me. They were going to have to put up with each other if they wanted to be around me. They glared at each other, then both broke eye contact.

Lilith focused on me. "God, Zaza, are you okay? Have you been *crying* ?"

"I'm fine," I said.

"It must have been awful," she said. "That weird man in your house. You must be so freaked out."

I nodded. She could think what she wanted.

"She's worried about Jason," said Toby in a flat voice.

Lilith met Toby's eyes, a look of concern on her face. "Really?" she asked.

Toby nodded.

Why weren't they at each other's throats? I hadn't heard them speak one civil word to each other in four years.

Lilith looked back at me. "Zaza," she said, "I thought I told you not to get attached to him."

"You did what?" demanded Toby.

Lilith looked back at him. "He saved her from Adam and Joe one day. She seemed ... I didn't know what to say to her."

"Adam and Joe," repeated Toby, confused. He turned to me. "Why didn't you tell me about that?"

I shrugged. That seemed so long ago. Like another life. What did it matter now, anyway?

"You shouldn't have done that," Toby said.

I glared at him. "I didn't want you to get like this," I said.

"I meant Lilith," said Toby, shooting her a loaded gaze.

"I guess not," said Lilith. "Didn't make any difference anyway."

There was something about their conversation that was strange, but I couldn't think about it, because I was still too worried about Jason. Even as I watched them talk, a new horror occurred to me. Maybe the man wasn't alone. Maybe there was a group of them. Maybe they would capture Jason and torture him and then hang him by his neck in the woods somewhere, and no one would find his body but the birds —

I gasped, covering my mouth with my hand, banishing the image from my brain. If anything happened to Jason, I didn't know what I'd do. I couldn't handle it. I needed to know if he was okay. I needed to be *doing* something. I was going to sneak out of school and go look for him. I had to. I couldn't stay here any longer. I was going crazy.

"She's right, though, Azazel," Toby said.

What? Right about what? What was he talking about?

"You shouldn't get attached to him," Toby said.

"I'm not attached," I exploded. "I'm just worried. He's a human being, for God's sake. I don't think it's criminal that I want him to be okay."

"You're a mess," said Toby. "You can't concentrate on anything." As if to prove his point, he nudged me forward in the lunch line.

I walked forward, annoyed. "Look," I said, "if this was happening to any of the guys, I'd be worried like this. They might be foster kids, but they're like my brothers." Even as I said it, though, I wondered if it were true. Was I a mess?

Was I unnaturally worried about Jason? I did care for him, very much. But were my feelings toward Jason really brotherly?

I didn't have time to contemplate it further, because our principal came into the cafeteria. He stood in the center of the room and motioned for quiet. It took several minutes, but eventually, a hush came over the cafeteria.

"I have an announcement," said the principal. "I know many of you have heard that one of our students, Jason Wodden, is missing. A team has been looking for him all morning. I'm pleased to announce that the search is over. Jason has been found and is currently in his foster parents' custody."

I started to cry again. I couldn't help it. I was so relieved.

The principal went on. "This means that all events cancelled by members of the search party are now back in session. Bus 56 will run as scheduled this evening on its regular route, since Mr. Gafferty won't be out on the search. Thank you."

They'd found Jason! They'd found Jason. I was so glad. All of that worry, and he was okay. He was at home. He wasn't dead. I'd never felt so grateful in my life. I closed my eyes, letting the tears rush out.

I realized I had to see him. "Toby," I said, "you have to take me home."

Toby didn't look pleased with my reaction to the news or my request. "It's the middle of the school day," he said.

"You're eighteen. You can sign yourself out," I said.

"But you're not eighteen. You can't sign yourself out," he countered.

"Who cares?" I said. "Let's just leave."

"If they catch us, we'll get ISS," he said.

"I don't care!" I said.

"No," he said. "I'm not taking you. Now, let's get lunch."

"Fine," I said. "Lilith, you take me."

Lilith bit her lip. "Zaza, I don't think that's a good idea," she said.

"Come on," I said. "Like you care about ISS."

She considered. "Usually, I'm all about skipping school, but I just don't think that you should rush home to see Jason. He's probably not in the mood for company, and—"

"I'll walk," I said. Both my boyfriend and my best friend were completely insane. Couldn't they see how important this was to me? And furthermore, didn't they care to see if Jason was okay? What was wrong with them?

"I'll take you," Toby said. He didn't sound happy about it though.

I hugged him hard. "Thank you," I said. "Thank you so much."

"And this is when you hug me," he muttered. "Great."

I stood on my tiptoes and kissed him. "You're the best boyfriend ever," I said.

"Because I'll help you ditch school to see another guy?"

I rolled my eyes. "You know it's not like that. I thought you were over this jealousy thing."

Lilith shook her head at him. "I can't believe you're doing this," she said to him.

"Shut up, Lilith," said Toby.

That was more like the Toby-Lilith exchanges I was used to. Jason was found and everything was back to normal. The world was perfect. I took Toby's hand. "Let's go," I said.

"Right now?" asked Toby. "But we haven't eaten lunch yet."

"I can't eat right now. I'm too excited," I said.

I was terrified teachers would stop us in the halls or in the parking lot. But both the halls and the parking lot were empty. Once we were in Toby's truck, the drive back to my house seemed to take hours and hours. I thought it would never end. On our way, I wondered how Jason was. Had he been hurt at all? Had he run away or had he been captured? If he'd been captured, had he gotten away? Would he look dirty and tired? Would he just want to sleep? Would he tell me everything?

Fat chance of that. Jason never told me *anything* .

Finally, however, we did make it back to my house. Toby didn't come in. "I'm going back to school," he grumbled. "Maybe if I go back, I won't get in as much trouble."

That was fine with me. Toby dropped me at the top of my driveway, and I ran all the way down the hill to the door. I burst inside.

My mother and father were in the kitchen with Sheriff Damon, two of the deputies, several members of the search party, and, yes, Jason. But Jason was handcuffed. There were scratches on his face. His clothes were a little worse for wear. And the expression on his face was not happy.

I didn't care. I was so happy to see him, I bounded across the room and flung my arms around him. He couldn't hug me back because his arms were handcuffed behind his back. But he did smile when he saw me.

"You're okay," I said. "I was so worried."

"I'm fine," he said.

I pulled back and looked into his eyes, shaking my head. "I'm so glad you're okay. You have no idea what I thought might have happened to you."

"Nothing happened," he said, and he grinned at me. His grin looked like the grin in the picture. A real grin, not like his usual brief one.

"What are you doing here?" asked my dad.

And both Jason's and my grins faded.

I turned on my father. "I had to see for myself," I said.

"You should be at school."

"Dad!" I said. "I risked ISS to get here. I'm willing accept the consequences of my actions, nonproductive as they may be."

"Your mother's taking you back to school," he said.

"No she's not!" I said. "I'm staying here. And why is Jason handcuffed?"

My father strode over to me, took my by the arm and led me out of the house. What was wrong with him? My dad never forced me to do things. My parents always wanted me to make my own decisions. And I'd made my own decision.

They couldn't make me go back to school!

But they did.

* * *

Later that evening, I was sprawled on my bed in my room working on the French assignment I couldn't get done earlier. Someone knocked on my door.

"Come in," I called.

Jason came into my room. He sat down on the bed next to me. Startled, I sat up straight. He was very close to me, and my eyes settled on different areas of his body. His shoulders were broad. His forearms were covered in downy dark hair. His fingers were thick and powerful. I shook myself. Forced myself to look at his face. "Hi," I said.

"Azazel, you have to help me get out of here," he said.

"What?" I said. "No." After all of that, after I'd just gotten him back, there was no way I was helping him leave again. I wanted him as close as possible. I couldn't handle the worry.

"You don't understand," he said. "It's not safe for me to be here. If anything happened to you—to your family—I wouldn't ever be able to forgive myself."

I hadn't had any time to talk to Jason. Dinner had been a boisterous affair, full of the regular noise my large family made. Somehow, the subject of Jason's escape had been avoided over mounds of spaghetti and meatballs. We hadn't talked about my leaving school early to come see him either. Instead, my mother had dominated the conversation, asking the guys all about their schoolwork. Since that was the last thing they actually wanted to talk about, they'd tried to change the subject often, without much success. My mom was persistent. After dinner, I'd gone back to my room to work on the huge pile of homework I had. Now I had Jason to myself. "What happened, Jason?" I asked. "Did you run away? Did that man take you away?"

"I left," he said. "I haven't seen Hallam since last night."

"Hallam?"

"That's his name," said Jason.

I nodded.

"Sheriff Damon says that no one else has seen him since yesterday either, but that doesn't mean anything," said Jason. "He's out there. And he's not going to give up until he finds me. That's why you have to help me get out of here."

"I'm not helping you run off so that man—Hallam—can get you," I said. "If I did that, and something happened to you , I wouldn't be able to forgive *myself* ."

He sighed. "I can look after myself," he said. "I'd be fine. But here ... I'm like a trapped rat."

It was true. Jason was practically on house arrest. He could go to school and come home. That was it. "Even if I wanted to," I said, "I couldn't." I gestured to Jason's ankle, where he wore an ankle monitor.

Jason glowered at the little black device. "Sheriff Damon was excited about putting this on me," he said. "Apparently, the department never gets to use it."

If Jason went anywhere besides school, the ankle

monitor would send a signal to the police. It also transmitted his location, so that they could track him down.

"How would you get around the monitor?" I asked.

"I'd have to get it off," he said. "If I could do that, would you help me?"

"How would you get it off?"

"It's not indestructible. Of course, after I took it off, they'd know and come for me immediately." He ran a hand through his hair in frustration. "Maybe you're right. Maybe it's hopeless."

Another thought occurred to me. "Do you want to leave?" Maybe Jason just didn't like it here.

He turned to me. "No," he said. "I don't want to. I wish I could stay here forever."

So did I. "So, stay," I said.

"But Hallam—"

"Let the police deal with Hallam."

"They'd be no match for him," said Jason, shaking his head.

Really? I believed Jason when he said that Hallam was dangerous, but the idea of one guy overtaking numerous police officers? It seemed unreal. I caught Jason's eyes with my own. "I don't want you to leave," I said.

Jason gazed into my eyes. His lips parted slowly. Our faces were so close. I looked at his lips. I thought about—

And then I tore my gaze away from Jason. What was wrong with me? Frantically, I looked around the room for something else to talk about.

"We finished *1984* today in English," I said. "You missed it." I still didn't look at him.

"That's too bad," said Jason. "I really like that book. Orwell is brilliant."

"Yeah," I said. "He really is."

We were quiet. I still wasn't looking at Jason.

"Should I go?" Jason asked.

I swung my eyes back to him violently. "No! I don't want you to leave. I don't know how to make that clearer to you!"

"I meant your room," said Jason.

"Oh." I felt stupid. "No, you can stay. It's fine."

"Okay," he said.

And then we didn't say anything for a long time.

"Um ..." I floundered. "Do you read stuff like Orwell for fun?"

"Sure," said Jason. "I guess. It's been a while since I read anything for fun. What about you?"

"I like Dan Brown," I said. "I think stuff like that — like secret societies and the Illuminati — is interesting."

"If you like the Illuminati, you should read Robert Anton Wilson," said Jason.

Book recommendations, huh? I liked Jason. There were so many layers to him. I just wanted to unpeel them all. He was so enigmatic, like a puzzle. I wanted to solve him. Understand him.

Jason looked serious again. "I can't stay, Azazel," he said.

"In my room? Sure you can. I mean, I do eventually have to get back to my French homework, but —"

"I mean here. I mean in your house. I can't be here."

"You have to," I said. "How are you going to leave?"

He made a face. "I know," he said. "And all of that is just strange. I'm not allowed to leave." He pointed at the ankle monitor. "This is overkill, don't you think?"

It did seem like everyone was trying very, very hard to keep Jason from going anywhere. I was grateful, but I did think they only gave ankle monitors to criminals.

Jason stood up. Faced me. "When Sheriff Damon found me hitchhiking, he handcuffed me and threw me in the back of his car."

"Well," I said. "You are my parents' foster child, legally. They have a responsibility to you. Technically, you're legally bound to be here."

"I guess," said Jason. "But there was a search party, and everyone was on red alert to find me. That doesn't make any sense."

Sure it did. We'd all been worried about Jason's safety. Well, I'd been worried about Jason's safety. I guess everyone else had too. Was he right? Was it too much? "Maybe you're just not used to what it's like for people to care about you," I said.

"Maybe," said Jason. "But I don't think so. Something weird is going on in this town."

* * *

As I was falling asleep that night, I couldn't help but

think about what Jason had said. Was something weird going on in Bramford? Things had gotten strange after Jason arrived, but I couldn't put my finger on why exactly that was. For the most part, things were going on exactly the way they had been. Nothing was strange.

Nobody liked it when I spent time with Jason. Toby was jealous of him. Lilith had told me to stay away from him. My dad had made a comment that I'd been spending too much time with him. But maybe they were all just concerned about my safety. If Jason were tied to some dangerous group of people who were tracking him, it made sense that they wouldn't want me to be around him all the time.

There was also the fact that Lilith and Toby had both said something about not being allowed to tell me things or to do things with me. Who was telling them that? Who said they weren't allowed? And today in the lunch line, they'd been almost civil to each other for a second. Then they'd been talking about something they both understood, but I didn't understand. What was it that Toby and Lilith had in common? How could they have anything in common? They hated each other. They'd hated each other for years. I didn't understand. That was definitely weird.

But it didn't really mean anything, did it? There were lots of reasons why Lilith and Toby could say they weren't allowed to do something. It was probably unrelated. I was worried because I'd been talking to Jason. Jason was paranoid, with good reason. I could tell that he hadn't had an easy life. He probably saw conspiracies and danger under every rock. Talking to him was making me paranoid. That was all there was to it.

Then there was the mystery of Jason himself. He appeared out of nowhere, running for his life from an unseen person or group of people. He claimed the people after him were dangerous. That they were fanatics — Freemasons with guns. Jason was usually composed and unemotional, but he knew how to fight. I'd watched him incapacitate at least three guys who looked bigger and stronger than him. He was very well educated. He'd read all kinds of things. He was smart. He could out-argue my dad, and Ms. Campbell was dazzled by his brilliance.

Hallam — the man who'd come after him — had claimed Jason was his brother, and there'd been a certain sincerity to what he had to say. I'd almost wanted to believe him. In the picture he'd brought, Jason looked happy. Jason made his past sound like it had been horrible. Had it always been horrible? At one point, when that picture had been taken, he'd been happy. I had to consider the possibility that Jason wasn't telling the truth. What had happened to him? Why was he running? And were we all in as much danger as he claimed? I didn't know the answer to any of those questions.

I did know something else, though. Something unsettling. There was something to Toby's accusations. Earlier that night, when Jason had been sitting on my bed, so close to me, I'd looked at his face, and I'd thought about kissing him. I'd been out of my mind with worry when I thought he was in danger. And I liked being around Jason.

The thought of being around him for an indefinite period of time sounded like a wonderful idea to me.

It wasn't too serious. I still loved Toby. Toby and I had been through a lot together. He was the person who I wanted to lose my virginity to. I wanted us to be together for a very long time. I'd never do anything to hurt him. I knew that.

But Jason was beautiful and mysterious and kind of dangerous. He'd saved me. And when I was around him ... But none of that meant anything. I didn't want to worry about it too much. I had a crush on Jason. That was all. I had to be careful, because I owed it to Toby, to the man I loved, to be faithful. These feelings I had for Jason would fade away eventually. But I did have to acknowledge they existed.

morningstar68 (06:24:16): we almost lost him. it's been a terrifying 24 hours. sorry I haven't been in touch.

michaela666 (06:24:57): it's understandable. but you're certain he won't be escaping again.

morningstar68: (06:25:08): Impossible. we've got him under lock and key.

michaela666 (06:25:35): and the man who seems to be pursuing him? is there a chance of rescue?

morningstar68: (06:26:12): he seems more scared of them than he is of us. or, more accurately, he isn't frightened of us at all. he has no idea what we're planning for him.

michaela666 (06:26:45): Good.

morningstar68: (06:27:10): samhain is days away. It's almost over.

After being so honest with myself, I didn't know how to be around Jason anymore. At breakfast, our hands brushed when we reached for the same cereal box. I recoiled as if he'd stung me. He shot me a strange glance, but I avoided his eyes. When Toby arrived to pick me up, I felt strange around him too. I felt guilty when I got into his truck. Here was Toby, a gorgeous boy, like an angel or something. He was blonde and tan and strong. He was a Ken doll. How could I be finding another boy attractive when I had this? He leaned across and kissed me, and I felt horrible.

In English, I found myself staring at Jason across the classroom. He talked so much that it seemed normal to watch him. Even after missing a day of school, he was caught up on the reading. He offered his viewpoint on the poem by Robert Herrick we were discussing.

Ms. Campbell said, "It's hard to explain the word 'coy,'" she said. "I think the best modern equivalent is that it means a girl is being a tease."

Jason raised his hand. "I don't think so," he said.

Ms. Campbell spread her hands. "Okay, Jason. What do you think it means?" she asked.

"If the virgins in the poem were being a tease, then it would mean that they truly wanted to get married as Herrick urges, but they were just playing hard to get." Jason was so dark. His hair fell into his huge dark eyes. His face was shaped like a heart.

Ms. Campbell nodded. "I've always read it that way," she admitted.

"Don't you think that implies a little bit of cynicism on Herrick's part?" Jason asked. "If they're all just teasing these guys, then they're sort of, well, they're more world wise than innocent."

"If Herrick didn't think the virgins wanted to get married, would he be telling them to do it?" Ms. Campbell asked.

"It's a didactic poem," said Jason. "Herrick is giving fatherly advice. He's telling the virgins what he thinks would be good for them, because he doesn't think that they know what it is."

I looked from Jason, who was animated and engaged with Ms. Campbell, completely invested in the meaning of a poem from hundreds of years ago, to Toby, who was flipping idly through the textbook as if he were too bored to be bothered. Toby was the all-American boyfriend. He was what every girl should want. Jason was odd. He was the antihero. He was the guy in the movie that pined over the popular girl, but never got her. Why did I find him so appealing? What was wrong with me?

"If what you're saying is true," said Ms. Campbell, "then the poem takes on dirty-old-man overtones. Now, Herrick is telling a bunch of teenage girls who haven't given marriage a second thought to get married?"

"No!" said Jason. "No way. I just think everyone's motives are pure in the poem. I don't think the girls are trying to lead anyone on."

And then our eyes met. Damn it. Was that some sort of hidden message? Was Jason saying that I was leading him on? Anguished, I turned away from him. I gazed at Toby.

"What do you think, Azazel?" asked Ms. Campbell.

"What?" I said.

"Your expression," she said. "I thought you had a thought."

"I think ... I think that the virgins do want to get married, in some way. But that they also recognize that the alternative is what they know. And they're used to that. So maybe they don't want to seize the day just yet."

Ms. Campbell nodded. She paused. "Azazel, would you mind talking to me at the end of class? It's nothing bad, I promise."

"Okay," I said, terrified, even though she'd said it wasn't anything bad.

Ms. Campbell addressed the class. "Come on, people, don't let Jason take over the conversation. What do you think?" No one said anything. "Thinking is cool, I swear," she said. "I'm not going to stop trying to convince you guys of this."

At the end of class, I approached Ms. Campbell's desk. It was covered with stacks of papers, and she was going through them, as usual. She looked up and saw me. "Oh Azazel," she said. "Thanks for staying. This will only take a minute."

"Okay," I said.

"Don't look so scared," she said. "I told you it wasn't anything bad. I, um, I've noticed you've been a little distracted lately."

She said it wasn't bad! "I'm sorry," I said. "I'll try to do better."

"No, that's not what I mean," she said. "Since Jason got here, I know things have been kind of tumultuous in your home life. It's understandable. I'm not a counselor, so I'm not qualified to give advice or anything like that. But I just want you to know that I am here, if you need someone to talk to. Someone that's outside of the whole situation."

"Really?"

"Really." She smiled. "You're a bright kid, Azazel. And there are other things in life besides English that are important." She considered. "Well, not many. But a few."

"Thanks, Ms. Campbell," I said.

French class was easier because Jason wasn't there. I tried not to let my thoughts wander, but I felt like I couldn't help it. The worst thing about all of it was that I might hurt Toby. I didn't want to do that. I cared so deeply about Toby. I didn't want him to be hurt. And I didn't want him to hate me. For the first time, I wondered if it wouldn't be easier if Jason just wasn't there. But I knew that wasn't true. I couldn't sacrifice Jason's safety, because I was confused about my love life.

Still, after French, I just couldn't bear the thought of facing him in history class. I knew my dad would notice if I wasn't there. I knew I was going to get in trouble. But I didn't care. I told Toby I was going to the bathroom, and then I just left the school.

Bramford High was situated on a hill that looked down over Route 50. Behind the school, there was a wooded area. There was a path through it. We'd gone walking on it in tenth-grade science when we were learning to type trees from their leaves. I walked out the doors by the gym, crossed the parking lot, and went into the woods. I just needed to be alone. I needed to think. There had to be some way that I could just erase the feelings I had for Jason.

I couldn't have them! They were ruining everything. I tried to think of ways that I could stop thinking about Jason.

Maybe I didn't have a crush on him anyway. Maybe I just needed to know who he was and where he came from. Maybe I couldn't get him out of my head because he was a mystery that I couldn't solve. Maybe if I figured it out, all of these weird, annoying feelings would just dissolve.

But I didn't know how I was going to do that. I wandered aimlessly down the path, staring at the trees. It was a gray day. The sky hung oppressively over the woods. The trees were losing their leaves. Just a few weeks ago, they'd been alive with brilliant reds and yellows. Now the few that were left were mostly brown. The atmosphere mirrored my mood. Bleak. Colorless.

I couldn't get Jason to just tell me about his past. He was way too tightlipped for that. And I didn't know of anyone else who could fill in the missing pieces for me. Even if understanding Jason would banish the feelings, I probably would never be able to understand him.

And what was worse, I didn't even know if that would work. Jason was entrenched in my subconscious now. I didn't know if I'd ever be able to stop thinking about him.

I was so engrossed in my thoughts that I didn't even hear him approach. I didn't see him.

He was just behind me suddenly, one arm around my waist, his hand over my mouth. "Don't scream," he whispered in my ear.

I knew his voice. The British accent. It was Hallam. The man from my house. The man who'd showed me the picture of Jason. I tried to scream anyway, but his hand muffled my voice. I bit his hand.

He yanked it away, letting go of me for a split second. I tried to scream then, tried to run, but he was too fast for me. Lightning fast, he pinned me against a tree, his hand at my throat.

"Don't scream," he said again, and there was menace in his voice now.

My mouth went dry. What was Hallam going to do to me? Maybe Jason was right. Maybe it was dangerous for him to stay in Bramford. Then again, maybe I was an idiot for wandering around in the woods by myself. Was I crazy?

"Okay?" Hallam asked.

His hand barely let me breathe. I nodded.

Slowly, Hallam removed his hand. I didn't scream. I didn't move. I hoped he would not hurt me.

Hallam stared me down. He looked very similar to the last time I'd seen him. He was wearing the same clothes. But he still looked very proper and tailored. Every inch an English gentleman. His appearance clashed with the way Jason reacted to him. Jason said that Hallam had committed such atrocities that Jason couldn't speak about them. Which was real? The clean-cut, well-dressed man or the terrifying, dangerous tracker?

"I'm not going to hurt you," said Hallam.

I didn't know if I believed him.

"I've been watching Jason. I've been watching him with you. He seems happy here."

I didn't know what to say.

"Do you think he's happy?"

"He's—he's afraid. Of you," I said. But maybe I shouldn't have admitted that. Maybe it made Jason look weak. Oh God, what was Hallam going to do?

"But that's the only thing that's making him unhappy? Me?"

"I-I guess so."

"I want you to give him a message," said Hallam. "From me. Will you do that?"

So he was going to let me go? Good. "Yes," I choked out. As long as he wasn't going to hurt me or torture me or kill me or—

"Tell him that from now on, as long as I can help it, he's got a clean slate. He'll know what that means. Will you do that?"

I nodded.

"All right, then," he said. "You can go." He stepped back from me.

I was stupid. I was crazy. I was begging to be flayed alive. But I couldn't help it. The question ripped out of me. "Is he really your brother?"

Hallam laughed. "In a way," he said.

That had gone okay. "What way? Who are you? Who's after him?"

Hallam didn't laugh again. Instead he leaned close to me. His voice was deep and rumbling, with a tinge of threat, "Run away, little girl. You don't want to spend any more time with me than you already have."

I didn't have to be told twice. I flew out of the woods, over the parking lot, and back into the school.

Once inside, I didn't know what to do. I'd skipped history, but I'd only been gone for fifteen minutes. What was I going to do now? Should I go back to class? I didn't know if I'd feel safe anywhere else. I stood inside the door, breathing heavily, totally undecided about my next course of action. In a flash of inspiration, it came to me.

I went to the nurse. "I've been throwing up in the bathroom," I said, "but I feel better now. Can I have a pass to class?"

She eyed me a little suspiciously, but she did what I said.

Clutching my pass, I slid into history class and handed my father the slip of paper the nurse had written for me. He gave me a concerned look, but didn't make an issue out of it.

At lunch, I found Jason immediately. He was sitting alone at a table, the way he usually did. I sat down with him.

"What are you doing here?" he asked me. I never sat with Jason at lunch.

I told him about meeting Hallam in the woods and what Hallam had said. I left out why I'd skipped history in the first place. I didn't want Jason to know I had a crush on him. Jason probably didn't think of me in that way anyhow. I was sure that Jason would want to be with a girl who was deeper and smarter than me. He deserved someone of the same caliber as himself.

Jason reacted angrily when he found out that I'd seen Hallam, but after I told him what Hallam had said, he got quiet.

"What does that mean, a clean slate?" I asked.

"He's telling me that they're going to leave me alone," Jason said. "I don't know if I believe him."

* * *

Jason asked me not to say anything about meeting Hallam in the woods. He said it might worry other people, and he said it might make it more difficult for him to do anything. According to Jason, if it came down to a fight, he was the only one who stood a chance at winning against Hallam. He needed to be free to do what he needed to do. I asked him if he was planning on leaving. He said he was going to give it some time. He needed to see what happened before he could be sure.

"But," he said, and there was so much hope in his eyes, it hurt, "if he's serious, then I could stay."

We didn't talk about why Hallam might leave Jason alone. I didn't ask, even though I was dying to understand. I knew that Jason wouldn't tell me anyway.

The Homecoming Dance was Friday, only two days away. Halloween. In a strange twist of events, the school had decided to schedule the Homecoming game for Saturday, the day after the dance. Students speculated this might be an attempt on the part of the administration to keep football players from getting into too much trouble at the dance. If they wanted to play well the next day, they couldn't be hung over. I thought it was a good theory. I'd never heard of having the dance before the game though. It wasn't the typical way of doing things — that was for sure.

I had my costume ready, thanks to my shopping day with Lilith. Toby was still set on being Michael Myers, which was fine with me, as far as that went. The only thing that I didn't like about the costume was that he'd be wearing a mask. It was going to make it difficult to steal kisses on the dance floor.

There was some debate at home about whether Jason should be allowed to go to the dance. He said he didn't care one way or another. In the end, my parents ended up having to chaperone, and so they wouldn't be home. There was no way they were leaving Jason at home alone, so he had to go to the dance, and so did the guys. There was some grumbling about that. Cameron thought Homecoming Dances were "gay." But they were all going, and they all had to scrounge up costumes at the last second.

In the whirlwind of preparation, it would have been tough for me to think much about either my feelings for Jason or my confusion about what was happening with Hallam and Jason's safety. But something happened on Thursday night that wiped everything from my mind. Toby was driving me home from school, and we were quiet, as usual. I still felt a little guilty about my stupid crush on Jason. And with all the tension between Toby and me lately, it had been hard for us to have a conversation about anything. Most of the time when we were together anymore, we didn't talk. I was getting used to the silence.

When Toby pulled up to my house to drop me off, I

leaned over to kiss him goodbye and then started to open the door of the truck to get out.

"Wait," said Toby.

I looked at him. "What's up?" I asked.

Toby looked nervous. "My parents are going to a Halloween party tomorrow night," he said. "They told me today that they're going to be out all night."

That was cool, as far as that went. "Lucky you," I said.

"You don't have a curfew anymore, right?" he asked me.

"No," I said. "Are you gonna have a party?"

"No," he said. "Of course not. I have the game."

"Right," I said.

"I thought maybe ... you could ... we could ..." he trailed off.

Toby was turning into Jason. He wasn't finishing his sentences, and he wasn't telling me everything. "What?" I asked.

"Do you want to stay with me tomorrow?" he asked. "All night?"

My jaw dropped. Did he mean ... ? "Are you saying what I think you're saying?" I asked.

He nodded. "I'm ready."

"Oh my God," I breathed. "Of course. Absolutely."

And then we kissed. It was a heavenly kiss, full of promise and excitement. It felt like orchestras and fireworks underscored it. When we pulled away, our faces lingered close to each other.

"I love you," Toby whispered.

"I love you too," I told him.

I walked back into my house dreamily, in a cloud of love. I was going to lose my virginity. And it was going to be to the most perfect guy ever. And we were in love. And it was perfect. And how many other girls my age could say the same thing?

Of course, I immediately called Lilith.

"Hello?" she said when she picked up.

I squealed. "Toby and I are gonna do it!" I said.

"Wow," she said, "that's great. When?"

"Tomorrow!" I said.

"Cool," she said. "I'm happy for you, Zaza."

But she didn't sound as excited as a best friend should be.

"Look," she said. "I'm swamped with homework. I'm really sorry, but can we talk tomorrow?"

"Sure," I said. But I didn't want her to hang up. She was my best friend. She was supposed to ask me to go over the details of how he'd told me. She was supposed to help me figure out what kind of underwear to wear. She was supposed to give me tips, considering she was wiser than me in the ways of sex, and had already done it a zillion times. Besides, it wasn't like Lilith to be overly concerned with homework.

I felt confused and a little hurt, but overall, I was too excited to dwell on it. I had so much grooming to do. I had to shave. I had to figure out what to do with my hair. I'd planned something for the dance, but now that it was going to be such a significant night of my life, I had to do something completely different. This was epic. This was the only time this could ever happen to me.

God. It was forever until Friday night, wasn't it?

I started my search for the perfect hairdo on the family computer. After searching through pages of different pictures, I had about ten different ideas, all of which I'd printed out. The next step was going to be locking myself in the bathroom and attempting to duplicate all of them. I would take a picture of each, then look at them to decide which one I'd do tomorrow. I wasn't going to be able to help my mom with dinner, but this was really, really important. Really important.

I thought about Toby, and I sighed, a silly grin taking over my entire face. I was so lucky to be dating him. I wondered what he was doing right now. Sometimes he was online in the early evening. I pulled up AOL instant messenger, but somebody else was already logged in. Huh? Who in my family called themselves morningstar68? That was a weird name.

I couldn't imagine any of the guys in the house used it, and my parents were hopeless about computers. I didn't think they even know what instant messenger was. Did they?

Whatever. I logged morningstar off and logged myself in. Toby wasn't online. Oh. Well. That was fine. I'd be seeing a lot of him tomorrow. Then I giggled as I thought about the full implications of that statement. I was going to have sex! I couldn't believe it.

I bumped into Jason in the hall after finishing the last of my hairstyle choices. I wasn't looking where I was going because I was flipping through the pictures on our digital camera. I couldn't decide which hairstyle I liked the best.

"Sorry," I said to Jason.

"You've been in the bathroom for a really long time," he said.

I showed him the pictures. "I'm trying to figure out my hair for tomorrow."

He took the camera from me and flipped through the pictures himself. "They all look the same to me," he said, handing it back.

Boys! They were completely and totally different hairstyles. There was nothing about them that was even remotely similar. "So which I one do you think I should do?" I asked.

He shrugged. "Like I said, I can't tell the difference."

"Well thanks for nothing," I said, sidestepping him to go to my room.

"But if you really want my opinion," he said.

"I do," I said.

"Then I think you should wear your hair down," he said. "It's, um, pretty like that."

"Oh," I said. "Thanks."

He half-smiled at me, and I made the mistake of looking into his big, brown eyes. Bad idea.

Toby, I reminded myself. My boyfriend. Who I was

going to have sex with. "I have to go," I said to Jason, and hurried off.

* * *

Friday afternoon, I was surprised when I got home from school and my two big brothers, Noah and Gordon, were there. I hadn't seen them since sometime over the summer. They didn't come home too often, and I was really happy to see them.

"What are you doing here?" I asked them, after I'd given both of them enormous hugs.

"It's Homecoming," said Gordon. "We came home."

"Besides," said Noah, "we wouldn't miss your big night for the world, Zaza."

My big night? My brothers didn't know I was going to have sex with Toby, did they?

My mother decided to order in Chinese food, since we all had to get into costumes and get ready. That way, none of us had to worry about cooking or cleaning up. My dad and Chance went to pick up our enormous Chinese order. When they came back, they needed help to cart all the food back inside.

Spreading all the food out on the dining room table, I was reminded of how wonderful my family was. We were loud. There were a lot of us. And we weren't your traditional family. But there was so much love and laughter in my house. Noah and Chance were fighting over egg rolls. Cameron and Nick were making bets on who could eat the most rice. Jason and I helped my mom pour iced tea for everyone. My father roared at everyone to sit down.

We did. Everyone grabbed for the Chinese carton containers and began opening them up. It was pandemonium.

"Who got orange chicken?"

"That's mine!"

"No, it's not. It's mine."

"Here's another orange chicken. Calm down."

"Where's my crab rangoon? Don't tell me you forgot the crab rangoon."

"No, I ordered it. It's in here somewhere."

"Where?"

"I don't want to eat with chopsticks!"

"So get yourself a fork!"

"I need rice."

"Who ordered this? What is this?"

"Here's your crab rangoon. Hope you're happy."

And on and on it went. We traded food. We chattered happily. I realized that I might be angry with my parents sometimes, but that I really and truly loved them, and I loved my home. We were so happy together. Everything we did was part of our own little ritual. Our own way of doing things. I felt like I was contained in bubble full of happiness.

As I ate my pork fried rice, I thought about how wonderful our family was, and I thought about why my parents had decided to be foster parents. My mother hadn't thought she'd be able to have children. She and my dad started out their relationship on their own, just the two of them. My dad's parents had died when he was in his early twenties. My mother's family hadn't approved of dad, and my grandmother had resolved not to have anything to do with my mother after that. My grandparents had a lot of money, and dad was too poor for them. They'd told my mom that if she continued to date my father, they'd cut her off. She'd chosen my dad over her family. She had one older sister, my Aunt Stephanie, who had tried to keep in touch with mom. I remembered seeing her once when I was very young, and we sometimes got Christmas cards from her. But Aunt Stephanie wasn't much of a force in my mom's life, either.

So there they were, a young couple, all alone, and probably going to be childless. They'd decided to adopt. After adopting Noah and my other older brother Gordon, my mother had gotten pregnant with me. She said I was her little miracle. But even though their home had now been full of children, my parents hadn't stopped. They'd wanted to open their home to as many children as they could. And that was why we were the way we were.

It might have been annoying sometimes. It might have meant that people teased me at school. But in the end, it was a great way to live. I loved my family. I sat at our dining room table, watching everyone interact. Watching the teasing. Watching the good-natured arguing over food. Even listening to the deafening noise. It was all amazing. I wouldn't have it any other way.

After dinner, we tossed the empty containers and stored

the leftovers in the refrigerator. Then we went to put on our costumes. Last night, I'd decided on a complicated up do, my hair twisted into an intricate bun on the top of my head. But as I stared at myself in the mirror, I thought about what Jason had said and changed my mind. Instead, I just pulled up a few strands at the front of my head. I left the rest of it down. If Jason thought my hair was pretty down, then maybe Toby would too. I curled the ends of my hair a little bit, so that it floated around my shoulders. I put on the dress I'd gotten from Goodwill. I applied makeup.

Surveying myself in the mirror, I decided I looked fresh and innocent, which was how a Vestal virgin should look. I hoped I looked good enough for what was about to be the most important night of my young life. I couldn't believe I was actually going to lose my virginity to Toby that night. I was too excited for words.

As I preened, my mother knocked on the door. I let her in. "Oh," she said when she saw me. "Azazel, you look beautiful."

"Thanks," I said, grinning. "I'm excited for the dance."

"Yeah," she said. "It's a big night."

Why was everyone calling this my big night? I hadn't told my mother about my plans with Toby.

"I brought you something," she said. "For your costume." She held up a necklace. Dangling from a silver chain was circular pendant. Inside, connecting the circle, were the points of a star, only the top point of it faced downwards.

"I don't know if it's period, mom," I said. "I'm supposed to be from ancient Rome."

"Just try it on," she said, moving behind me to clasp it behind my neck. I held my hair up for her. She was right. The necklace was the perfect length for the costume. It settled just above my cleavage—which wasn't overstated. There was a dress code for this dance, after all.

I touched it. "It's pretty," I said.

"It's very old," she said. "I received it right before I got pregnant with you, from Mrs. Cantle. You remember her?"

"Kind of," I said. Mrs. Cantle had died a few years back. She'd been really old, over a hundred. She'd lived in Bramford her entire life. Everyone thought she was kind of strange. I remember that in kindergarten, a few of the kids said that she was a witch.

"Well, she gave this to me, and she told me to wear it, and a few weeks later, I found out I was going to have you."

"Neat," I said. I liked the necklace more and more.

"It's good luck," she told me. "And I think tonight is a good night for you."

What *did* my mom know?

My mother hugged me. "Oh, Zaza, you look so grown up," she said. "I can't believe that you're already seventeen. I feel like I was holding you in my arms just days ago."

I fought the urge to roll my eyes. Didn't adults know this kind of thing was totally cliché? Why did they say the same things over and over, anyway?

"Listen," she said. "You're ready."

Ready for what?

"I know you're going to do a wonderful job. I might not feel ready to let you go. You're my little girl. But I know you can do it. I know you won't let anyone down."

"Mom," I said, confused, "what are you talking about?"

She laughed. "I'm sorry, sweetie. You'll find out soon. I love you so much."

Chapter Nine

Toby picked me up in his truck. His Michael Myers mask was on the seat next to him. When he saw me, his eyes lit up. "You look amazing," he said.

I wished I could say the same thing, but Toby was wearing an old blue jumpsuit, and he was carrying a fake knife as a prop. He hadn't felt the need to look nice for what was going to be the biggest night of our relationship. Still, he was gorgeous as always, and I was too excited to breathe.

We drove to the dance, both of us nervous and excited. We kept attempting to start conversations, talking over each other, then dissolving into laughter. In the parking lot at the school, he leaned over to kiss me. We started making out heavily. If it had been up to me, it probably would have happened right then and there. Toby started putting his hands places he'd never put them before, and he didn't fight my hands when I put them between his legs. We got a little sweaty and a little out of breath and were in danger of starting to lose our clothes. But Toby stopped me.

"Patience," he said to me.

"God," I groaned. "I've been having patience forever."

He laughed. "We've got a long night. We've got to go to the dance."

"Do we?" I asked. "Can't we just go to your house now?"

He chuckled. "It's the Homecoming Dance of our senior year. You really just want to miss it?"

So, I took a deep breath, composed myself, and reapplied my lipstick. Toby picked up his mask, but didn't put it on. He took my hand, and we walked to the dance together. The gym had been transformed for the Homecoming Dance. There were banners on the walls. One said, "Happy Homecoming." The other said, "Happy Halloween." Tables lined the walls, covered with black tablecloths. There were orange and black streamers covering the ceiling. The lights were off in the gym, and the entire room was lit by electric candelabras, which had been attached to the walls. The atmosphere was spooky and a little cheesy, but it had a certain charm.

Once inside the dance, I spotted Lilith. I couldn't tell what her costume was supposed to be. All I could tell was that it had a plunging neckline, and you could see half of her very ample breasts. I was amazed she hadn't been kicked out for violating the dress code. Once I saw her, I wanted to go and say hi, but I didn't want to leave Toby, so I just waved.

"Go talk to her," said Toby, nudging me.

"I don't want to leave you," I said, looking up into his eyes.

He smiled down at me. "I'm not going anywhere. Go on. Go say hi to Lilith."

"Okay," I said.

We kissed. "I love you," he said.

"I love you," I said.

I didn't drop his hand until we were too far away to hold on anymore. And when I walked away, Toby pulled his mask over his head.

Lilith hugged me when I got to her. "I'm sorry I was such a bitch last night on the phone," she said. "I'm getting my period, and I haven't gotten laid in forever, and I was a horrible best friend."

"It's okay," I said, forgiving her instantly.

"It's so not. You needed me last night, and I let you down," she said. "So ... what kind of underwear are you wearing? Thong?"

"Eew," I said. "Like I want dental floss up my butt."

"Thongs are sexy," she said.

"I'm wearing lacy boy shorts," I said.

She considered. "With a matching bra?"

"Of course."

"Nice," she said.

"You think? It's not too, I don't know, girly and innocent?"

"Considering Toby's made you wait this long, he probably likes girly and innocent," she said.

"I hope so," I said. "I'm so nervous."

"It's gonna be great," she said. "You'll see. You're never going to forget this night as long as you live."

I took a shuddering breath. "I know. Oh my God!"

"Oh my God!" said Lilith, and we both squealed, hugging each other.

And I looked across the room, just in time to see the guys come into the dance. Chance and Nick had gone for easy costumes. They had on scary rubber masks with jeans and a t-shirt. Cameron hadn't done much better. He was dressed as a Jedi, which meant he was wearing a dark bathrobe with a plastic lightsaber tucked into it. But Jason ... Jason was dressed as a pirate. He had a huge flowing white shirt, which was open at the collar. His black breeches were tight against his legs. His hair was hidden under a bandana and he wore an eye patch. And, as usual, I couldn't stop staring at him. Dammit.

I resolved to pay no attention to Jason. Instead, I spotted Toby across the room, said goodbye to Lilith, and went over to him. I was going to be attached to Toby for the rest of the night. I wasn't even going to *think* about Jason.

And for the most part, I did a good job. I danced with Toby. I talked to our friends. I took particular pleasure in the moment when Eve and Sherry were looking over my costume. "What are you dressed as?" asked Sherry.

"A Vestal virgin," I retorted.

They actually looked ashamed. Good. Bitches.

And as midnight neared, when the dance would be over, I began to get more and more anxious and more and more excited. I knew that once the dance was done, Toby and I would go to his house. I wondered what it would be like. I wondered if Toby had made a trail of rose petals or something ridiculous like that. I wondered if it would hurt. I'd read romance novels. I knew that there was sometimes blood involved in this entire thing. But I also knew that most people didn't have hymens in this day of tampons, and I wasn't too worried. Still.

I thought about going to talk to Lilith. Asking her a zillion questions. But then, I didn't. I wasn't sure I wanted to know. What happened between Toby and me would be our thing. It wouldn't be what had happened to every other girl. It would be my story. My first time. And I loved Toby, and he loved me. So it would have to be perfect. Because too many things had gone wrong for this to be ruined. I deserved one perfect high school memory.

Even though I'd promised not to think about Jason or look at him, every so often, I'd caught sight of him as the dance wore on. He was always alone, sitting at a table by himself, the way he did at lunch. I felt bad about that. But I didn't know what to do. I couldn't leave Toby to hang out with Jason. Not on this night of all nights.

Around eleven o'clock, Toby and I were dancing. His mask was ridiculous and not a little creepy, and I wanted him to take it off. When I'd asked, though, he said he didn't have much of a costume without it, so I'd dropped it. Because I didn't feel like looking at a mutilated William Shatner face, I was looking over Toby's shoulder at the rest of the dance. And I saw that Eric Nelson had approached Jason.

"Uh oh," I said.

"What?" asked Toby.

I pointed.

Toby sighed. "God," he said. "It never fails, does it? Jason has to ruin everything."

"It's not his fault," I said.

"Spare me," said Toby. "You take Jason, I'll get Eric."

We hurried over to the two of them.

I could hear Eric talking as we approached. "I'm ready, anytime, anywhere," he was saying. "Just say the word, dumbfuck."

Toby and I intercepted them. Toby put his arm around Eric and led him away. I looked at Jason. "Sorry about Eric," I said.

He shrugged. "Guy's a jerk."

"Yeah," I said. Jason wasn't wrong.

"You don't have to hang out with me," said Jason. "You

166

look like you're having a great time."

"You look like you're not," I said. "And Toby's going to be busy talking Eric down anyway."

"I'm fine," said Jason. "It's just cool to actually be at a high school dance. I never thought I'd get to do anything like this."

"But you're just sitting here alone," I said.

"You wanna go for a walk?" Jason asked.

"You mean leave the gym?" I said. "That would be against the rules."

Jason smirked. "Yeah," he said.

"Sure," I said.

We walked past the bathrooms. The hall was dark and empty. Jason rounded a corner and pulled me after him. Now we were alone in a different dark hallway. No one could see us, and we couldn't see anyone else. Occasionally, we heard chattering as girls left the bathroom or entered it, but other than that, we were alone.

Jason took off his eye patch. "Thing's annoying," he said by way of explanation.

We'd stopped walking. Instead, we stood facing each other. The wall was behind me. I backed up, trying to put some distance between Jason and me. Jason just moved closer. I swallowed. I was beginning to think this was a bad idea.

I could see Jason's dusky skin through the opening of his collar. It looked soft, like velvet. His dark eyes glowed intensely through the darkness of the hallway. And he was really, really close to me.

"Um, Jason?" I said.

"No," he said. "Don't say anything. I want to talk to you."

I didn't say anything.

"Why are you with Toby?" he asked me.

Oh God. This was a bad conversation to have.

"And don't say it's because you love him," said Jason, "because I don't think you do."

"Of course I do!" I protested. Now more than ever, I did. "I love Toby."

"Do you really?" Jason asked, and he was closer now. I hadn't thought it was possible for him to be closer, but he was. We were practically touching.

"Why are you asking me this?" I said, trying to will myself to push Jason away. Unfortunately, I didn't really think I wanted him away. I liked being close to him like this.

"Cameron said you were really freaked out when I was gone," said Jason, his voice lower and deeper.

"I was worried," I said.

"When I got back, you hugged me in the kitchen." There was a husky edge to his voice.

My breath caught in my throat. "I was glad to see you," I said, hating how breathless my voice sounded.

"Were you?"

I fought with myself. Clenched my fists in determination. And with every shred of strength in my body, I squeaked out, "You're too close."

Immediately, Jason backed up. There was at least a foot of space between us.

I took a shaking breath. Good. That was good. Wasn't it?

"Maybe I'm wrong," said Jason. "But when I saw you in the kitchen, you put your arms around me, there was something in your eyes." He wasn't looking at me anymore. He was looking at the floor, at the wall, everywhere except my eyes. "Believe me, Azazel, if I didn't think there was a chance that ... If you hadn't told me what Hallam said, if I didn't think that there was a possibility that I'd be here for any period of time, I wouldn't be doing this."

He looked at my face again. "But I watched you tonight, with him. And I've heard people saying things, like you two are going to ..." He didn't seem to be able to say it. "... tonight. And if I'm going to stay here, and I'm going to have to see you every day, I can't watch you with him knowing that I feel the way I do, and I never said anything."

Oh God. "Jason—"

"No, let me finish," he said. "Before you say whatever you're going to say, just let me finish. You're the most beautiful girl I've ever seen in my life, Azazel. And you're so smart and determined and stubborn. And he's not good enough for you. He's a dumb jock. He doesn't see what he has. I'm not saying I'm good enough. I'm ... there are so many things wrong with me that—"

"There's nothing wrong with you," I said, and my voice shook.

"Don't do it," he said. "Don't leave with him."

169

So Jason liked me, huh? This was bad.

"Listen, Jason," I said. "I think that you are really, really ..."

Jason put his arm against the wall, leaning over me. "Yes?" he said, waiting.

I didn't finish. I looked up at him. His face dipped down, closer to mine. His eyes caught my own, and I felt like I was drowning in their depths. His lips were so near. And they were full—fuller than Toby's, but somehow more masculine. And before I knew what I was doing, I was cupping Jason's heart-shaped face in my hands, and I was pressing my lips against his.

My eyes squeezed shut, the world exploded like a bomb had gone off. His lips were electric. Tingles started at the top of my head and shivered their way through my limbs, out my fingers and toes.

I ripped my lips away from his, shoved him away from me.

And I ran out into the hallway and into the girl's bathroom.

Locking myself in a stall, I rested my forehead against the cement wall. I wanted to scream, but I didn't. Instead, I just grimaced as hard as I could.

What had I just done?

How could I face Toby?

How could we ... how could we have sex after what I'd just done?

Well, the answer to that was simple. We couldn't. We

wouldn't. I clearly didn't love Toby as much as I had thought. If I loved Toby, I wouldn't have kissed Jason like that. I was going to have to go to Toby. I was going to have to tell him what happened. I pictured the look on his face. He was going to be so hurt!

How could I have done this to him?

I sat down on the toilet, pulled my knees up to my chest, and wished I could cry. But my eyes were dry. I just sat there, horrified with myself.

Someone was entering the bathroom. I could hear voices.

"Lock the door," said one of them. A guy's voice.

A familiar voice.

"Wait," said a girl's voice, also familiar. "Let me make sure no one's in here."

Maybe she looked under the stalls. I couldn't tell. But she seemed satisfied. "We're safe," she said, and then I recognized her voice.

It was Lilith.

Oh God. I was going to have to listen to Lilith have sex with some guy in the girl's bathroom, wasn't I? Could this night get any worse? Maybe I should show myself? No. Lilith would never forgive me for ruining her moment. Of course, I could never tell her I'd been here, or I'd heard this.

"Why did you bring me here?" asked the guy. Who was it? I knew that voice.

"I just can't handle it," said Lilith. "It's been hard enough, pretending for all these years, but I did it, because it was asked of me. Now, though, with what's going to happen tonight, I just ... I don't want you to."

This was a weird conversation to be having before getting it on. What was Lilith up to?

"We don't have a choice," said the guy. "You know that as well as I do."

"We always have a choice," said Lilith. "Isn't that what they tell us? Isn't that what we believe? Our choices make the world?"

"This is too important," said the guy.

"Don't do it."

"I have to."

"You don't, though. We could just leave. Both of us. We could go somewhere, and we could actually be together. I love you. I can't stand watching you with her anymore."

Lilith loved someone? Who was that? And this guy was dating someone else?

"I love you too," said the guy, "but you know we can't be together. I have a role to play. I'm honored to have been given that role. And I have to do this."

And then I recognized the guy's voice. I recognized it when he said, "I love you." And I'd been wrong. The night could easily get worse. And it just had.

I pushed out of the bathroom stall, glaring at Toby and Lilith.

Now, I could cry. Finally. "How long?" I asked them.

"Zaza," said Lilith.

"How long?" I repeated.

"Look," said Toby, "you don't understand. I don't know

what you just heard, but—"

" *How long* ?"

They were quiet.

"Summer after eighth grade," said Lilith. "We were dating before you guys started seeing each other."

I shook my head. "Then, why, Toby?"

"It's complicated," he said.

"Are you fucking her?" I asked.

"Azazel," he said miserably.

"Are you? Is that why you wouldn't have sex with me?"

"This is all going to be explained," said Toby. "Just please, calm down, and we'll figure it—"

"You are, aren't you?" I said. "You guys are having sex. You've been doing it all along. Haven't you?"

"Listen, Zaza," said Lilith. "I'm really sorry. You need to understand that—"

" *Haven't you* ?" I demanded.

"Yes," Lilith whispered.

I shook my head, shaking in rage and crying all at the same time. "Fuck you both," I rasped. I tore out of the bathroom, slamming the door after me.

I strode down the hallway, back through the gym, and out the door into the night air. I didn't look at anyone. I didn't care if anyone looked at me. I just needed to get ... away.

It all made sense now. Why Lilith and Toby didn't seem to like each other. It was their cover. So I wouldn't suspect them. It made sense why Lilith never really had a boyfriend and why she was so bitter about men in general. The guy she was in love with was dating another girl. No wonder she was so screwed up. And Toby. How had I been so blind to the fact that he was such an asshole? Why hadn't I been able to see it?

I felt sick. I wanted to vomit. To think I'd been about to have sex with him. Jason was right. Toby didn't deserve me. Lilith didn't deserve me either. I'd been a great girlfriend and an excellent best friend. They'd betrayed me. Both of them. Ugh. It was disgusting. To think of all the times I'd put my lips on Toby's lips. The same lips he used to kiss my best friend!

How horrible. How completely and totally screwed up. I hated them. I hated them both. I couldn't believe this had been happening for so long, and I'd never noticed.

I raced through the parking lot, not sure where I was going. I felt like if I ran far enough, maybe I could run away from this. From all of this.

"Azazel!" called a voice from behind me. "Wait!"

I didn't. I didn't even look back. I didn't know who it was, and I didn't care. I ran forward blindly, but my legs got caught in my skirt, and I tripped.

I fell. Huddled on the pavement, my dress dirty and torn, tears streaming out of my eyes, I couldn't find the will to get up.

Someone knelt next to me.

"I'm sorry."

It was Jason.

I looked at him dully. Why was he sorry? Did he know about Lilith and Toby? Had he heard? Did everyone know? Was everyone laughing at me behind my back?

"I should never have said those things to you," he said.

Oh. Right. I'd kissed Jason in the hallway. That seemed like light years ago. "That's fine," I managed. "That's fine now."

It was, I guess. I didn't have to feel guilty about kissing Jason anymore. Compared to what Toby had done to me, it was nothing. I laughed suddenly. Bitterly. Hysterically. I couldn't stop.

"Are you okay?" asked Jason.

"No," I said, between giggles. "I'm really not."

He pulled me to my feet. "What's wrong?" he asked.

I just shook my head, trying to stop laughing. "It's cold out here," said Jason. "We should go back inside."

Oh, no way. I wasn't going back in there. You couldn't pay me enough money to do something that stupid. No, I was going to start walking, and I was going to walk until I fell down from exhaustion. There was just no way I could even take the thought of being alive right now. Everything was ruined. Everything was destroyed.

Jason put his arm around me, trying to pull me back towards the school. "Come on," he said.

I stopped laughing. "No," I said.

Other people were leaving the gym. A group of guys. One of them was Toby. He was wearing his Michael Myers mask again. He walked towards Jason and me, flanked by half of the football team. Almost all of them wore monster masks too. It was like legions of the undead were descending on us or something. A pack of demons was advancing on us.

Why was Toby coming after me with half the football team? Did he think that was going to make anything better? He was delusional.

I looked at Jason. "I need to get out of here," I said.

But Jason didn't have a car. And neither did I. He'd come with my parents. I didn't know how I was going to leave.

Toby and his pack of jocks stopped in front of us. They folded their arms over their chests.

"You both are going to have to come with us," said Toby from inside his mask.

"I'm not going anywhere with you," I said.

"I'm afraid you don't have a choice," said Toby, and the football team swarmed us.

Five of them jumped Jason. They knocked him to the ground. Two of them stood on his back while he struggled. They tied his hands behind his back.

I looked at Toby with uncomprehending eyes. "What's going on?" I asked.

Toby reached for me. I backed away from him, but I backed into another football player's arms. He held me fast. Toby wrenched my hands forward, tied them together. He dragged me towards his truck.

The other players picked up Jason and forced him to

walk forward. They shoved him into the back seat of a car. Toby pushed me into his truck. It occurred to me at this point that maybe I should scream.

So I did. As loud as I could.

Toby just chuckled. "Nobody's coming to save you, Azazel," he said. "Save your breath."

Toby started the car. He pulled out of the parking lot and the car containing Jason followed him. I stared at Toby, his face obscured by that stupid mask. What the hell was going on?

Chapter Ten

I don't usually share my visions in this forum, considering I feel that visions are a personal experience, generated mostly for my own spiritual growth and edification. However, since there has been so much talk about the vision I received years ago, especially recently, I want to detail it here.

In my vision, I saw a teenage boy who had been raised by the agents of Order to take over the world. I saw this boy rise to power. I saw him take away the rights of choice and decision from countless numbers of people. Then I saw a girl, filled with the spirit of Azazel, come from the depths of the woods. She carried with her a spear of fire. And she smote the agent of order, and Chaos reigned again in the world.

© Michaela Weem, www.thegreatgodazazel.com

Trees streamed by outside the window of Toby's truck as I struggled against the rope he'd tied my hands with. Toby drove recklessly fast, his mask still on. I didn't think he could see with it over his eyes. I strained, yanking my wrists away from each other as hard as I could. But the rope held. I wasn't doing anything except giving myself rug burn.

I glared at Toby. "Where are we going?" I asked. Was this some kind of practical joke? If it was, it wasn't funny. I really wasn't enjoying it.

Toby just laughed from behind his mask. He didn't answer.

"What are you doing with Jason?" I asked.

Nothing from Toby.

I was flabbergasted when Toby pulled his truck into my driveway. He was taking me to *my* house? Why were we here? Toby got out of the truck and came around to my side. Roughly, he pulled me out. I stumbled as I tried to keep my balance while he yanked me forward. Behind us, I could see the car that Jason was in. He was getting similar treatment. The football players, still wearing their masks, were dragging Jason along with them.

"Toby, what is going on?" I demanded.

Toby cocked his head at me. From behind the mask, he looked so blank. "Oh, come on, Zaza," he said. "We're going to consummate our relationship. Isn't that what you've wanted all this time?"

I winced at the ugliness of his voice. And what the hell was he talking about? If Toby thought I still wanted to have sex with him after what had happened, he was a mental patient. I didn't want to look at Toby ever again, let alone touch him.

He dug his fingers into my arm and tugged me forward. I had to go with him. If I resisted, I'd just fall down.

The lights in my house were all off, but the kitchen door was open. We all went inside. Toby led the group of masked madmen through my dining room and living room, to the door to the basement. He opened it.

The soft light of candles greeted us. Our basement wasn't much. It wasn't finished. It was just a concrete hole in the ground. It always smelled musty down there, and no one went into it except to get our washer and dryer.

But someone had been in the basement recently. A tea light candle blazed on each step of the stairs leading down into its depths. Toby forced me onto the first step. I tried to resist, but he was strong. Carefully, we descended into the gaping mouth of the basement, one step at a time. As I got lower and lower, I could see that the entire basement was covered in candles. They were clustered in every corner. They sat on tables, which surrounded the room. Each table was covered in a black velvet tablecloth. The washer and dryer had been similarly covered in black velvet, and candles of various heights and widths placed on them.

All of the candles were black.

On one of the tables, many silver chalices sat next to a decanter of wine. There was also a loaf of bread next to them. It sat on a silver platter. In the center of the basement, there was a bed. It was covered in black silk sheets. From the steps to the bed was a trail of black rose petals.

I nearly gagged. What was this? What had Toby planned? It was like an inversion of everything he'd ever said to me. Black rose petals? A bed with silk sheets? Me tied up? Half of the football team?

I was started to feel very, very frightened.

"We're a little early," said Toby to the rest of them. He pulled some rope from his pocket and tossed it to his friends. "Tie Jason to that pole," he ordered, gesturing with his head.

The football players dragged Jason to the pole and began lashing him to it. His arms. His feet. His neck. Jason caught my eyes. I looked back at him. I could tell he was trying to figure out a way out of this.

"I'll get Azazel ready," said Toby, his voice cruel and determined.

Toby took me to the bed. He made me sit down. I realized that not everything silk on the bed was a sheet. There were also two black silk hooded robes sitting next to us. They looked like something off the cover of a death metal album. What was this? What was going on? My heart beat in my chest loudly. It pumped blood against my temple. I was freaking out.

I tried to smile at Toby. "Okay," I said. "This was funny. I'm laughing. You can stop now, though. Really."

Toby sighed. "It wasn't supposed to be like this Azazel. I didn't want to have to tie you up. But after you heard Lilith and me, I didn't know what else to do. The ritual has to go on as scheduled, whether you're willing or not."

Ritual? What ritual? I was terrified.

"I'm going to have to untie you for a minute," said Toby. "But you can't try to run away or anything, or else I'm going to have to get some of the guys over here to hold you down. And I really don't want to do that."

Okay. Maybe I wouldn't run.

Toby fumbled in his back pocket for a pocketknife. I shied away from it as he opened the blade. But he just cut the rope holding my wrists together.

Toby surveyed the marks on my wrists that I'd made trying to get free from the rope. He touched them almost tenderly. "You shouldn't have struggled," he said. "You're just hurting yourself." He looked into my eyes. "This is really an honor, you know. You're going to become so powerful."

Powerful? Honor? Hadn't Toby said something about an honor in the restroom earlier? Oh God. There was more to everything than just Toby and Lilith having sex. They'd said all kinds of weird things. And they both had said things about not being allowed. This was connected to that, somehow. Somehow.

But how?

Toby reached around me and put his hands on the zipper of my dress. He started to unzip it. He was going to take my dress off?! In front of everyone?!

"No!" I said. I put both of my hands on his chest and pushed him as hard as I could. He grabbed my wrists, irritated.

"Don't struggle," he said. "I'm just trying to put the robe on you."

"Toby, don't," I begged suddenly. "Don't." I looked deep into his eyes, and shook my head, trying to find some piece of the boy I thought I knew in there.

"Don't look at me like that," he yelled. He dropped my hands and took a step back, disgust all over his face.

I pressed my advantage. "Toby, you can let me go," I said. "You can just let me go. I won't tell anyone. I'll just walk away, and I'll—"

"It's not supposed to be like this," he said.

"Please Toby," I said.

He reached over and balled up one of the robes in his hands. He shoved it at me. "Put on the robe," he said, his voice shaking. "Just take everything off and put on the robe."

A little sound escaped my mouth. Take everything off? I didn't want to—I *couldn't* think about what was going to happen to me.

Jason looked at me from where he was tied to the pole. His face was unreadable.

"Do it!" Toby screamed.

I couldn't. I couldn't just take off my clothes.

Toby turned around. He glanced over his shoulder. "Don't try to run," he warned me.

The other guys on the football team were standing around Jason, watching Toby and I.

"Turn around," Toby ordered them.

Silently, they did.

"And Jason," said Toby. "Close your eyes."

Jason closed his eyes.

But I couldn't move. I looked at the crumpled robe in my lap, and I couldn't move.

"Hurry up," growled Toby.

And because I didn't know what else to do, I did it. I unzipped my dress. It fell off me, pooled around my feet. There I was in the lingerie I had put on for Toby to see. I nearly gagged in revulsion. But I took it off. And I put on the robe. It buttoned up, and I buttoned every button, but I still felt very, very exposed.

"I'm done," I whispered.

Toby turned around. He looked me up and down. "Good," he said. Then he tied my hands again. He walked me over to the football players, threw me into one of their arms. "Hold her," he said. "I'll be back with the rest of the coven to do the Invocation."

Toby swept up the stairs. One of the football players had me in a bear hug. There was nothing between my skin and his body except the stupid, flimsy robe. I started to think about what was happening to me, to speculate about the near future. Then I decided it was a bad idea, and so I stopped. I just concentrated on breathing.

In a few minutes, the door at the top of the steps opened and a long line of people in black robes like mine came down the steps. Their hoods were over their heads and they stared at the floor. I couldn't see their faces in the scant candlelight.

They formed a circle. One of them came for me, pulled me into the center of the circle.

Now that he was close, I could see it was Toby.

"Why are her hands tied?" asked one of the hooded people. The voice sounded familiar, but I was sick of identifying voices tonight. I knew who it was, but I didn't want to know, so I just tried not to.

"Complication," said Toby. "Let's just get on with it."

"Untie her," ordered another hooded person. I knew that voice too.

No. No. No.

No.

I struggled for other thoughts, and there was only one. No.

Toby fumbled with the knot at my wrist. I had started to shake. My teeth were chattering. I couldn't believe this was happening to me. I couldn't believe it. Maybe, if I tried hard enough, I'd just faint. Couldn't I just faint? Couldn't I just make this not real, somehow?

One of the hooded people advanced to help Toby. I could tell from her hands that she was a woman as she deftly untied the knot at my wrist. I purposefully didn't look at her face. I tried so hard not to, but ...

She cupped my chin in her hands. "Zaza, it's okay," she said.

And then I lost it. I started sobbing. And I said the only word I knew to identify the woman with. The only thing that sprang to mind. My voice broke with the betrayal of it. "Mommy," I sobbed.

My mother gathered me into her arms. "Why are you crying, sweetie?" she asked me.

Why was I crying? Was she insane? My own parents had set me up to be in some sort of cult ritual where my boyfriend ... raped me, and she wanted to know why I was crying?

Still, I clung to her as my body was wracked with sobs

185

that I thought would tear me apart. She was the only ghost of comfort left in a world that had been completely and utterly turned upside down, ripped apart, ruined.

My mother clutched me, stroking my hair. She turned to another hooded person. "Daniel, I told you she wasn't ready," she said.

My father lowered his hood. He looked at us sympathetically. "It has to be tonight," he said helplessly. "The next night of power isn't until the solstice. We can't wait that long."

My mother nodded. She turned back to me, wiping at my tears, brushing my hair out of my face. "Okay, then, Zaza," she said. "You're just going to have to be strong, okay? Can you do that for me? Can you be my strong girl?"

No, I couldn't be strong! What did she want from me? I just shook my head violently, back and forth. I couldn't do this. I couldn't do this.

Around me, all of the hooded people were lowering their hoods. Lilith. Sheriff Damon. His wife. The principal of my high school. Mrs. Clem, the dean of students. Mrs. Zimmerman, my French teacher. Sherry Astor. My older brothers, Noah and Gordon. I knew them all. I gazed around the circle, and I saw the pillars of society in our town. I saw people from my high school. They were all part of this. Whatever this was. I didn't know. And I didn't think I wanted to know.

"This is all going wrong," said Sheriff Damon. "What did you do, Toby?"

Lilith stepped forward. "It's not Toby's fault, it's mine," she said. "Let me talk to her." She walked up to me and took my hand. "Upstairs, Zaza," she said.

Confused, I let Lilith drag me upstairs.

Once through the basement door, she shut it after us. She looked down at herself. "God, these robes are so unflattering," she said. "You'd think they'd at least let you wear a bra under them, you know? But it's all, 'The host has be defiled through sexuality, blah, blah, blah.'"

What was she talking about?

"You're probably wondering what's going on," she said.

That was an understatement.

"It's weird, I know," she said. "When it happened to me, I was totally freaked out, too."

"This happened to you?" I asked in a small voice.

"Well, sort of," she said. "It's supposed to happen on your eighteenth birthday, and there's supposed to be a little more lead up to the whole thing, like a couple hints and a test."

"A test?"

"Not like on paper, but someone from the coven like grills you on choice and chaos and junk. You didn't get that because you've been chosen from birth to be the vessel or whatever, and they had to rush the whole thing, because Jason showed up, so they have to do the Invocation and the Entering of the Circle all on one night. Which incidentally is almost over. We've got like fifteen minutes until midnight, so I've got to talk fast."

"What?" I said. But I was starting to calm down. Sort of. At least Lilith seemed like herself still.

"We're Satanists, Azazel," said Lilith.

Satanists?! I considered bolting for the door right then. But I was only wearing a flimsy black robe, and practically everyone I knew and would ask for help was already in my basement. Besides I couldn't leave Jason down there with them.

"I mean, kind of," said Lilith. "We worship Azazel. The demon you're named after."

"Oh God," I moaned.

"Yeah, don't say that. That's like blasphemy," she said. "Okay, so, see Azazel is an incarnation of what most people would identify with Satan. But we worship Satan, or Azazel, because he symbolizes the ability of people to have free will and to be individuals. We worship Chaos because it isn't stifling, and it doesn't assume that people need order enforced upon them to function properly in society."

She sounded like she was reciting something.

"So we reject the incarnations of order, including Christianity and other organized religions, because they impose a set of rules and values onto people which is ... stifling. You following me?"

"Kind of," I said.

"Okay, so, when you're eighteen, you Enter the Circle by participating in a Black Mass. Which is like a perversion of a traditional Mass. So we take the host—or communion or whatever—and then everybody has sex."

"Eew," I said.

"Not in front of each other. And usually with their husbands or wives or boyfriends. Usually. And the initiate — in this case you — has sex with someone in the room with it all set up like it is."

"Why?" I said.

"It's just a ritual. I don't know. I think because everyone in town is horny," she said.

"And the initiate is a virgin?" I asked.

"Not usually. I mean, I wasn't. Most eighteen-year-olds have gotten it on, you know what I mean. But you like had to be, because you're the vessel. And so, they made Toby date you and not have sex with you, so that you'd be pure."

"But you said that you and Toby started dating after eighth grade," I said. "I thought you didn't find out about this stuff until you were eighteen."

"Our parents bribed us," said Lilith. "They gave Toby that truck so he'd date you. And my parents gave me my computer. It was important that you didn't have sex."

"This is gross," I said.

"When you think about it, it's not really that much grosser than thinking communion wafers turn into someone's body in your mouth," she said.

That *was* gross. "But what do mean, I'm the vessel?" I asked.

"Oh," she said. "That. Well, see this other Satanist chick who runs this online forum or something had a vision of Jason, like seventeen years ago, before he was born. And in her vision, a girl filled with the power of Azazel vanquished him. I'm not sure how they know this, but she confirmed that was you, after you were conceived. So, they're gonna do an invocation to Azazel, and the spirit of Azazel will fill your body, and then ... you'll kill Jason."

"What?!" the words exploded out of me.

"I know," said Lilith. "I mean, I'm kind of on board with the whole let's-be-free-and-have-lots-of-sex thing. And the black robes aren't even all that bad. But this is kind of ... I don't know. I mean, they say that Jason really isn't a person, because he's an agent of Order or whatever, and he's destined to like enslave the entire human race, but ... I mean, didn't they say that about Jews during the Holocaust or black people when they were lynching them?" She looked very thoughtful. "I don't want to go against the coven, but I just kind of feel like it would be ... wrong to kill someone."

I covered my face with my hands. Lilith was stupid, I realized. I had no idea how we'd been friends for as long as we had. Had I never noticed what an idiot she was? But I had to get Jason and me out of here. Somehow. Because there was no way I was killing him. "So," I said, "what order is this going to happen in? I mean, Invocation first or Entering the Circle first?"

"Invocation," she said. "We have to. It's practically midnight. So, I figure, they'll invoke Azazel, then everybody will get busy, and then we'll all get back together so that you can kill Jason."

"Okay," I said. I could work with that. So they were

going to invoke the spirit of Azazel into my body, huh? I could handle that. Especially since I didn't believe Azazel existed. While they were doing that, I was going to have to come up with a plan that didn't involve my getting busy with anyone and also involved my getting both Jason and I out of here alive. "Let's get this over with."

"Really?" said Lilith. "I didn't think you'd want to kill Jason."

I shrugged. "I'm the vessel," I said. "I guess some part of me's always known this is what I was born to do."

Lilith shrugged back. "Cool." She smiled. "That didn't take nearly as long as I thought it would." She paused. "Oh, and Zaza, I'm really sorry about sleeping with Toby. I really am."

"Save it," I snapped. "We'll talk about that later." If I'd actually been planning to stick around, I would never have forgiven her for that.

Lilith led me back down the steps triumphantly.

"I'm ready," I said.

My mother put her hand to her chest and breathed a sigh of relief. "Oh thank Chaos," she said. "I was so guilty, Zaza. I really didn't want to push this on you."

"It's fine, Mom," I said. I'd think about the fact that my mom was a demon worshipper later. Right now, I had to save Jason.

He was still tied to the pole. Hoping no one would notice, I winked at him. If Jason saw, he didn't acknowledge it with his face.

191

I rejoined Toby in the center of the circle. They all raised their hoods again, so I did too. Toby took my hand. Oh yuck. I did not want to hold Toby's hand. But I had to play along, at least for a little while.

Suddenly, everyone in the circle began intoning some kind of chant in a language I didn't understand. I peered out from under the edge of my hood. Weird. Creepy.

My father stepped forward. He approached me and lifted his hands up to the ceiling. "Great God of Chaos, Azazel, I invoke thee," his voice rang out, echoing off the walls.

He nodded at me. "Repeat that," he said.

Sure, whatever. I raised my hands questioningly. My dad nodded. "Great God of Chaos, Azazel, I invoke thee," I said and really hoped my voice didn't sound sarcastic.

My mother approached, holding an ornate silver chalice. She handed it to my father. He held it in front of me. "Fill your vessel as this liquid fills her body." His voice still had that ringing quality. It was kind of scary.

My father handed me the chalice. I took it. "Repeat," he said.

I hesitated for a second. What if I was wrong, and Azazel really was real? What if I really did get filled with the spirit of a demon?

I chewed on my lip, undecided.

No. There was no way that demons were real.

"Fill this vessel, as this liquid fills my body," I said. This time, there was definitely a cocky edge to my voice.

"Drink," said my father.

I put the chalice to my lips. I drank.

"Finish it," said my dad.

I didn't really know what I was drinking. It tasted alcoholic, but it wasn't beer. Was it wine? I chugged it, grimacing from the taste.

Silence.

Well. Nothing was happening. Maybe they'd done it wrong.

But everyone seemed satisfied. A hooded person, I couldn't tell whom, was gathering the less ornate silver chalices I'd seen on the way in and handing them to each person. Behind them, another robed person offered them the loaf of bread. Each person silently ripped off a hunk of bread. Once they had bread and wine, they started up the steps in pairs. I guess this was the defiling of the host part of the Black Mass. All in all, I was finding it pretty anticlimactic.

Finally, there was no one left but Toby and me. We were each handed a wine glass, and we each took our bread. Then the people who'd given it to us also went up the steps. Toby and I were alone, except for Jason, who was still tied to the pole.

Toby stuffed the bread into his mouth and chewed. I did the same thing. Then he drank his wine in one gulp. I drank mine too. That was definitely not the same stuff that had been in the chalice. What had I drunk? I desperately hoped it wasn't something disgusting like animal blood.

Now, here was the problem. We'd done the Invocation, and were somewhere in the middle of the Entering the Circle, and I still hadn't come up with a plan to save Jason.

Toby advanced on me.

Great. What was I going to do? What was I going to do? I glanced around the basement, hoping for inspiration. All I saw were candles and Jason.

I made a face at Toby. "Do we have to do this with him watching?" I asked.

Toby looked over at Jason.

I didn't think. I just acted. I grabbed onto Toby's shoulders and kneed him as hard as I could in the crotch.

Toby howled, doubling over in pain.

I ran to Jason, fumbling with the knots behind his hands. I couldn't get them undone! What was I going to do?

Toby was still bent over, moaning.

I dashed over to the washer and dryer and grabbed a candle. Back behind Jason, I used the flame to burn the rope.

Jason made a noise when I burned him.

"Sorry," I said.

But he snapped the rope that held his hands.

Toby was gagging on the other side of the basement.

"My neck," said Jason. "Get the one at my neck!"

I held the candle higher. Jason held the rope away from his skin so that it was easier for me to burn it. The smell of burning rope filled the room. Jason pulled at the rope. It snapped too.

Toby was getting up and lumbering towards us.

194

Apparently, he'd recovered from the kick I'd given his balls.

Panicking, I knelt down to get the rope at Jason's feet.

Toby advanced.

Jason knelt down too, holding the rope in the same manner as he had before.

Toby came closer. He reached for Jason.

Jason balled up a fist and punched up into Toby, catching him in the stomach.

Toby stumbled backwards.

Jason yanked hard on the rope at his feet, and it broke as well. He was free.

But Toby was on his feet again and coming for Jason.

Like the time in the alcove, Jason moved fast. He punched Toby's face twice, hard — one-two. Toby's nose started to bleed, but he kept coming. He threw a punch at Jason, which Jason easily sidestepped.

Toby's punch left his midsection open. Jason's fists collided with Toby's stomach again. Toby fell back again, and tried to grab at Jason, use his momentum to topple both of them.

Instead, Jason kicked Toby's feet out from under him. Toby hit the floor hard. Jason didn't stop, even though Toby was down. He kicked him in the face. Once. Twice. Three times. He kicked until Toby stopped moving.

Then he looked at me. "You're okay?" he asked.

I nodded. "Mostly," I said. "You?"

"Never better," he said tightly. He looked around the basement. "Where'd the others go?"

"They're busy," I said. I didn't even want to *think* about it. Yuck. "Come on," I said, reaching for his hand.

I pulled us up the steps and out into the living room. There were robed people lying horizontal on the couch. I didn't look. I didn't want to know who it was.

We raced through the dining room. There were robed people on the dining room table. Oh, gross, gross, gross!

They noticed us flying past. "Hey," said a male voice.

We darted through the kitchen and outside. We ran up the driveway. Then I realized the hole in my plan. How were we going to get away? And where were we going to go?

I stopped, but Jason dragged me forward. There were tons of cars in the driveway, all belonging to people who were inside, I guessed. Jason started trying door handles. They were locked.

"Help me," he said.

I went to the first car I saw and yanked on the door handle. Locked. Second car next to it. Locked.

"Got one!" Jason called. I looked up. He was several cars down from me, standing next to the open door of a glossy black Nissan. I ran to him, opening the passenger's side door.

"You know how hotwire a car?" I asked.

"I do," he said, "but lucky us, the keys are in the ignition." And he started the car.

As Jason backed the car out of the driveway, robed people began filtering out of the house, running towards their cars.

We pulled onto the road, and Jason sped away from my house, going as fast as he could around the curves. I reached for my seatbelt. I hoped we weren't going to die in a car wreck. "They're going to follow us," I said to him.

"Yep," he said. "And that's not our only problem."

"What?" I said.

"I'm still wearing the goddamned ankle monitor," he said.

"Fuck!" I exclaimed.

Chapter Eleven

To: Hallam Wakefield (hwakefi@risingsun.org)
From: Alfred Norwich (anorwic@risingsun.org)
Subject: (none)

We've tried to reach you repeatedly since we discovered that you weren't in New York. You were never in New York. All we can determine is that you were lying for some reason unknown to us. Since we cannot be sure of your motives, and we cannot get in touch with you, you should consider yourself excommunicated from the Sons of the Rising Sun, effective immediately. I do not need to remind you of the consequences of a decision like this.

On a more personal note, I wish to say that if you showed good faith and turned yourself in, I would argue to the Council on your behalf. Until this little stunt, you have been an asset to the Order. I am saddened to be writing this.

Alfred

A high-speed chase through the back roads of West Virginia was nothing like a high-speed chase on the movies. For one thing, all the roads only had two lanes, and there weren't very many passing zones. Jason wasn't used to driving in the mountains, and though he tried to go as fast as he could, the Satanists behind us were gaining on us. We got stuck behind a really slow car on Route 50, and they were right on our tail.

I was screaming. Jason was swearing. The car was ramming into the back of our stolen Nissan. Overall, everything looked bleak.

Then Jason passed the car in a no passing zone. Another car appeared around a blind curve.

We were in their lane.

If it were possible, I screamed harder. I just knew we were going to have a head-on collision.

But the car swerved into the guardrail on the side of the road, and Jason jerked us back into our lane, nearly grazing the car we'd just passed.

I looked over my shoulder out the back window. The car that had swerved lost control and rammed into one of the Satanist's cars.

Lucky us, again. There was a four-car pile up, blocking any pursuit of us.

I stopped screaming and stared forward. "I hope no one died," I said.

But we weren't too lucky. After all, they could still find Jason with his ankle monitor. And we had nowhere to go. No one to help us.

"I have to get this monitor off," said Jason. "I'm going to pull over."

It made me nervous to be stopped, but Jason was right. Wherever we went with that thing on him, we'd have a homing beacon.

Jason pulled the car over onto the shoulder and switched

on the overhead light.

"How are you going to take it off?" I asked.

"I could do it with scissors," he said. "How likely is it that there are scissors in this car?"

I searched the glove compartment. "There's a nail file," I said.

"Give it to me."

Jason struggled with the monitor for a long time, but only succeeded in breaking the nail file.

"I need something stronger," he said, looking around the car. "What's in the glove compartment?"

"Tissues. Owner's manual. Ice scraper."

"How big is the ice scraper?"

I showed it to him. It was one of those plastic hand-held kinds. It said "World's Greatest Dad" on it. It was maybe eight inches long.

"I'll try it," he said. He took the ice scraper and wedged it between the monitor and his leg. "See, I think if I could just apply enough pressure, I could snap it off," he said.

Instead, the ice scraper snapped in two. "Damn it!" said Jason. "There anything else in there?"

"A mini-maglite," I said.

"Yes," he said. "That."

At first Jason couldn't get the maglite flashlight between the monitor and his ankle. But then he forced it in, and when he did, the monitor's rivets popped away from the bracelet and the monitor fell off his leg. "Success!" said Jason, high-fiving me.

I grinned.

Jason got out of the car and placed the monitor under one of the wheels. Then he got back in and ran over the thing. We heard it crunch as we pulled away.

"Now," said Jason. "You need clothes, and we'll eventually run out of gas, and then we won't have a car. So ... basically we need money."

Suddenly, I knew where we could go. "I have an idea," I told Jason.

* * *

When we pulled into Ms. Campbell's driveway all the lights in her apartment were off.

"I can't believe you know where she lives," said Jason.

"It's downtown Bramford," I said. "Everybody knows where she lives."

"I still think this is weird."

"She said I could come to her," I said. "And she wasn't at the crazy ritual-thing tonight, so we know she's not a Satanist. She can get us help."

"I think we should just hold up a convenience store for cash," Jason said.

"That will get us arrested," I said. "Let's not break the law, okay?"

"I just crushed an ankle bracelet in case you don't remember," he said. "I'm pretty sure that's gonna get us arrested."

"Whatever," I said, getting out of the car.

Jason followed suit. We climbed the steps up to Ms.

Campbell's front door and rang the doorbell. For a long time, nothing happened.

Then a man opened the door. He wasn't wearing a shirt, just a pair of jeans with holes in them.

Jason looked at me, as if to say, "Are you sure we have the right house?"

I didn't know either. As far as I knew, Ms. Campbell didn't have a husband. "Um," I said, "we're looking for Ms. Campbell."

"Jenna!" called the man over his shoulder. "I think some of your students are here."

Ms. Campbell appeared at the top of a staircase, which was visible from the door. She was wearing a long t-shirt that came to her knees. It said in upside down letters, "If you can read this, put me back on the bar stool." Ugh. Ms. Campbell drank? I guessed she really wasn't that old. "Azazel? Jason?" she said. "What are you doing here?"

She hurried down the steps, pushing the man out of the way. "Well, come in," she said. "Jesus, Azazel, what are you wearing?"

She ushered us inside and pulled the door closed after us.

"We're sorry we woke you up," I said.

"Oh no," she said. "We were awake. We were—no, we were asleep. We were very asleep." She looked flustered. "This had better not be some sort of Halloween prank. I will flunk you both, don't think I won't."

"Not a prank," I said. "We're really sorry."

"Well, it's okay. I guess. Are you two okay?"

"Not really," said Jason.

"No, huh?" She nodded. "Let's sit down."

She flicked on some lights and led us into her living room, which was a total mess. There were clothes strewn over the couches, dirty dishes piled on the coffee table, a bag of chips sitting on the floor. Ms. Campbell started picking things up off the couches so that we could sit down.

"I wasn't really expecting company," she said.

"It's okay," I said.

"Sit down," she told us. "I'm gonna go put on some pants."

She disappeared out of the living room for a second.

We were left with the shirtless guy. "I'm gonna go with her," he said.

Alone, I made an apologetic face at Jason. "Maybe this wasn't a good idea," I said.

"Why, because we probably interrupted Ms. Campbell and her boyfriend?" he asked. "You didn't think she was a nun, did you?"

"Ugh." I shuddered. "I just don't want to think about anybody else having any sex tonight at all."

"Noted," said Jason.

Ms. Campbell reappeared. She was wearing a different shirt and a pair of jeans. The man was wearing the shirt she'd been wearing. They sat down on the opposite couch from us.

"So," said Ms. Campbell. "What's up?"

"Everyone in town is a Satanist," I said.

"You said this wasn't a Halloween prank," she said.

"It's not," I said. "They forced me to wear this robe and made me drink weird stuff out of a chalice and tried to force me to ritualistically kill Jason."

Ms. Campbell sat back on the couch. She turned to her boyfriend. "Kevin?" she said. "Can you get me another beer?" She looked at us. "You guys want ... ? No, wait. You're underage. I shouldn't be drinking in front of you."

"It's okay," I said.

"Really," said Jason. "This whole night has been too weird for anything to shake us."

"Well," she said. "Since I'm already kind of drunk anyway ..."

Ms. Campbell was drunk? Was nothing sacred?

Kevin went into the kitchen and came back with two open beer bottles. Ms. Campbell took a long swig. "Okay, then," she said. "So, you were captured by Satanists."

"I didn't know they were Satanists," said Jason. "And they were trying to kill me? Really?"

I started at the beginning. Told them all the whole story, including the fact that I'd found out Lilith and Toby were screwing around behind my back. When I was finished, Ms. Campbell was on her second beer.

Jason looked appalled, and Kevin was staring at me like I was from another planet.

Ms. Campbell stood up. "Okay," she said. "Okay. Um, first, Azazel, I'm gonna get you some clothes. They'll probably be big on you, but they'll be better than that robe thing."

While I changed in Ms. Campbell's bathroom, I could hear her talking in the living room.

"What am I gonna do?" she was saying. "I don't know what to do. I mean, who do I call? I can't call her parents. They're the ones who are doing this crap."

I emerged from the bathroom in a slightly baggy pair of jeans and t-shirt. Ms. Campbell had given me a sports bra, which fit me okay. I felt much better now that I was clothed.

"I'm sorry," I said to her. "We never should have come here." In the classroom, Ms. Campbell had seemed like an authority figure, with power. Now, I realized she was just a person, and that she was only six or seven years older than us. She was just as floored by all of this as we were.

"No," said Ms. Campbell, "you did the right thing. I'm a teacher. You trusted me. You came to me for help. That's good. It means I'm doing my job, I'm just ..." She trailed off. "You mean your dad, Daniel Jones, and the principal, and like the entire administration, they're all Satanists?"

I nodded.

"Actually," she said, "that explains a lot." She shook her head in amazement. "Okay," she said. "I'm gonna make some calls. You guys sit tight. Um, I think I have some stale chips somewhere if you're hungry." And she disappeared into the kitchen.

Finally, she returned. "It's okay," she said. "Some people are coming. Authority-type people who deal with this kind of thing. We'll get this figured out."

Maybe it hadn't been a horrible idea coming here. Maybe everything was going to work out.

"I should get rid of the beer bottles," said Ms. Campbell, gathering them up.

"So," said Kevin to me, "you've lived in West Virginia you're whole life?"

I nodded.

"People really are whack-jobs, here, huh?" he asked.

Jason shrugged. "Well, they seemed very nice at first."

"Right," said Kevin.

Ms. Campbell came back into the living room. "God," she said. "My apartment's a wreck. This is so embarrassing." She peered out her window. "Oh, I think a police car's pulling up already. That was fast."

"Police?" I said. " *Local* police?"

"I guess so if they responded so quickly," she said.

"Who exactly did you call?" Jason asked.

"Um, I called Cora. Cora Ridgely, the counselor at our school," she said.

"Oh no," I said. "She was there, tonight. She's one of them."

Ms. Campbell shrugged. "Well, we weren't all there tonight, Azazel," she said. "I hadn't seen Kevin in weeks, and it was Halloween."

"We?" I said, a sinking feeling developing in my stomach.

Kevin spread his hands. "Hail Satan, kids," he said,

grinning.

No. No, this was not happening.

I looked at Jason. His face was strained. I had to be the stupidest person on earth.

"It's everyone in town, isn't it?" I said.

"Yeah," said Ms. Campbell. "Hey, for what it's worth, you've probably had so much luck so far because you're imbued with the spirit of Azazel. You may not think that ritual worked, but—"

"Shut up," said Jason. "And Robert Herrick was not a dirty old man, okay?" He grabbed my hand. "Back door," he said.

And we were running.

We burst through the back door of Ms. Campbell's apartment and into the alley behind it. Jason gripped my hand as our feet pounded against the pavement. Jason ran fast. I struggled to keep up.

They were pursuing us. Though I didn't look back, I could hear the screen door of Ms. Campbell's back door slamming and the footsteps behind us.

Jason darted down streets, taking turns at random, still holding onto my hand tightly. He was trying to lose them. Trying to take so many turns that they couldn't follow. But they were right behind us, and it wasn't working. I was out of breath. Jason was in much better shape than I was. I felt like an iron fist was closing over my lungs. I didn't know how much longer I could keep this up.

"Stop or I'll shoot!" called a voice behind us.

Shoot? Would they really shoot us? I was the vessel, wasn't I? That had to count for something.

Jason abruptly turned onto a side street, pulling me with him. However, instead of continuing to run, he flattened us against the side of a house. Jason stood at the corner, his face trained on the street.

What was he going to do?

I tried not to breathe too loudly, but I couldn't help it. Jason didn't seem to notice my noisy panting. He was too busy watching the street.

Within a few moments, one of the deputies rounded the corner.

Jason dashed towards him. The deputy was startled to see Jason coming at him. He'd thought we were still running up the street. Jason tackled him. The deputy went down. There was a frenzied struggle, a tangle of limbs—Jason's and the deputy's.

Then Jason got to his feet, holding the deputy's gun. He leveled the gun at the man.

"Jason!" I said.

Jason pulled the trigger anyway.

The deputy screamed.

I covered my mouth in horror.

Jason came for me again. "I just shot his leg," he said in answer to my expression, tucking the gun into the waist of his pants.

And we were running again.

A police car raced by on the street perpendicular to us,

its sirens wailing. Another car screeched to a halt at the end of the street we were running down, blocking our exit.

Jason turned left, down a different street, but there was a car blocking the end of that street too.

We stopped.

They were blocking us in!

We ran back up the street and back the way we came, but there was the police car I'd seen racing by us.

Jason's eyes swept the area. I could tell he was searching for a way out, the way he always did. He didn't see one. Cars blocked off all of the streets around us. "Damn it," said Jason.

He pulled out the gun he'd stolen from the deputy.

"Jason, what are you going to—"

"They're trying to kill me," he said. "At this point, it's all self-defense."

"Don't," I said. I didn't like the idea of Jason with a gun, even though he seemed to know what he was doing with one. He looked comfortable with a gun in his hand, as if he'd held guns tons of times before.

Jason kept me close. One hand held mine. The other held the gun. We stood in the intersection of two streets, and watched as people got out of each of the cars that were parked at the end of all of our exits.

They were coming at us from four directions. Jason pivoted, leveling his gun first at one direction and then at another.

"Don't shoot anyone," I begged him. I didn't know why.

These people were clearly crazy. But they used to be my family and friends. And shooting people was ...

"Azazel, do you want to get out of here alive?" asked Jason.

"Yes," I said.

"Okay, then," he said. And he shot someone.

Down one of the streets, I saw a figure crumple.

"Oh my God," I whispered.

"All of you stop," yelled Jason, aiming his gun at another approaching figure.

They kept coming.

"Did you ... kill him?" I managed.

"No," he said to me in irritation. "I've been shooting guns since I was five. Give me some credit."

Five?

"I'll shoot someone else," Jason threatened in a loud voice.

The man who Jason had his gun trained on stopped.

The other two figures were closer now. I could see that one was Sheriff Damon. The other was my dad.

Sheriff Damon had his gun out as he approached.

Jason pulled the trigger again. The figure who had stopped cried out and fell.

I couldn't help it. I screamed.

Sheriff Damon and my dad stopped.

"Jason," called my dad, "let's talk about this."

Sheriff Damon was aiming his gun at both of us.

Jason pointed his gun at my dad.

"Jason!" I cried. I didn't want him to shoot my dad. My dad might be a crazy Satanist, but I didn't want anyone to shoot him.

Jason ignored me. "You could try shooting, Sheriff," said Jason. "But can you be sure you won't hit the girl?"

What was he doing? Why was he taunting the sheriff like that? And would Sheriff Damon shoot me? I hadn't exactly been cooperative.

"Tell him to lower his gun, Daniel," said Jason to my dad.

My dad's voice was hoarse. "He doesn't answer to me," he said.

"He might shoot your daughter," said Jason. "You better make him answer to you."

"Jim," said my dad, his voice still hoarse.

I glanced back and forth between the sheriff and my dad. The sheriff still had his gun on us. My dad's face was twisted in fear. So, he still cared about me. Weird. He had a funny way of showing it.

"I won't hit her, Daniel," said Sheriff Damon, not taking his eyes off Jason and me.

"You can't shoot him," said my dad. "The ritual has to be performed by the vessel, or it won't work."

Did they really still think they could convince me to kill Jason?

Sheriff Damon's hand wavered, as if he were hesitating. Then he seemed to get hold of himself, tighten his grip on the gun. "She's not going to do it, Daniel," he said. "We have to take him out."

This wasn't going well at all. Now, right in front of my eyes, Sheriff Damon was going to kill Jason. None of my plans to save him—to save us—had worked out very well. Maybe Jason was right to be shooting people.

Jason looked at Sheriff Damon, his gun still pointed at my dad. "I didn't want to have to do this," he said.

Oh God, what was he going to do?

In one fluid movement, Jason pulled me into his arms, so that his stomach was against my back. One arm pinned me against him. The other snapped the gun against my temple.

I whimpered in surprise.

"Trust me," Jason breathed in my ear. To Sheriff Damon, "Put the gun *down* !"

Sheriff Damon lowered his gun immediately.

"On the ground," said Jason. "Carefully, slowly, put it on the ground."

Sheriff Damon hesitated.

"For Chaos' sake, do what he says!" screamed my father.

Sheriff Damon knelt and placed his gun on the ground.

"Slide it to me," Jason ordered.

Sheriff Damon complied. The gun skittered across the pavement and rested at my feet.

"Pick it up," Jason told me. I knelt down to get it, Jason still holding his gun against my head. Jason took the gun from me and put it in the waist of his pants. His arm wrapped around me again, pulling me tight against him.

I wasn't afraid of Jason, but I was really thinking this

strategy was going to backfire if they called his bluff. Certainly they knew that Jason wouldn't hurt me. Of course, I guess they also thought he was an agent of Order who was going enslave the entire human race. Maybe they thought he was pretty much capable of anything.

And, as frightened as I was, I kind of liked the way it felt to be this close to Jason.

"Okay," said Jason. "Here's what's going to happen. I'm going to take Azazel, and we're going to get in a car. We're going to drive away. If I hear or see anyone following us, I will put a bullet in your precious vessel's skull, got that?"

God. His voice sounded so hard and cruel. He was good at this.

"We understand," said my dad. He was gazing at me helplessly, like he desperately wanted to help me and didn't know how.

But he'd betrayed me. They all had. Everyone had. Everyone I trusted. I was alone now. And the only person I did trust had a gun to my head.

"Good," said Jason. "Somebody bring me some keys."

My father stepped forward, pulling his keys from my pocket. "You can take my car," he said.

But Jason didn't have a hand to take the keys.

"Azazel, take the keys," he told me.

I held out my hand and my dad placed his keys in it.

"Zaza, baby," said my dad. "I'm so sorry."

"Don't talk to her," Jason ordered.

But what was he sorry for? Sorry that he wasn't saving

me from Jason? Sorry he and his goons had pursued me all over town, trying to take me somewhere against my will? Sorry that he'd arranged the way his own daughter would lose her virginity, like he was my pimp not my father? What was he sorry for? Could he ever be sorry enough? Somehow, I doubted it.

I didn't look at him.

Jason and I inched down the street to the waiting car. He shoved me in the driver's side door. I had to climb across into the passenger seat. Jason got in after me. He pulled the driver's side door shut.

"You okay?" he asked.

"Yeah," I said. Even though I wasn't. My entire world had been shattered over the course of several hours. I didn't know if I'd ever be okay again.

"Good," he said, starting the car.

As we pulled out onto the streets of Bramford, heading for Route 50, Jason shot a glance in his rearview mirror to make sure no one was following us. No one was. "Well," he said sardonically. "So much for a normal life."

Part Two

"And what rough beast, its hour come round at last,
Slouches towards Bethlehem to be born?"

-William Butler Yeats, "The Second Coming"

Chapter Twelve

Missing Person Notice
Name: Jones, Azazel
Race: White, non-Hispanic
Age: 17
Height: 5′6″
Weight: 125 pounds
Hair: brown
Clothing: Grey short-sleeved t-shirt, light blue baggy jeans, and brown sandals.

Azazel was last seen in her hometown of Bramford, West Virginia, getting in a green Chevrolet Cobalt with a seventeen-year-old white male with dark hair and eyes. She may be traveling with him still.

Anyone with information should call the Bramford Police Department at (304)555-8392.

Jason and I drove through the night, out of Bramford and through the winding roads, tree branches like skeletal limbs hanging in our path. The moon was barely a sliver in the sky. I felt the darkness pressing around me from all directions. It was going into my mouth. It was going into my eyes, my nose. I was drowning in it. When dawn began to burn across the sky, it banished the darkness, but not the feeling I had. I could hardly breathe. It hurt to exist.

I didn't look back, not literally, but as we drove my father's car farther and farther away from my home and my family, I felt like that was all I did. I sifted through my memories of the past few weeks. It seemed so obvious now, how everything had fallen apart. The moment when Jason appeared in my life, my world had cracked. I hadn't seen it, but with every moment since the first time I'd seen him, the crack had widened and splintered my foundations. It was no wonder everything had come crashing down. I felt almost stupid that I hadn't seen it before.

Jason's jaw twitched in the driver's seat. He gazed at the road. I wanted to be angry with him. I thought, "If Jason had never shown up, none of this would have happened." But when it came to Jason, I just didn't think clearly. I recognized that now. Looking at him made me dizzy. His dark, intense eyes. His powerful shoulders. I couldn't think clearly when I stared at him. How could I be angry? In fact, I was grateful. All I'd left in Bramford was dust. Jason was the one real, brilliant thing in the world right now. I had nothing left. Except Jason.

"You're quiet," Jason observed, after we'd been driving for over an hour.

I *was* quiet. It was hard to breathe. It was hard to think without running into jagged edges in my brain. All my thoughts hurt right now. Everything was wrong. How could I possibly speak when I wasn't even sure how to exist anymore? "Sorry," I mumbled.

"You don't have to talk," he said softly.

I nodded once, a lump forming in my throat. It was all I could do to stare forward.

"Sometimes," Jason said. "Sometimes it helps to just focus on surviving."

Surviving? Was I still alive? Did I exist in this world where nothing I knew was the way I thought it would be?

"For instance," he said. "We do need money. You wanna help me rob a convenience store?" He smiled at me.

I tried to smile back. The corners of my mouth felt too tight.

Somewhere between Winchester and Martinsburg, Jason took an exit off the interstate. It was nearly desolate, so early in the morning, just a country 7-11. Nothing else around but mountains and trees. I stayed in the car, unable to help. I remembered that some part of me thought that stealing from people at gunpoint was wrong. I wondered why I didn't feel guilty now. It took Jason less than five minutes, and he returned to the car with a handful of bills which he made me count.

We'd stolen a little over three hundred dollars.

"Now we're criminals," I said. Funny. It didn't upset me.

"Don't worry about it," said Jason. "The Sons cover up whatever I do. I'm their problem, really. Besides, officially, I don't exist."

I remembered that my family hadn't been able to find any record of Jason anywhere when he'd moved in with us. Then I remembered something. "You do!" I said. "My parents got you registered with the state so that you could be their foster kid." I winced. I hadn't wanted to talk about them. My parents.

Jason shook his head. "I don't buy that. They were planning on killing me, so they had me registered with the state? Besides, that whole process was way too easy. I signed some papers. It was a smokescreen. They were just trying to keep me from being suspicious. Damn it if it didn't work."

Devious people, my parents. Something else Jason had said, though. It was my way out. Something to focus on. The Sons. That was it. Who were the Sons? And how did they cover this stuff up? "What do you mean, the Sons?" I asked.

Jason just shook his head. "Nothing."

"Jason," I said. "I think I deserve some answers if I'm going to be helping you commit armed robbery."

He considered. "Okay," he said. "Okay. Soon. Just not now. I'm too exhausted to get into all of it now."

* * *

We ditched my dad's car in Baltimore and took a bus to New York City. We both napped on the four-hour bus ride. The bus let us off at Penn Station. We were in New York, because Jason claimed he had a contact there. It was where he'd been heading before he'd had what he called his "little pit stop" in Bramford.

I'd never been to New York City. I was so astonished by what I saw, it was easy to put aside thoughts of Bramford and gape at the sights. Jason laughed at me as I gazed up at the towering skyscrapers, my mouth hanging open. The city was tall and breathtaking, but it was also dirty, crowded, and small. The streets seemed narrow, the sidewalks hardly big enough for all the people who strode through them.

Mostly, I was simply floored by the sheer number of people. I'd just never seen so many people all together in one place who had nothing in common. They weren't here for a sporting event or a rally. No, they were just going about their lives, walking to or from work, to the store, to a restaurant. None of them paid each other any mind. I could hear them talking loudly on their cell phones. There were simply people everywhere.

Once off the bus, Jason found a payphone and called someone on it.

He stood at the payphone, one hand shoved his pocket, cradling the phone with one hand. He looked nonchalant. Like he knew what he was doing. I realized Jason was more in his element here, on the run, than he had been back at home. He knew how to do this. He didn't know how to be a normal teenager and go to school.

"November One," he said into the phone. He paused, waiting as someone said something on the other side. "Yeah, it's me ... . Right ... . I'm going to need to double the order. I've got someone with me ... . Female." He looked at me as if he were sizing me up. "Uh ... 5'5 or 5'6, maybe ..." he covered the mouth piece with his hand. "How much do you weigh?"

"What?" I demanded. How rude!

"It's for an ID," he said.

Oh. "A hundred and twenty," I said, lying a little.

He relayed my weight. "Brown hair, green eyes," he continued. "When can we pick it up? ... Great, then." He hung up the phone. "Let's go," he said.

Jason walked like a New Yorker. Like he knew where he was going. I followed him as close as I could. Now that we weren't running for our lives, he didn't hold my hand. I thought back on the dance, which seemed as if it had happened sometime in the 1700s, and wondered how he felt about the fact that we had kissed. I wondered how I felt about it. There were so many other things to consider right now, like the fact that I was homeless, that worrying about whether Jason still liked me seemed petty and pointless.

We treaded over the sidewalks for blocks and blocks. Everything looked the same. Little shops, restaurants, pizza stands. There were hot dog vendors on every corner. I wanted to stop at one, because I never had, but I felt stupid asking Jason if we could. So I just trailed after him, trying to keep up as he walked with confidence through the big, big city.

I was getting breathless.

Jason noticed. "Sorry," he said. "I guess we could have taken the subway. I just like walking in New York."

"Yeah," I gasped. "It's great."

"Do you want to slow down?" he asked, laughing.

I nodded.

He slowed his pace. "Next time, say something," he said.

I didn't feel like I could say things like that to Jason. I didn't want to be in the way. I didn't want to bother him.

Even though I'd known Jason for nearly a month, my knowledge of him had expanded so much in the past twenty-four hours. Now Jason wasn't just some mysterious, smart boy who appeared in Bramford. He was a gun-wielding dangerous man who could shoot people without qualms and rob convenience stores. And while Jason had seemed brooding and silent in Bramford, he seemed to get happier and noisier with every violent incident we lived through. Was this the kind of life Jason was used to?

And what had I gotten myself into? Not that I had a choice. It was either stay in Bramford with the crazy Satanists or run away with Jason. Still, I was beginning to feel that danger followed Jason around like a hungry wolf. From the moment he'd come into my life, it hadn't been the same. And now my life was turned completely upside down. I had run away from home. I was in New York City. I only had the clothes on my back and some cash we'd stolen. Who was I? What was happening to me?

"We're almost there," said Jason.

"Where is there?" I asked.

"My ID contact," said Jason. "I said I'd be in town within the next few months to pick one up. That was like three months ago. Anyway, I've been expected. Don't worry. It's safe."

Safe? Was anything safe anymore? I'd thought Bramford was safe. It showed how much I knew.

We rounded a corner, and Jason pointed to an apartment building a few buildings down. "That's where we're going," he said. All of the buildings on the street were brick and rectangular. They each had fire escape steps climbing up the sides. They were shoved against each other, like they were all one building. Air conditioners jutted out of some of the windows, even though it was late autumn. Mostly, the apartment buildings just looked a little ... rundown.

We walked through the front door and into the elevator. Jason punched the button for the sixth floor. Once out of the elevator, he strode confidently down the hall, with me trailing behind him. He knocked on a door that had a welcome mat sitting out in front of it.

What was the point of a mat outside an apartment? Were one's feet really that dirty by the time one got up the elevator?

The door opened and standing inside was one of the most beautiful women I've ever seen. She was tall, with smooth, cappuccino-colored skin. Her hair fell around her shoulders in tiny braids. Her eyes were light brown and almond shaped.

"Jason Wodden," she exclaimed. She had a British accent.

"Hey Marlena," he said, grinning.

She looked him up and down appreciatively. "You've grown up," she said, her voice was a little too sultry for my tastes.

This was Jason's contact? He might have mentioned that she was a beautiful woman.

She gave Jason a huge hug. "Well," she said, "come in. Come in."

Jason and I went into her apartment. We entered a living

room, decorated in reds and browns. Tapestries were thrown over the couches and the coffee table, which was decorated with candles. Incense was burning. The room was separated from the rest of the apartment by a beaded curtain.

"My God," said Marlena, "it's been ages. You were like twelve the last time I saw you."

"And that would have made you like thirteen?" said Jason, grinning.

"Joker," said Marlena, poking him. She shook her head at him. "Are you legal yet?"

He laughed. "I didn't think you much cared for legalities," he said. And then he grabbed my arm and pulled me close to him. "This is Azazel."

"Fine," said Marlena, laughing. "Point taken. Of course you'd want an age-appropriate girlfriend."

"Oh," I said. "I'm not—I mean—" I looked at Jason.

He dropped my arm.

Oops. This was awkward. I didn't know what I was supposed to say. I *wasn't* Jason's girlfriend. Was I supposed to lie? Did Jason want me to be his girlfriend? Before, he'd said ... But a lot had happened since then.

"You guys have a seat," said Marlena, gesturing to her couches. We sat down. "You want anything? Tea? Coffee? Marijuana?"

I shot Jason a horrified look, but he just laughed. "Coffee's fine. Azazel?"

"Um," I said. "Coffee. Sure."

Marlena disappeared through the beaded curtain.

"How do you *know* her?" I whispered to Jason.

"She was a friend of Anton's," he said. "Used to do favors for him. We can trust her."

If he said so. There wasn't much about Marlena that I thought was trustworthy. She had to be at least twenty-five, and she was totally flirting with Jason. And I didn't like that. I didn't like it at all. Maybe that was stupid. After all, I had no claim on Jason. Still, the thought of it just made me feel a little uneasy.

Marlena reappeared with two cups of coffee, which she handed to us. Then she ducked back out of the room to return with cream and sugar, in little packets like you get at a restaurant.

"Still stealing from fast food restaurants, I see," said Jason.

"You have no idea how much money I save on ketchup packets alone," said Marlena, settling down on a chair that faced us. "So," she said, suddenly all business, "your ID is finished, Jason, but since I've had such short notice for Azazel, it's going to take me another day. And I should get a picture of her."

"Another day?" asked Jason. "I wasn't planning on sticking around that long."

"No?" Marlena looked disappointed. "Where are you planning to go?"

"You know I'm not going to tell you that," said Jason. "Okay, another day. We can do that. We'll find a hotel that will take cash or something. Unless—what about the credit cards I asked you about?"

"Oh," said Marlena, remembering. "Got you one." She held up her index finger. "Five thousand dollar limit."

"Great!" said Jason.

"But they track those easy. You know that."

"First they've got to connect it to me," said Jason. "They don't even know where I am."

"I don't think you should use the credit card in the city," said Marlena. "They might track it to me, and as much as I love you, Jason, I'm not going down for you."

Jason sighed. "Then I guess just don't worry about Azazel's ID. We'll leave tonight. No hotels."

"Don't be silly," said Marlena. "The two of you should stay here for tonight."

Stay here? I didn't want to stay with Marlena.

"I don't want to endanger you," said Jason.

"Don't be ridiculous," said Marlena. "You're perfectly safe here, if it's only for one night. And I can have Azazel's ID for you in the morning."

"Okay," said Jason. "But we're gone first thing tomorrow."

"Of course," she said.

* * *

Marlena went out for a few hours to "take care of things," as she put it. Jason and I were left alone in her apartment. Jason easily made himself at home, raiding Marlena's pantry for pretzel sticks and sprawling out on the couch in front of the television.

I just sat next to him, wondering at this new turn of events. We were staying at woman's house who made illegal IDs, could get Jason a credit card, and also probably smoked marijuana. It didn't seem like a particularly safe place to be. Plus, for some reason, I just didn't really like Marlena. She seemed a little too cavalier about what was happening to Jason. Of course, maybe she was used to interacting with Jason when he was in mortal danger. Maybe Jason was in mortal danger all the time.

Nothing was happening. When nothing was happening, it was too easy for me to think about the mess my life was. I didn't want to go back to the way I'd felt in the car, like I couldn't think or breathe. I began to panic, wishing I could distract myself easily the way Jason did. But I couldn't focus on the TV. What could I focus on? Then I remembered. Jason had promised to explain things to me. Now was as good a time as any.

"Jason," I said, "you promised to tell me who the Sons were later. It's later now."

"I guess I did," said Jason, and he shut off the TV. He took a deep breath. "I don't know where to start."

"How about with your mother?" I said. "Sheriff Damon said she was killed by her husband."

Jason looked confused. "When did he say that?" he asked.

"I overheard him talking to my parents once, right after you were found." Actually, now that I thought about it,

228

Jason had apparently told my dad his mother had died in childbirth. Maybe I shouldn't have started with that little revelation.

"I never met her," said Jason. "Anton told me her name was Marianne Wodden and that she died right after I was born. That's all I ever knew." He looked thoughtful. "Killed by her husband? So I guess that's a matter of public record?"

"I don't know," I said.

Jason disappeared behind Marlena's beaded curtain for a few moments and returned with her laptop.

"She doesn't care if you use that?" I asked.

"Marlena's like my big sister," said Jason. "Or as close as somebody like me gets anyway." He flipped open the laptop. He was quiet for a few minutes as he searched. Then he sat back.

"What?" I said.

"All this time," he said, "and I never even once thought to just google her name."

"It's true?"

"Yeah," he said. He turned the laptop screen so that I could see. The screen was filled with a graphic of two big golden angels holding a banner that said, "In Memory of ..."

Underneath the text read, "Marianne Rachel Aird Wodden, 1973-1991. Our beloved sister and aunt. Shot to death at the hands of her husband, Ted Wodden, who then being the coward that he was, turned the gun on himself. Nothing can bring her back, but she is in our hearts and prayers forever."

I scrolled down the page.

There was another entry. "Jason Edgar Wodden," it read. "Unborn child of Marianne Wodden. Marianne was pregnant when she was killed."

"Oh my God, Jason," I said. "Look at this."

He moved the screen back.

"That's you," I said. "You're supposed to be dead."

"Well, I'm not," he said. "Weird." He shrugged, closing the laptop. "Well, anyway, about the Sons of the Rising Sun."

I wanted to know about the Sons, so I didn't want to stop him, but I couldn't help but wonder, "That's it? You aren't more concerned about your mother?"

"If she's even my mother," said Jason. "Maybe Anton pulled a name off some website like this to name me in the first place. Who knows where I came from."

"They didn't have websites in 1991," I reminded him.

"Whatever," he said.

Okay. He really wasn't concerned. "Jason, if this is true, your mother had a sibling and that sibling had kids. You have a family."

He was quiet for a second. Then he shook his head. "No, not really, I don't. Let's not talk about this part anymore. I can tell you about what I know. I don't know anything about my parents."

"Okay," I said. "Who are the Sons of the Rising Sun?"

"They're the people who raised me," said Jason. "They're a huge, huge group of men who have influence all

230

over the world."

"Like the Illuminati," I said excitedly.

He grinned. "Yeah, you and your Illuminati. I guess sort of."

"You're the one who called them Freemasons with guns," I pointed out.

"Okay, it's true that the Sons have members high up in every major world government. It's true that they affect global policies and all kinds of stuff I don't understand. I know that much. I just don't know how they do it. Because there are members of the Sons who are out in the public like that, but there are also the Brothers, the other members of the Sons. Anton was a Brother."

"And you were raised by these Brothers?" I asked.

"I was raised by Anton. I saw other members. Sometimes. Not often, at least not when I was young. Anton was in communication with them. It was his job to keep me out of sight and safe. And to teach me and train me, in preparation for ..." Jason trailed off.

"For what?"

"Well, you know, at first I didn't know what they thought I was," Jason said. "I didn't have any real idea of the way the rest of the world worked. My earliest memories are of Anton. I remember being a really little kid, maybe three or four, and Anton reading to me before I went to sleep. We always slept in hotel rooms. We were always moving. I remember things like Anton teaching me how to tie my shoes. I remember playing games with little men, which he had helped me make out of toothpicks. I remember eating in diners and fast food restaurants. I remember all kinds of little things like that. And at the time, I was too young to know that wasn't the way everyone lived. It's the only time I was ever really happy, I think. Because by the time I was just a little older, I began to realize that there was a whole other world out there that I didn't understand and wasn't part of. And that everybody else was part of it. And I hated that.

"But back then, I didn't know that things were weird, and so I didn't bother to ask why we did things the way we did. When I was older, when it started to become clear to me, I did ask Anton. I wanted to know why we didn't live in a house. And why we always traveled. And why I didn't have a mom and a dad like everybody else.

"Anton said that I certainly had a mother and father, but they were dead. He said that we traveled, because there were bad people who wanted to find me and hurt me, and we had to stay away from them."

"Did he tell you why people wanted to hurt you?" I asked.

"Well, back then, Anton just said I was special. And I was five years old, so I believed it. Who doesn't think they're special when they're five?"

"Five? And that was when you started shooting guns?"

"Yeah, definitely. Anton always had guns. We shot cans off railroad tracks in southern towns. We always traveled through the south when I was a kid. A couple times he took me to a shooting range. He taught me guns were tools. That they were powerful. That they could cause all kinds of damage. They weren't toys. Anton was very serious about everything. It made for a kind of solemn childhood."

"Was that one of the things that made you think your life was strange?" I asked.

"Not really. In a lot of ways, everything I knew about the world, I got from watching television shows in hotel rooms. Everybody had guns on TV. No, I thought guns were normal."

I shivered. What a way to grow up! "So you've spent your whole life traveling from place to place?"

"No, not my whole life. The first ten years of my life pretty much. We were always running from one place to the other. The first time I think I realized exactly why was maybe when I was seven. I think I was about that old. Anton and I were staying in a hotel somewhere in backwoods North Carolina. I woke up in the middle of the night to the sound of gunfire. They were shooting into our hotel room. The window shattered. There was glass everywhere."

I covered my mouth with my hand, horrified. But Jason's face was composed and unemotional.

"Anton made me hide under the bed. I wanted to help him. I remember I wanted to shoot with him. But he wouldn't let me. I had to hide. Anton took care of them. And we left in the middle of the night without paying for our hotel room."

"Did that kind of thing happen to you a lot?"

"Maybe four or five times before I was ten," said Jason,

thinking about it carefully.

I couldn't believe he was so unaffected by relating the story. That he couldn't specifically remember how many times he'd been shot at as a small boy. "Why were they shooting at you?"

"They were trying to kill me," said Jason.

"But why?"

"I didn't know at the time," said Jason. "Anton really wouldn't talk about it. He said that they were bad guys and that seemed to make sense in my way of viewing the world. There were bad guys on TV. The men were bad guys.

"Anyway, it started to get worse. The shootings were more and more frequent, so that was when Anton and I went to England. Anton was from England. And that was when I found out."

"You've been to England?" I said, astonished. I'd never been anywhere besides to Virginia Beach for vacation a few times. And my family didn't go on vacation too much. There were too many of us.

"Yeah," he said. "Not for long. We were maybe only there for a year. We went to visit the High Council of the Sons. At the time, Anton didn't tell me exactly why we were going. I was mostly excited because we got to ride a plane."

I'd never been on a plane! "Is that when you met Marlena?" I asked. "Is she British?"

"She is," said Jason, "but no. I met Marlena when I was really young. Um ... I don't know, maybe six or so. Her father was a car thief, and I guess Marlena's mother wasn't in the picture anymore, so he just kind of dragged his daughter around with him, stealing cars. After her father died, Marlena started doing forgeries instead. She'd always helped her father with that kind of stuff, I guess. Titles to the cars and things. I don't know. Anyway, Anton and I were often in the need of untraceable transportation. Marlena's dad was one of his contacts."

"Oh," I said.

"So, Anton and I went to England," said Jason, picking up where he'd left off, "and when we got there, we went to stay in this strange old castle. It was really weird. The walls were made of stone. And it was drafty. There were all these very serious British men wandering around, and they were all really interested in me. They asked me all these questions all the time, and anyway, we had to go to these meetings, where we sat in front of the Council, and they questioned Anton, and without anyone really explaining it to me, I sort of figured it all out.

"The Sons of the Rising Sun, like I said, have these branches. So some of them are businessmen, and some of them are politicians, and I'll bet there's some feeder fraternity in some colleges somewhere, God knows. But like I said, Anton was a Brother. And the Council is made up of Brothers. And Brothers are kind of like monks or spies or something. They're like Jesuits mixed with James Bond." He grinned at me.

I laughed. "Okay."

"So, they're celibate. And they devote their lives to

235

pursuing the Purpose."

"What's the Purpose?" I asked.

"Oh, come on, this should be easy for you, Miss Illuminati," he said.

I looked at him blankly.

"You even said that stuff to your dad about the dollar bill," he said.

"Novus Ordo Seclorum?!" I gasped out. No way!

He applauded. "And she comes out swinging. Exactly. New World Order. I guess, technically, they just want to establish a global government. More accurately, they want me to establish a global government."

"You?"

"Haven't you guessed?" Jason said, spreading his hands. "I'm the freaking messiah."

I snorted. "What?"

He laughed too. "No lie," he said. "That's totally what they basically said."

"I don't get it," I said.

" *You* don't get it? Think how I felt." He took a deep breath. "Basically—well, it's too complicated to explain basically, because they have pages and pages of stuff on all of this crap—but, the gist of it all is this: Many ancient religions talk about the return of a deity. Christianity obviously talks about the return of Jesus. Norse Mythology has the return of Balder after the earth has been recreated after Ragnorak. In Indian mythology, Vishnu is going to return in his final avatar. Then there's just the dying gods of

236

the mystery religions, who die and return in cycles. Mithras. Dionysus. Osiris. Um, beyond religion, there's talk of the return of King Arthur, when England needs him most. So, the Sons of the Rising Sun believe that this super being of some kind is going to descend on the earth, and they scoured texts from various religious and mythological backgrounds to come up with a list of trillions of signs and wonders leading to the return of what they call the Rising Sun." He pointed at himself.

"You? But why you?"

"Well, when I went to England with Anton, they were not sure it was me. There were maybe two other contenders. And that was why we were getting shot at. Because proponents of the other possible Rising Suns didn't want me in the way of their guy. So, we went there because Anton was like, 'You guys asked me to keep this kid safe, and we're getting shot at by other members of the Sons. I want better protection.' Anyway, it turned out while we were there, one of the other contenders died in a car accident, so it was just me and this other guy.

"And the Sons decided that they'd call the other guy to England as well, and they'd just figure out which one of us it actually was."

"How'd they do that?"

"It was like a trial. We had to go sit in front of the Council and hear people bring evidence forward, most of which had to do with the list of trillions of signs and wonders leading to the return of the Rising Sun."

"So, you fulfilled these signs and wonders?" I asked. I was confused.

"Well, we both did," he said. "At least we both fulfilled some of them. A lot of them contradicted each other. This guy was older than me. He was maybe fifteen. And he hadn't been raised by a Brother like I had. He had a family, I think. I don't know what happened to him. Anyway, they picked me, because I was born in 1991, clearly an auspicious year since it's the same backwards and forwards." He made a face to show how silly he thought that was.

"I was born in 1991, too," I said.

"Yes, but you're a girl," he said. "And there are no women in the Sons of the Rising Sun. It's very sexist. Plus they'd have to change the name to Sons and Daughters or something."

I laughed. "Okay, so why else did they pick you?"

"I can't remember every reason," said Jason. "Um ... I remember the biggest deal was this verse in the Bible, Genesis 49:10. It says something like the power of Judah won't be restored until Shiloh comes. And I was born in Shiloh. Of course, the verse might have meant Shiloh, Israel. Or it might have just meant the messiah. Anyway, Shiloh, Georgia was good enough for them. And there were lists of lists of things besides that, all from different religious traditions. So, in the end, they decided it was me."

"That's crazy," I said.

He nodded. "Yeah. It is. And can you imagine what it was like, to come back to America, an eleven-year-old kid, thinking that you're like the savior of the world?" He laughed. "Do you have any idea how much pressure that is?"

I didn't.

"Everyone's careful of you. No one lets you experience anything, because they're afraid it will ruin you for your higher purpose. You live a half-life, not a real one."

Wait. That did kind of sound familiar. I shrugged. "I was groomed my whole life to be the vessel," I said.

He laughed. "Yeah. That's got to be why I like you so much. You kind of understand."

I had another thought. "Wait," I said. "You're supposed to impose a New World Order. Like ... you're an agent of Order, sent to enslave the world?"

"What?"

"The language of the Satanist vision," I said. "It was kind of right about you."

"I'm not going to do any of that, Azazel," said Jason. "Why do you think I ran away?"

"But how did that woman who ran the online forum have a vision of you? And how was she right?" I asked.

"What are you saying?" Jason said, a grin breaking across his face. "Are you saying you're really filled with the spirit of an ancient demon?"

"No, of course not," I said. "It's just weird, don't you think?"

"It's a coincidence," said Jason. "I've spend my entire life around people who read stuff into coincidences. Things are what you make them. That's all there is to it."

And I agreed with him. But I still found that somewhat disconcerting. What if there was something to what the Satanists had to say? What if ... I shrugged it off. "So you came back to America when you were eleven?" I asked.

"Yeah. And we went to live in a Society of Brothers of the Sons, which was located in Tennessee somewhere. It was an old building where a bunch of celibate men lived and tried to further the Purpose. There were some guys closer to my age there. It was the first time I really ever hung out with other kids. That was where I met Hallam."

"The guy who came to Bramford?"

"The very one. He's only a few years older than us. He was studying to become a Brother. In the Society, the High Council would send down orders to the Brothers telling them to carry out certain missions. That was how Anton had ended up being my guardian. It was his assignment. Anyway, these orders were sometimes kind of dangerous, and there was never any rationale given to them. So, the Brothers didn't know why they were doing it. They just did it, because they trusted the Council. As I got older, they started to give me orders to carry out as well. I always had to stay back. I never got to really be part of the action, because it was important to keep me safe.

"Sometimes, the orders made sense. Once I remember we infiltrated a suicide cult and took down the head of it before he could make all the people, you know, kill themselves. Sometimes, they just seemed really random. We got in the middle of a gang war once. We were supposed to protect one side, instead of the other. No one knew why. No one could tell a difference between the sides. It was bloody and scary and violent, but they were already fighting, so it didn't bother my conscience too much.

"But sometimes, the orders were not only just random, they seemed downright, well, wrong. Hallam and I were sent once to a ..." Jason trailed off. He took a deep breath. "To a sorority house. The girls there were basically prostituting themselves for extra cash. It was a bad scene, for certain. It was illegal. But, um, they told us to go in and ... kill everyone."

We were both quiet. I didn't know if I wanted to know this about Jason. I almost told him to stop, but I didn't. I couldn't speak. I just watched him.

Jason's Adam's apple bobbed. "I couldn't do it," he said, looking at his hands. "I tried, because I thought it was my duty, but ... But Hallam. He ... Sometimes I have nightmares about that night. I see Hallam's face. Blood's spattered all over it. And he's screaming. I can't tell if he's screaming because he's horrified, or because he's having a really good time. And I'm just standing there. Watching him. Not stopping him, just watching."

I reached over to touch Jason's shoulder, wanting to comfort him. Jason had been through so much. It made everything I'd seen him do make so much more sense. I didn't relate. I couldn't. But I ached for him. I wished I could make it better somehow.

Jason shook himself. "Anyway," he said. "It was stuff like that that made me want to leave. But in the end, I left because of what happened to Anton. Anton had always believed everything that the Sons said, hook, line, and sinker. He believed that I was the Rising Sun. He believed that the Sons had the best interests of the world in mind. He believed that there were prophecies. He believed in a right and wrong, and he wanted me to be on the side of right. So when stuff like that started happening, Anton got kind of confused. He had a code of ethics. Shooting college girls, whether or not they had turned into hookers, was not part of his code of ethics. He started doing some research and looking into what the Sons were asking us to do. And I don't know what exactly he found out, but I think it was that the Sons don't care anything about right and wrong or a peaceful New World Order. Basically they just care about making money and having power over people. I think Anton was going tell all the Brothers and start a revolution of sorts.

"He asked me to come see him in his room one night. He said he had something he wanted to tell me. I went there, and by the time I got there, they'd already gotten to him. He was lying on the ground, bleeding from multiple gunshot wounds. He wasn't conscious, but he was breathing. And I just held him in my arms until his lungs filled up with blood, and he drowned on it. "

Jason stopped for a second, studying his fingers.

He looked up at me. "And then I took some guns and

some money, and I just left. They followed me. I ran. I ran
and ran until you found me.

Chapter Thirteen

From: Renegade Son (settingsun007@yahoo.com)
To: Gerald Masterson (geraldm@christisking.org)
Subject: Headed your way
Father Gerald,

I'm headed your way, and I think J is too. Unfortunately, without the resources of the Sons, I've lost tabs on him. He seems to have run out of West Virginia, where I thought he'd be safe. We're both on the run, but I sincerely believe J will be heading back south. I hate to do this to you, but I'm calling in a favor, and I need you to hide me.

Send word to this new email address if there's some reason you can't.

-H

Marlena called to tell us that she would be back late, but that we should make ourselves comfortable. There was food in the refrigerator, there were blankets in the hall closets, and the couch in the living room pulled out into a bed. She said not to wait up. She had no idea how long she'd be gone.

Jason and I raided the refrigerator. There were some vegetables and eggs, so I made us omelets, even though it was dinnertime. Jason pronounced them delicious. Since my mom had done most of the cooking in my house, I realized I really didn't know much about cooking. The omelets were edible, however.

After Jason's story, we didn't talk much. I tried a few times, but Jason didn't really seem in the mood for conversation. Instead, we watched some television until we were both yawning. The only sleep we'd really gotten had been on the bus to New York, and we were tired.

As we got the blankets from the closet, Jason suggested that I sleep on the pullout couch and he sleep on the other couch. The other couch was a loveseat. There was no way he would fit. I told him not to be ridiculous. There wasn't any reason we couldn't both sleep in the same bed. Then, of course, I blushed to the roots of my hair.

Jason didn't argue with me. We made the bed. We switched out the lights. And then we both got on opposite sides of the bed. We were very careful to stay on our own side, each of us curling up on our sides with our backs to each other.

"Jason?" I whispered in the darkness.

"Yes?" he said.

"Are we going to be okay?"

He didn't answer for a minute. Then he said, "You can trust me."

And I did. I knew Jason could take care of himself. But what if I ruined everything? What if I was just too slow? Too clumsy? What if ...

In horror, I realized that I could get Jason hurt. "Jason?" I said again.

But Jason was asleep. I could tell because he started to

snore gently. It wasn't so loud that it disturbed me. It was actually kind of cute. Knowing he was asleep, I rolled over on my back and stared at the ceiling. I was exhausted, but I didn't feel like I could sleep. My mind was churning with all of the things that I'd found out over the past two days.

First of all, there was the story Jason had told me. I hadn't imagined the depth of his life before he'd come to Bramford. Compared to my life, Jason's had been so difficult. I could tell that he'd loved Anton. That he'd been crushed when Anton was killed. When I thought of him, basically all alone in the world, trying to deal with something like that, my heart broke for him. Jason had been through too much to have to go through any more pain, but it seemed like his life just wouldn't let up. All things being equal, the rest of his life should be easy, normal, and sane. But it didn't seem like that was in the cards for Jason.

The worst thing was, though, even though I felt sorry for Jason, my sympathy for him didn't compare to the aching hole I felt for my own losses. Just last night, I'd been sitting around the table with my family, laughing and talking. We'd been sharing our Chinese food. I remembered how happy and complete I'd felt. I remembered that I'd thought to myself that I wouldn't trade my family for anything. I remembered thinking how lucky I was.

But it had all turned to ashes. My family had been nothing like what they'd pretended to be. In the end, they'd wanted me to fulfill a role for them, not to simply love me. And they'd wanted me to do something unspeakable. They were all insane. Everything they'd taught me, everything I'd thought they were, it was a lie. I had been betrayed, and I had lost everything and everyone I loved.

I remembered my mother, stroking my hair in the basement, asking me to be her "strong girl." My mother had wanted me to be strong so that I could participate in ritual sex and then so that I could take someone else's life. The mother that I knew, that I thought that I knew, would never have asked me to do that. She would never have condoned such atrocities. My parents had always taught me to think for myself, to make my own way in the world. I couldn't believe that they had bought into that strange set of beliefs, so appalling and violent.

In some ways, I could hardly believe I'd managed to stay standing throughout last night. I had been driven by my desire to save Jason. That was all that had kept me upright. Because I had nothing left. All my hopes and dreams were shattered. I had no idea what to expect from the future. I had no idea where I was going or what I was doing. I was lost.

And I knew that in many ways, in every way, Jason's life had been so much harder than mine. But Jason was used to being adrift, to being cut free from ties, used to having no one to count on but himself. I didn't know how to handle it. I had no experience with feeling this way. So was it so wrong that I felt so sorry for myself?

And was it okay that I felt completely and totally terrified? I trusted Jason, but I didn't feel like I could lean on him in the way I wanted to lean on someone. I was used to having the structure and support of a loving family. Now, what did I have? I had Jason.

Sort of. Did I have Jason? How long was this arrangement between us going to last? Was he going to show me the ropes of running from place to place and then leave me on my own? Simply because he'd thought I was attractive in Bramford didn't mean he still did. I was a different girl, then. I was in my element. In Bramford, I was strong and sure of myself. Now I was floundering. I was pathetic and needy. What boy, especially a boy who was sure of himself like Jason, wanted to have a girl like that around?

But I realized that I wasn't just worried that he would find my lack of abilities unattractive. I was worried that I would hold him back. I knew Jason felt obligations deeply. I could tell from the way that he'd taken me along with him to New York that he wanted to make sure I was safe. But Jason was dealing with very dangerous men who were trailing him everywhere he went. Adding me to the mix just made everything harder for him. I felt sorry for myself and worried about what would happen to me. But when I thought about something bad happening to Jason, it felt like my intestines were being ripped out. I didn't think I be alive and know I was responsible for harm coming to Jason.

I rolled back over onto my side, prepared for my thoughts to continue chasing themselves back and forth in my brain, but sleep suddenly dragged me under, and I was mercifully lost in the blackness of dreamlessness for hours.

I awoke to the sound of a door slam. Marlena's living room was suddenly flooded with light.

Sleepily, I raised my head. Marlena was standing in at the door, her face sweaty, her eyes wide and alert. "Jason, wake up," she said.

Jason sat straight up in bed. He rubbed his eyes. "What?" he said, and I was startled that he sounded so awake, even know we'd both been roused from a deep sleep.

Marlena knelt in front of him, pressing several cards into his hands. The IDs, I guessed. "I was followed," she said.

"Followed?" Jason asked.

I sat up, trying to shake the sleep from my brain. I still felt very, very tired.

"Several men in suits," she said. "Short hair cuts. Reminded me of Anton. They didn't think I saw them, but I did. You've got to get out of here. They're right behind me."

Jason leapt to his feet, shoving the cards she'd given him in his pocket and collecting the two guns he'd stolen from Bramford. "Come with us," said Jason. "I don't want to leave you here if they're coming after me."

Marlena ducked behind her beaded curtain. "Jason Wodden," she said, reappearing with a rifle, which she was loading, "in all the years you've known me, have you ever had any reason to suspect I couldn't take care of myself?"

I wished I could take care of myself. I was like a damsel in distress, needing Jason to protect me all the time. I wouldn't even have been able to get out of Bramford without him.

"These aren't your typical thugs, you know," Jason said.

And someone knocked on the door. "NYPD," said a voice, but the accent wasn't quite right. It sounded sort of ... British.

"You're wasting time talking to me, when you should be going out the fire escape," said Marlena. "It's cute that you're being so gallant, but save it for your little girlfriend here."

God. I was just getting in the way of everything, wasn't I?

"Azazel's brave," said Jason. "And you be careful, Marlena."

The knock came again. "Open up, or we're breaking down the door," said the voice outside.

"Out!" said Marlena, pushing us through the beaded curtain and into her bedroom.

Jason opened the window. "You first," he told me.

I climbed out the window and onto the rickety metal fire escape. Jason followed me. Outside, the night air was cold. I shivered.

"Go, Azazel," Jason urged. "Down the steps."

And down I went, fast as I could, which apparently wasn't fast enough, because Jason was right on my heels. At the bottom of the steps, we had to jump about eight feet. I hesitated, only for a second, but Jason growled behind me, "Jump!"

I jumped. I stumbled when I hit the ground, catching myself with my hand and scraping up my palm. It hurt, but

I didn't say anything. I didn't want to be a huge baby. I couldn't keep slowing Jason down so much. Jason landed beside me. He took my hand the way he had in Bramford, and we started running. Was it wrong that I really liked how his hand felt holding mine? Was this completely the wrong time to have thoughts like that?

"Come on," said Jason. "There's a church just up the block."

Church? What did a church have to do with anything?

We rushed up the street, and sure enough, there was a beautiful building wedged between the rectangular apartment buildings. It had towering spires, which were dwarfed by the buildings around it. The doors were twice the size of regular doors, huge and wooden with iron hinges. Jason and I hurried up the steps and through the doors.

Inside, the church was silent, but all the lights were on. There were rows of wooden pews, which opened onto an ornate altar at the front of the church. Rows and rows of lit candles sat in front of an enormous statue of a crucified Christ. I felt a little awed by the atmosphere. I'd never actually been inside a church. I'd seen pictures, seen them in movies and television, but church wasn't something my family had ever done. Obviously, I guess, considering they were Satanists.

I shoved aside my reverence, and turned to Jason. "I don't get it," I said. "Why are we in here?" After all, the doors were unlocked. They sure as heck weren't going to stop some crazy agents of the Sons from getting in.

"Sanctuary," he said. "The Sons respect any place of worship as a place that should be free of violence. Any church, temple, mosque, sweat lodge, whatever. If it's a place of worship, the Sons see it as consecrated to the All-Father."

"All-Father?"

"God," said Jason. "Whatever you want to call him. The Sons believe in God."

"Really?" I said.

"Absolutely. They just don't think that humans have the capacity to truly describe him, so they don't believe in any one incarnation of God."

"And they call him the All-Father?"

"That's what Anton called him. It's what Odin is called in Norse mythology."

"Huh," I said. Weird. "So we're safe in this church?"

"As long as we're inside, we're safe," said Jason.

I realized Jason was still holding my hand. Cool. We walked up the center of the church, between the pews, hand in hand. At the front of the church, we craned our necks up at the statue of Christ.

"How did they find us?" I asked.

Jason sighed. "I don't know. Maybe they've been keeping tabs on Marlena. Maybe Hallam followed us from Bramford." His eyes looked hollow, trained on the large crucifix. "They always find me."

"I made it harder, didn't I? Harder for you to get away?"

Jason's eyes fell away from the statue. "It's always hard," he murmured.

"I'm sorry," I whispered.

"It's not your fault," he said. "When I think about what almost happened to you back in Bramford—" He broke off, shivering. "I was right there, in the basement. And I couldn't stop it. I thought I'd have to watch ... I couldn't have taken that. I wanted to protect you."

Because I was delicate. Because I was weak. Because I needed protection. I made things dangerous for Jason. Even more dangerous than they already were. I didn't want to, but I pulled my hand out of his.

Jason looked down at his empty hand and then up at me, his eyes large and luminous. Then he folded his arms over his chest.

It would be easier for him without me. I knew that. I had to let him go. For his own sake.

* * *

When a priest discovered us the next morning at dawn, huddled up asleep on separate pews, he politely asked us to leave, telling us the church sponsored a shelter just a few blocks away, where we could get food and blankets. Jason was cautious as we left the church, as if he were afraid that the Sons were waiting just outside the door to ambush us. But no one was there. The sun was just stealing into the sky, and above the buildings we could see the rosy fingers of dawn. As we walked out onto the streets of the city, for the first time since leaving Bramford, I felt free and buoyant.

Maybe it was sky. Maybe it was the brisk air, which chilled my nose. But I simply felt happy and grateful to be alive.

Jason and I went into a little restaurant for breakfast. We drank orange juice and coffee, and I felt very cosmopolitan and mature. While I was in the bathroom, Jason used a payphone to call Marlena. "She's okay," he reported to me. "They left her apartment a mess and figured out we'd gone out the fire escape but had no idea where we'd gone."

It was good that Marlena was okay.

"We need to get out of the city, though," Jason said. "Luckily, Marlena came through with the IDs and credit card."

The waitress brought our food then. I'd got pancakes. Jason had got eggs and bacon. We ate without speaking for some time. The pancakes were very good. I was hungry.

"So," said Jason eventually, his mouth full of bacon. "We should figure where we're going to go."

We. The buoyant feeling I had came crashing down. I didn't think "we" were going anywhere.

I took a deep breath. I didn't want to say this, because I was afraid for myself, but I felt like it needed to be said. I was slowing Jason down. I was in the way. He was in real danger from the Sons. I didn't want to make it easier for them to catch him. "Jason," I said, "I'm not sure if I should stay with you."

"What?" he said. "Where would you go?"

"That's not the point," I said. "The point is that I'm slowing you down. I literally can't run as fast as you. And it's got to be harder to hide two people than it is to hide one. If the Sons got to you because of me, then I'd feel horrible."

"Where would you go?" Jason asked.

He was concerned about me. That was sweet. I had to reassure him not to worry about me, so that he'd be able to take care of himself. "I'd figure something out," I said. "You wouldn't have to worry about me."

"Like what would you figure out?"

God, he was stubborn. "I would ..." I shrugged. "I don't know exactly."

Jason looked stunned. He sat back in his seat. "I can understand why you'd want to get away from me," he said in a quiet voice.

Of course he understood. He knew that I was weighing him down. My presence endangered him. "Good," I said. "So after breakfast, you should get out of the city, and I'll—"

"Wait," he said. "Okay, I know that it's dangerous for you being around me. And I appreciate your wanting to go someplace away from that and away from me. But I can't leave you in the city by yourself. There are other dangers besides the Sons, you know. You're just a girl."

Just a girl. That was it exactly. He even thought of me as something hard to protect and take care of. "No, Jason, I don't want you to have to try to take care of me anymore. That's the whole point. If you stay here and try to help me get safe, then the Sons will find you. We can't waste time."

"You want to get away from me that badly?"

What? Had he been listening to me at all? "It's not about

me wanting to get away from you, Jason," I said.

"That's what you just said," he said.

"No," I said. "I want to stay with you. I'm scared to be without you. But that's selfish of me, and I can't put you in danger."

Jason looked confused. He didn't say anything for several minutes. The waitress came back and asked if there was anything else we needed. "Just the check," said Jason. He shook his head at me, still looking confused. "You don't put me in danger," he said. "I'm always in danger. It's the way things are. You can't add to that in any way."

"I slow you down," I said. "I'm just a girl. I can't ... shoot guns or beat people up."

"Sure you can," he said. "You just don't know how yet."

The waitress brought back the check. Jason threw several bills on top of it and stood up. I stood up with him.

"So, let me get this straight," he said. "You do want to stay with me."

"Yes," I said. Maybe I shouldn't have admitted it. Even though Jason said I couldn't put him in any worse danger, I didn't know if I really believed him.

"And you aren't worried about what kind of danger I'm putting you in, you're just worried about me?"

"Yes," I said.

We left the restaurant. The sun had climbed a little higher into the sky. It was reflecting off the tall buildings that surrounded us, like it was splintered by thousands and thousands of mirrors.

"Azazel," said Jason, "as long as you want to be around me, I want you to be around me. Okay?"

I nodded.

Impulsively, Jason closed the distance between us in one quick step. His arms went around me, and he pulled me against his chest. His eyes searched mine questioningly, waiting for me to tell him to stop. When I didn't, he crushed his lips against mine.

We stood in the brilliant New York sunlight, cars honking on the street around us, people swerving around us on the sidewalk, ignoring us completely, and we kissed for a very long time.

* * *

Jason didn't let go of my hand as we walked to the subway station. He didn't let go of my hand while we bought our metro cards. And he didn't let go of my hand while we sat down in the subway car.

We grinned at each other as we sat next to each other. I watched the stone walls of the underground tunnels fly past us. Being with Jason like this, our hands entwined, so close, it just felt right. I'd never felt anything like this before. And I knew that from the first time I'd seen Jason, I'd begun to feel it. I pictured him, running out the woods, sweating and panting. He'd been so alive then. When he'd burst into my life, he'd kick-started something in me that hadn't ever woken up before. He'd brought me to life. Real life. All of the things I'd thought I'd felt for Toby had been adolescent and immature. They were products of living life with the mute button on, in black and white. Jason turned the volume up to eleven. He let the colors in.

Jason squeezed my hand. He leaned close. "So," he said, "this is what we'll do. We'll take the subway, and then we'll take the ferry over the Hudson into New Jersey. You ever been on a ferry?"

"No," I said.

"So that will be cool," he said.

New Jersey? I had a thought suddenly. "You know," I said, "my Aunt Stephanie lives in New Jersey."

Chapter Fourteen

To: Alfred Norwich (anorwic@risingsun.org)
From: Richard Durham (rdurham@risingsun.org)
Subject: Re: West Virginia
Alfred,

We've been monitoring the situation in West
Virginia, tapping the phones of the Jones family. It's
our feeling that if the family should come in contact
with Jason again, they would be an immediate threat
to his person. For now, we've just got them under
surveillance, but if they should make any moves, we
would recommend termination.

It's also my personal feeling that since Hallam was so
adamant we stay away from West Virginia, he knew
Jason was there the entire time. That means any place
he said Jason wouldn't be is probably where Jason is.

Yours in the pursuit of the Purpose,
Richard

It wasn't as hard to find Aunt Stephanie as I feared.
Jason and I just found an internet café and used the
computers to look her up on anywho.com. We got a phone
number and an address. Aunt Stephanie lived in Alpine, NJ,
which Jason said was good, because it was relatively close.
We were already in New Jersey, having gotten off the ferry.
We weren't sure if we should call Aunt Stephanie first. I'd
told Jason that my aunt hadn't really kept in touch with my

family and that she and my grandmother had disowned my mother for marrying below her station.

Jason wasn't sure it was a good idea for us to go to my aunt's house. I had to admit that my last idea of going somewhere for help (Ms. Campbell) had backfired completely. But he admitted that Alpine, NJ was the last place the Sons would look for him and that he didn't have any better ideas.

Apparently, Alpine was a community of really, really rich people. I hadn't known this. But all the houses there were worth millions of dollars.

"Your mother really did marry down," said Jason.

We decided to call her, because we were going to have to take a bus to Alpine, and if she didn't want us to be there, we'd have wasted all that money. I had to admit there were definite advantages to this whole metropolitan area thing. Public transportation was a marvelous thing. It was really cool getting around without a car. One less thing to worry about.

I dialed my aunt's number on a payphone (which was extremely hard to find in this day of cell phones. Neither Jason nor I had one). It rang and rang. I chewed on my lip nervously.

Finally, someone answered the phone. "Hoyt residence." That was my mother's maiden name. Aunt Stephanie had never married.

"Um," I said, "may I speak to Stephanie Hoyt?"

"May I ask who's calling?"

"It's her niece, Azazel," I said.

"Hold on," said the voice, but whoever it was sounded a little startled. I wondered who was answering the phone at Aunt Stephanie's house. Did she have servants or something?

I waited. Finally, someone picked up the phone.

"Azazel?"

"Hi Aunt Stephanie," I said.

"Is your mother with you?" she asked.

"Um ... I've kind of run away from home," I said.

"Of course you have. How could you live there with that woman?" said Aunt Stephanie. "Where are you?"

"In Hoboken," I said. That wasn't the response I was expecting.

"Oh my God," said Aunt Stephanie. "Alone?"

"N-no, I have a friend."

"Well, thank Heaven for that. I wouldn't want you all alone out there," she said. "I'm sending a car. Tell me exactly where you are."

After giving her a detailed location, I hung up the phone. "She's sending a car," I said to Jason. "She didn't seem upset that I ran away."

"Good sign," said Jason.

* * *

Aunt Stephanie's house was enormous. It had wings. It sprawled over an immaculately landscaped lawn. It looked too big for a family of ten. And Aunt Stephanie lived there alone? I was floored.

We pulled up in the car that she'd sent for us. Apparently, Aunt Stephanie had a chauffer. She also had a brand new black BMW. I felt out of place in it, as if I was afraid I might break something or spill something or that my very presence might somehow destroy it.

Aunt Stephanie met us at the door. I recognized her from pictures my mother had shown me, but she was definitely older now. She was a somewhat plump woman with short, brown hair. She wore a lot of makeup. But she had a big smile and a New Jersey accent, which I kind of liked. Vaguely, I wondered why my mother didn't have an accent.

"Oh my God," she said as we approached. "Look at you, Azazel. The last time I saw you, you barely came up to my knees. You are beautiful."

"Uh, thanks," I said.

She was sort of brash, but I liked it.

"Who's your friend?"

"This is Jason," I said. "He was a foster kid at my parents' house for a few months."

"So you ran away together, then," she said, ushering us into her house.

Inside it was even more breathtaking than outside. She led us into a foyer, tiled in white marble. There was a small table in the center, on which a large bouquet of white roses sat. Behind it was a massive expanse of space. The far wall was composed entirely of windows. Through them I could see a garden. It was fall, so not much was growing, but there were several very pretty evergreen trees and bushes.

"You poor things," Aunt Stephanie continued. "You have bags?"

"No," I said.

"Heavens! Just the clothes on your backs then?"

Jason and I nodded. I was glad to see that even Jason was a little taken aback with the surroundings and Aunt Stephanie. It was good not to be the only overwhelmed one.

Aunt Stephanie threw back her head and bellowed, "Marci!"

A tiny woman darted out into the foyer.

"Ms. Hoyt?" she said. Even her voice was tiny.

Aunt Stephanie waved her hands at us. "They need clothes," she said. "Marci, measure them. Get them something."

Marci pulled measuring tape out of her pocket and began measuring us. Jason and I exchanged glances over Marci's head. What was going on?

"Honestly," said Aunt Stephanie. "You look awful. Just awful. And you must be starving. I think Lydia's whipping up something for lunch in the kitchen, so at least you'll have something to eat, but my God, when was the last time you had a shower?"

"Um ..." I tried to think. It had been awhile. "Friday?" I said.

"No," said Aunt Stephanie, looking terrorized. "That's horrible. Just horrible. Well, don't worry, I've got bathrooms. Come with me."

She started walking away. Marci was still measuring us.

We didn't move.

Aunt Stephanie looked back at us. "Well?" she said. "What are you waiting for?" Then she noticed Marci. "Oh, enough already, Marci. My God, you and I both know you can look at someone and tell what size they are. Just get some clothes. Have them delivered. I don't care. But I want something here by the time both of them are done bathing."

Marci bobbed her head and darted out of the room.

Jason and I followed Aunt Stephanie.

She deposited us both in separate bathrooms on the same wing. Once inside, I didn't do anything for a few minutes. I just stood staring at the bathroom, gaping. This was a *guest* bathroom, and it was the size of my bedroom at home. It was all white like the foyer. It was too white. I was afraid to get clean in a bathroom like this. What if I got it dirty?

Before I'd even had a chance to undress, Aunt Stephanie knocked on my door with some clothes. "Marci's getting more," she assured me. "This is just a start. I don't know if you like them or not, or if they're in style. I don't keep up with that kind of thing, but Marci has impeccable taste, and I'm sure we can trust her to have picked out something nice."

She ducked back out of the bathroom without another word. I looked at the clothes. They were very nice. There was a pair of jeans and a peasant top. They still had price tags on them. I looked at the price tags. I gagged.

After showering, Jason and I joined Aunt Stephanie in

her kitchen "nook" (if this was what she called a nook, I'd hate to see what a cranny was) for lunch. Jason also had new clothes. Our clothes did seem to fit us very well. Apparently, Marci was talented.

For lunch, we all sat down to eat enormous chef salads. Aunt Stephanie barely had a bite swallowed before she began talking. "Now," she said, "you have got to tell me, Azazel, what happened? Why did you leave?"

I was hesitant. The last time I'd told this story — to Ms. Campbell — it really hadn't turned out well.

"Don't be shy," she said. "There are reasons why I don't speak to your mother anymore. And I told her that if she continued down the path she was on, she would lose her children. I warned her, but she did not listen. And so I just want to know exactly what happened, so that if I ever do see her again, I can say I told you so."

"Well," I said, still not reassured. This story was really weird. "My parents kind of surprised me on Halloween."

"Oh my God," said Aunt Stephanie, "she made you participate in a Black Mass, didn't she?"

"You know about that?" I asked.

"Well, why do you think we disowned her?" Aunt Stephanie asked.

I was shocked. "I always thought it was because dad was poor," I said.

"No, no. That was fine." Aunt Stephanie took another bite of her salad. "Everything was fine. Well, Mother was not exactly thrilled, but we dealt with that. I even tried to send your mother money, and, of course, she's stubborn, and she wouldn't take it. But when she found out she couldn't get pregnant, well, she just went nuts."

"What do you mean?" I asked. "My mother didn't get disowned until after she and Dad were married?"

"No. It wasn't until she started doing all those weird spell things to try to get pregnant," said Aunt Stephanie.

My hand went to my neck. I was still wearing the necklace my mother had given me on Friday. What had she said? Something about getting the pendant before she found out she was pregnant with me? From Mrs. Cantle, the woman who everyone said was a witch.

"And I guess they worked," said Aunt Stephanie. "I mean here you are, a medical miracle. But the price, I'm telling you. To lose my sister to the worship of Satan. My God. It just ..." For once, Aunt Stephanie seemed to be at a loss for words.

"So," I said, more to myself than anyone, "all of it was just to have me."

Aunt Stephanie nodded. "Yes." She turned to Jason. "So were you there when this Black Mass happened?" she asked him.

"Yeah," he said. "They, um, tried to kill me."

"Oh my God," said Aunt Stephanie. "You poor things. Well, look. Neither of you worry about anything. I am so happy you got away from that woman, from that place. You'll be safe here. Just consider yourselves at home."

* * *

It was a dream. It was a beautiful, wonderful dream. I couldn't believe it. I wished I'd thought of Aunt Stephanie earlier. We wouldn't have had to spend that terrible night in New York, sleeping on a pullout couch and running from the Sons. For the first time in my escape with Jason, I'd actually had a good idea. Finally.

The rest of the day, Jason and I lounged in Aunt Stephanie's den on lush, overstuffed couches, watching television and eating snacks.

I felt so relieved. Everything was going to be okay now. I relaxed. I luxuriated in our surroundings and soaked up the atmosphere. During a commercial break, I looked over at Jason, who was sitting very close to me on the couch. We'd started off sitting far away from each other, unsure if our touching would be rude to Aunt Stephanie. But as the afternoon wore on, we'd gotten closer and closer. Now our heads were inches from each other, resting on the back of the couch.

"If you could live anywhere," I asked, "where would you live?"

"The Sons wouldn't be chasing me?" he asked.

"Of course not," I said.

Jason considered. "I don't know," he said. "I never really thought about it."

"Never?" I asked.

"Where would you live?" he asked.

"Um ... by the ocean," I said. "Somewhere warm."

"Sounds nice," he said. "I don't know. All I've ever

wanted is to be normal. I wanted to go to school and play video games and think about things like girls and sports. Now, I only ever think about one girl."

I smiled, feeling my heart leap.

"So, I guess, if I could live anywhere, I'd want to live where you live," he said.

I couldn't help it. That was too sweet. My heart swelled, and I reached over and kissed him. "I want that too," I said. "I want to be with you."

He smiled and put his arm around me. He rested his chin on top of my head. "So, we'd live by the beach. In the evening, we'd walk on the sand barefoot, holding hands. And when we woke up, it wouldn't be because something was after us, and we had to run." Jason mused. "I could take you on dates. To the movies or to restaurants. Would you go on a date with me if I asked you?"

"Of course I would." He had his arms wrapped around me, and he had to ask?

I moved out of his embrace for a second so I could look at him. "You know, Jason," I said. "If things hadn't worked out the way they did in Bramford, if everything hadn't gone insane, I still would have ended up with you."

"You can't be sure of that," he said. "It's okay, you don't have to—"

"No," I said. "I mean it. When I kissed you at the dance, it was like everything lit up for the first time. Even if I'd never heard that conversation between Toby and Lilith, I never would have gone with him that night."

"Really?" Jason asked.

"What I feel for you is so much different than what I felt for Toby," I said. "I just feel ... drawn to you."

"Yeah," he said, recognition in his voice. "Like I can't look away, even if I want to."

I nodded. "Yes. When you're around, you're all I think about."

"When you're not around, you're all I think about," he said.

I settled back into his arms. "Mmm," I said. "I don't like it when you're not around."

"I don't like it either."

"We're together now," I said. "That's all that matters."

Then, of course, Jason had to ruin everything.

"You know I can't stay here, right?" he said.

I didn't know that. I had thought that everything was fixed. I had thought that we could stay here forever and that the nightmare was over. "What do you mean?" I asked.

"It's only a matter of time before the Sons track me down," he said. "I can't stay anywhere."

"But you said they'd never look for you here," I said.

"Maybe not for a while. But even in Bramford, they found me."

I remembered Hallam's hand on my throat. Remembered his cruel voice telling me to run away. Oh. I really didn't want to leave here. I liked it here. It was awesome here. "I don't want to go," I moaned.

"You don't have to," he said. "You should stay. She's

your aunt. You've got family. You'll be safe if I'm gone. I'll know you're all right. You should stay."

I pushed myself away from him. I gaped at him. "After what I just said, how could you think that I could do that?"

Jason looked away. "Maybe ..." he said, " ... maybe if things ever changed, I could come back."

"Jason, if you leave, I'm coming with you," I said. "I won't lose you. You don't know what it was like for me when you ran away in Bramford. I couldn't eat or think or concentrate. All I could think about was whether or not you were hurt or dead. You can't do that to me again. I won't let you."

"It won't be right away," he said. "I can stay here for a while. Let's not talk about it now."

"I want you to take it back," I said. "I want you to say you won't leave me."

"I can't say that," he said. "Azazel, I love you. I can't put you in danger. Not when there's some better alternative."

He loved me? I was shocked. My mouth hung open. Everything else he'd said was blotted out for now. "I love you too," I said. I knew it was true. Jason and I may not have had the longest courtship. We hadn't been traditionally together for more than a day or two, really. But there was something between us that transcended all of that. There was something about what we had that was too big for traditions. We were something incredible. We belonged together.

* * *

Late that night, I awoke to find someone in my room with me, on my bed, tying my hands to the bedpost. My legs were tied too. At first, I was too disoriented to completely understand what was going on, but as I woke up, I recognized my attacker.

I screamed. I screamed and screamed.

And Toby balled up the sheets on the bed and thrust them in my mouth. His face was bruised and purple. His nose was twice the size that it usually was. But I would have screamed anyway, even if he'd looked like the cherub he used to resemble. I had hoped never to see Toby again.

"Listen," he whispered. "It didn't work. The Invocation didn't work because you didn't join the Circle. We have to complete the ritual."

How had he gotten in here? Where had he come from? And what the hell did he think he was going to do to me? I spit the bed sheets out of my mouth.

"Toby, you are not going to complete any kind of ritual with me, okay?" I said.

He looked apologetic. "I don't really want to do this either, Azazel. I don't want you to be all struggling and screaming and ... It makes me feel really bad. But we have to do this. It's important."

"How did you find me?" I demanded.

"Your aunt called your mom to gloat," said Toby.

What?! Aunt Stephanie had betrayed us? She clearly didn't understand the seriousness of the situation.

"We drove all night. All of us," said Toby.

"All?" I said.

"Yeah. Me, your mom, your dad, my dad, my mom, some other people."

"And you're all here? In this house?"

"Yes."

"And Jason?"

"Will be waiting for you to complete the ritual as soon as we're done here," said Toby.

Oh my God. This was awful. Going to Aunt Stephanie's house had not been a great idea. It was not a beautiful dream. It was just another chapter in the nightmare that had become my life.

And now Toby was going to ... I felt sick just thinking about it.

"Look, Azazel, I know you don't want to do this with me anymore," said Toby, "but if you lay still and don't ... well, I think it'll be better. Just don't fight me."

Don't fight him? How could I? My arms and legs were tied down. Couldn't fight physically. And they already had Jason. There was no one to hear me scream. What was I going to do? I could beg Toby not to, but I didn't think that would work. I could ... God what could I do?

Toby began pushing my nightgown up, over my legs.

I could tell Toby I had AIDS. Except he'd know that was a lie, because he knew I was a ... Wait.

I had an idea. "Toby?" I said.

"Yes," he said.

"For the ritual to work, didn't I have to be a virgin?" I

asked.

He looked at me. "Yeah, you did, but why would that matter?" He made a face. "Why did you say 'did?' Past tense?"

"I'm not a virgin anymore," I said.

"What?" he said. "Of course you are."

"Not," I said. "I totally did it with Jason last night."

"No way."

"Yes way," I said. "Twice, even."

"You're lying," he said. "You're just trying to keep me from doing this."

God. He could see through me so easily. I told myself to stay strong. "I'm not lying," I said. "Ask Jason."

"Well, he's not in here, and if I leave you, you'll figure out some way to get untied, and you'll run off," he said. "I'm just gonna have to do it anyway."

No! "What if I'm right though?" I blurted out. "You already said you didn't want to do it. Think how much effort and discomfort you'll have to go through for nothing."

He considered. He started to untie me. "Fine," he said. "We're gonna go downstairs and talk to your dad about this. And when he finds out that you had sex with that ... thing, he'll probably kill Jason himself and save you the trouble."

Oh please God, no. Maybe this had been a bad idea.

Everyone was in Aunt Stephanie's massive dining room. They sat at the long, long polished wooden table, still decorated with a bouquet of white roses. Behind them, a huge picture window looked out onto Aunt Stephanie's

273

elaborate gardens. Aunt Stephanie, Jason, her cook Lydia, and Marci were all tied to chairs and gagged. My mother, father, Sheriff Damon, his wife, and several other members of the community were all seated in chairs around the table.

"That was fast," said Sheriff Damon when Toby and I appeared.

"I didn't do it," said Toby. "She says she had sex with Jason. And the ritual won't work if she's not a virgin. I didn't know what to do."

As Toby predicted, my dad was angry. He got up and ripped the gag out of Jason's mouth.

"Is that true?" he demanded of Jason.

Jason was trying hard not to laugh. "Yes," he said. "That is true." He winked at me. "Twice."

I grinned at him. It was like we could read each other's minds! He was never allowed to leave me. I wouldn't let him.

My dad backhanded Jason.

"She might be lying," said Toby.

"Might be," said Sheriff Damon, "but how do we know?"

My mother spoke up. "Zaza, baby, just be truthful with us. Tell what really happened."

"Why should I tell you anything?" I said to her. "You turned to Satanism so you could get pregnant with me."

"Oh sweetheart, did Stephanie tell you that?" my mother asked.

I nodded.

"I wanted you so badly," she said. "And the coven needed a vessel. And it was the only way."

This just got worse and worse. "So you had me specifically to be a vessel for a demon which you then named me after?" I demanded.

"Satanism is about the individual," she said. "I already believed that. Your father and I both already believed that. You were born with a specific purpose. We raised you to end the suffering that Jason will cause. Why can't you see what he is?"

"I do see what he is," I said. I gazed at Jason. "He's amazing."

Jason smiled at me.

"Stop trying to reason with her, Jodi," said my dad. He turned to Toby. "Toby," he said. "Didn't you have gym class with Jason?"

"We all had gym together," said Toby.

"Ever see him in the shower?" asked my dad.

Oh God. Where was this going?

"Azazel," said my dad, "is Jason circumcised?"

Damn it! And how disgusting was it for my dad to ask me something like that? My parents were horrible, horrible people. Well, I had no idea.

I looked at Jason. He looked at me. I tried to find some clue in his eyes. I sifted through everything I knew about him. The Sons of the Rising Sun were religious and religious people got circumcised, so, "Yes," I said.

Jason winced. He shook his head.

Damn it. So much for reading each other's minds.

"No," said Toby. "He's not. I *knew* she was lying."

I felt my heart sink. What were we going to do? I could see that Jason was struggling against the ropes that held him to his chair, but he wasn't having any luck. There wasn't any hope for it then. What I'd thought I'd escaped in Bramford had come for me in Alpine, New Jersey. And here in this lush house, I wasn't going to be able to stop Toby from doing what he came to do.

Toby grasped my arm and turned my body around. I stiffened. I wasn't going to walk with him. If he was going to try to do this, I was going to struggle every step of the way. There was no way I was making it easy for him.

I looked at his face, those blue eyes I used to think were so beautiful. Now there was only a twisted expression on his face, something hovering between disgust and hatred. Toby had become a monster.

Unexpectedly, the picture window behind everyone shattered. Pieces of glass rained down, clattering against the marble floor. And Aunt Stephanie's throat blossomed with blood. She gargled through her gag, her eyes wide. Then her head slumped down.

I was stunned and scared. What?

I heard them then. They sounded like muffled missiles, tearing through the air. Gun shots. From guns fitted with silencers. They were swift. Efficient. There was no time to think. No time to evaluate. Just the images, one after another, burned into my brain. My mother — blood trickling between her eyebrows. My father—his left ear exploding in gore. Toby—his face going blank, blood seeping out of his mouth—dropping to the ground next to me. All of them—Sheriff Damon, his wife, my aunt's servants, the rest of the coven.

All dead. In a matter of seconds.

And then they were swarming in through the window. Five men dressed in black, carrying guns. They stepped over the bodies like they were old pieces of furniture. One knelt behind Jason to untie his bonds.

"What about the girl?" asked one of the men, who had a British accent.

And then I understood. The Sons of the Rising Sun. They were here.

The man came for me, his gun raised, waving it in my face. Maybe I should have run. I was frozen.

Jason was free from his ropes. He moved so fast, he looked blurred. He elbowed the man who had freed him in the face. Kneed him in the groin. Wrested the gun from the man's hands. And pointed it at the man who had pointed a gun at me.

During all this, another man was answering the first man's question about me. "Waste her," he said.

And Jason shot the man who was pointing his gun at me.

His shot was eerily similar to the shots the Sons had inflicted on my family. The man's temple erupted, blood pouring out. He crumpled to the ground.

I wanted to scream. I wanted to be horrified. But ...

maybe it had just been too much. Maybe there was nothing left inside me to horrify. Or maybe I was in shock.

"Get his gun, Azazel," said Jason.

And it seemed like the most natural thing in the world to reach down over the body of a dead man and take the gun out of his hand.

I held it up, staring at it. I didn't know how to use one.

The other four men were on guard now, shifting their guns back and forth between Jason and me. My brain was still working somehow. I didn't know how. It should have turned off a long time ago, but it hadn't. I was thinking that I was in more danger than Jason because they wouldn't seriously hurt the Rising Sun. They needed him. I was, however, expendable. It was important that I figure out how to use the gun.

Jason was still shooting. I wasn't paying attention. I was looking at the gun.

Since the man had been shooting before I'd taken it from him, that must mean the safety wasn't on, so I shouldn't have to worry about that. It should be as easy as pointing and shooting.

I held it in both hands. It was a little heavy. I leveled it at the man in front of me. I rubbed the trigger with my forefinger.

And Jason shot him.

Jason had shot all of them.

Jason had *killed* all of them.

I surveyed the dining room, now littered with bodies.

Jason came over to me. "You all right?" he asked.

"Yeah," I said. I felt very, very calm oddly.

Jason also seemed calm. "Good," he said. "Go back to our rooms and pack us some clothes. I'm going to find some cash and the keys to a car."

I guess it wasn't really stealing since my aunt was dead.

"Meet back here in five minutes?" I asked.

"Seven," he said.

We parted. I changed out of my nightgown. I didn't think about how sad I was to be leaving this huge closet full of clothes. I definitely didn't think about how Aunt Stephanie couldn't ever get any more clothes. Or how I'd never even talk to Aunt Stephanie again. I didn't think at all. I just pulled clothes out of my closet and then out of Jason's. I couldn't find anything to put them in, so I shoved them in an empty garbage bag that I found in a trashcan.

Jason was waited for me when I returned. We didn't look at the bodies. Instead, we went directly to the garage and slid into the Beamer we'd come into the house in earlier that day. Jason pulled out, and we drove. I watched the huge, million dollar houses go by our windows. Alpine was a beautiful place. The homes were absolutely gorgeous.

When we were finally out of Alpine, I stared straight ahead. Neither Jason nor I spoke.

Chapter Fifteen

To: Jason Wodden (jwodde@risingsun.org)
From: Renegade Son (settingsun007@yahoo.com)
Subject: Risky business
Jason,

You probably don't even check this email anymore, but I have no idea how to get in touch with you. And it's not safe for me to be exposing myself in this email to you. We're both on the outs, if you know what I mean. Listen, there are things you need to know. Things that I've figured out. I need to show them to you.

Bethlehem. As soon as you can.

P.S. Sorry about the lack of a clean slate. I tried.

We drove through the morning and the afternoon. Jason asked me once if I wanted to stop for food. I wasn't hungry. We didn't stop. As the sun began to grow heavy in the sky, we stopped at a hotel somewhere in Pennsylvania. The woman at the desk was chewing gum and had teased her unnaturally red hair to heights I didn't think possible. "We only have rooms with one bed open," she said.

"That's not a problem," I told her.

Jason was standing behind me, but he had apparently decided to leave the negotiation of a hotel room up to me.

"How old are you kids?" the woman asked.

Kids? We weren't kids. We were the vessel of Azazel and

the Rising Sun respectively. We killed people. "I gave you my ID," I said to her.

"It says you're twenty-one," she said.

"That's right," I said.

The woman slid us our key. "Don't cause trouble," she said.

We'd sure try not to. But trouble seemed to follow us everywhere we went.

Inside our room, I dropped our garbage bag full of clothes on the floor. There were orange curtains drawn tight against the large window next to the door. The bedspread on the queen-sized bed was a loud geometric pattern of oranges and reds. It was stained. When I flicked on the light in the bathroom, a loud fan came on that rattled. It sounded like the fan was just going to fall out at any second.

I came out of the bathroom to find Jason standing in the middle of the room, his hands jammed in this pockets, staring blankly into space.

There was a ratty easy chair in a corner next to the bed. I sat down in it.

"The BMW's conspicuous," said Jason suddenly. "We should probably see about getting another car. Maybe tomorrow sometime."

"Okay," I said.

Jason didn't move. I didn't either.

Minutes ticked by. It was too early to go to sleep. I was tired, though, I realized. I hadn't had an uninterrupted night of sleep since Thursday night. What day was it now?

Sunday? Three days? That was funny. It felt like longer. Much longer.

Jason abruptly walked to the bed and sat down stiffly. "So," he said. "I shot five people in the head." He looked at me.

"You saved my life," I said. "Again." It had happened. It was over. Thinking about it might make it seem too ... "Besides, they killed my ... They killed everybody else."

"I couldn't handle it if anything happened to you," he said.

He stood up again. He was doing everything in jerky movements, like he was a robot. He came to me on the chair. Held out his hand to me. I took it, and he pulled me to my feet. I stood next to him, facing him, our bodies inches apart. Jason swallowed. His eyes looked empty and hollow.

Then his arms were around me. He was kissing my forehead and my cheeks and my neck. His hands slid up my shoulders, tangling themselves in my hair. And between kisses, he was talking, his words tumbling out over top of each other, like he'd unleashed a torrent within himself. "When I knew you were with Toby, I thought ... I was so worried. I thought—and if something had happened to you, I don't what I would have done. If you were—" He pulled back a second, looking into my eyes, his face so earnest.

"Jason," I whispered, putting my hand to his cheek.

"I'm sorry," he said. "I'm sorry about your parents."

"Don't," I said. I didn't want to think about that. If I closed my eyes, I could still see their faces, their eyes unseeing and staring and ... dead. And the images were all that I could process right now. I couldn't process words or emotions or thoughts. I kissed his lips, trying to wipe away the entire incident.

For a few minutes, it worked. Jason's lips and Jason's tongue were all I could think about. He was warm and soft and solid, and it was all I wanted.

Jason pulled back. He needed to talk, for some reason. I didn't want to talk! I'd be fine if we never talked about it, any of it, ever. "When I saw him pointing the gun at you, I didn't really think. It was like something took over. Something I learned somewhere. I just moved. I just pulled the trigger. I just ..."

I knew what he meant. I'd felt it too. I remembered coldly assessing the gun, figuring I didn't have worry about a safety, leveling it with both hands, my finger tensed against its trigger. I'd been about to shoot someone. But Jason had beaten me to it. I knew that I should comfort Jason. I should tell him he was okay, that he'd done the right thing. The necessary thing.

But comfort wasn't something I could really do right now. It was too warm. There wasn't anything inside me except a cold, stiff hole. If I tried to let warmth in, I'd fall apart. I'd have to *feel* things. I didn't want to do that. I needed to stay in control.

So, instead I said, "You've never killed anyone before?"

"No," said Jason, his voice ragged.

I kissed him. I didn't know what else to do. I didn't have

words to say. I didn't have anything for him.

When I kissed him, I realized his face was wet. Jason was crying.

The right thing to do when someone was crying was to comfort someone. I tried to remember things you said to comfort someone. "It's okay," I said.

And Jason started to sob. His body shook. His strong, huge shoulders, his muscular back. I held him. Rubbed his back gingerly. But I couldn't quite connect. I was there physically, but this outpouring of emotion was foreign, frightening to me.

Maybe Jason could tell that I was holding back. Maybe it made him angry. Maybe he wanted to force a reaction out of me. But he started kissing me then, kissing me through his tears, kissing me fiercely, as if he had to throw the force of his emotion into something else.

He threw me back on the hotel bed and he was on me like a wolf, his mouth on my mouth, on my neck, my throat. His hands were inside my clothes, thrusting them out of the way, exposing me. He ripped at the bra I was wearing. I heard the fabric tear. Felt the air against my bare skin. Felt Jason's hands on me, squeezing, twisting, and ... it *hurt* .

It was the pain that woke up the human part in me. The pain forced me back into my body, forced the flood of feelings to wash over me. Tears sprang to my eyes, and I put my hands on either side of Jason's face and made him look at me. "Not like this," I said.

Jason flung himself away from me. We lay on our backs

next to each other, not touching. I listened to Jason's rasping breath.

My parents were dead. They were gone. At the end, they'd been tyrannical. They'd put me in situations that I should never have had to face. They'd introduced terror into my life. But at one time, I'd loved them. And I think, in their own perverse way, they'd loved me too. And they were gone.

I reached for Jason. "You can cry," I whispered. "It's okay to cry."

He propped himself up on his elbow. Looked at me. "I'm sorry," he said.

"You did what you had to do," I said, not sure if I was talking about killing the men or the way he'd attacked my body. In some ways, I guess I meant both.

"The right thing to do was to —"

"Sometimes there isn't a right thing," I said. "Sometimes there are only wrong things, and you have to pick whichever one you think is the least wrong."

His eyes were filling back up. "You sound like your parents."

"They're dead," I said helplessly, feeling my own voice fill with tears.

And so we clutched each other and cried. We lay on the stained hotel mattress and stained it with our tears. And when we couldn't cry anymore, we both fell asleep, our limbs entangled, half on the bed, half off.

Sometime in the middle of the night, I woke up,

uncomfortable because my legs were hanging off the bed. The lights were still on in the hotel room, and my clothes were in disarray. I rearranged my shirt and shook Jason awake.

He was alert immediately. "What happened?" he said, sitting up straight.

"Nothing," I said.

He let out a breath.

"I just thought we should get under the covers," I said. "Maybe put on pajamas."

He laughed. "Yeah. Okay. Pretend we're living actual human lives?"

I smiled. "Yeah."

I went to the garbage bag and began going through it, but it was difficult to find anything in it, so I just dumped the clothes on the floor, and sat on my knees, sorting through them. I looked at Jason apologetically. "I seem to have forgotten the pajamas," I said.

"It's fine," he said. "I can sleep in jeans."

"No," I said. And I took a deep breath. "But you could ... take them off."

Jason raised his eyebrows. "After the way that I ... After what happened earlier, I wouldn't think you'd really want to touch me again."

He was stupid. He was so stupid. I'd already forgiven him for that, or had he missed that? I got up and walked to where he sat on the bed. I kissed him. "I was sleeping in your arms, you idiot."

He touched my face. "Azazel, I don't know what I'm doing," he said.

"And neither do I," I said. "But look, Jason, this can't be the day that I lost my parents, and you killed someone for the first time. That can't be why we remember this day. So, let's make it the day that we ... made love for the first time."

I kissed Jason again, lingering on his full lips.

"You're sure?" he breathed.

I nodded.

We fell back on the bed.

It wasn't like I imagined. It wasn't like two souls melding into each other. It wasn't like we were connected and had somehow become one being. But it wasn't like the horror I'd heard some of my friends tell either. There wasn't any blood. There wasn't any pain. If there was anything wrong with it, it was just that it was new and confusing and a little awkward. We giggled a lot. We bumped heads a couple times. But when it was done, and I was lying in Jason's arms, tucked under his chin, against his body, his smooth, smooth skin touching my own, it felt like ... well, something had happened. It felt like we belonged to each other. Like we'd cemented a bond. Like a physical declaration of the feelings we already knew we had for each other.

As I drifted off to sleep for the second time, Jason murmured, "I love you."

I said it back, but he was already snoring.

* * *

When morning came, we ate the continental breakfast in the hotel lobby. In the corner, there was an internet-enabled computer, and so we both checked our email. I didn't know why I did. I didn't really know if I wanted to be reminded of my old life. There weren't any new messages in my inbox, but there was a message from Lilith on myspace. She went on and on about how sorry she was. I couldn't finish it. I didn't care that Lilith was sorry. Toby was dead. It didn't matter anymore. She was going to have to deal with that, now. And besides, I was never going back to Bramford.

Jason checked email next. He said that before leaving Bramford, he'd been in touch with a guy somewhere in Texas, and maybe we could head there next. I let him go to the computer and began eating my Danish.

Jason called me over the computer. "Read this," he said.

It was an email message. I read it. It didn't make much sense. It was like it was written in code. But when I got to the last sentence, I gasped. "Hallam?" I said.

Jason nodded. "I don't usually check my email account with the Sons, but I did because I still think it was weird that they found us in New Jersey. And how did the Satanists get there?"

I told him that Aunt Stephanie had called my mom.

"Oh," said Jason. "You know, I bet the Sons followed your parents. That must be how they found us. But anyway, I thought maybe there'd be something in my account that would give me a clue. There wasn't. There was just this."

"What's it mean?" I asked.

"I don't know. He's not sending it from his email account with the Sons. And he doesn't use his name. And he says he's on the outs like I am. And none of that stuff in West Virginia ever made any sense. Like the clean slate comment."

"Didn't make sense?" I said. I wasn't following.

"If the Sons had found me in Bramford, they should have done basically what they did to us last night," said Jason. "So that was why I ran when I found out Hallam was around. I figured they'd break into your house and start shooting. But they didn't. Which never made any sense to me. It didn't make sense that Hallam said I had a clean slate."

"Yeah, what exactly does that mean, anyway?" I asked.

"It's a reference to a conversation we had once," said Jason. "After the incident with the sorority house, Hallam and I talked. I said that sometimes I wished I wasn't the Rising Sun. I said I wished I had a clean slate, that I could just walk away and be normal."

I nodded. "Okay. So he was saying that you had the chance to be normal when he talked to me in the woods in Bramford?"

"Yeah," said Jason. "And the only way he could have done that is if he were working against the Sons. So they must have figured out that he was doing that. And now he's on the run."

"Wait," I said. "Hallam was *helping* you?"

"I think so," he said.

"This is the guy who you said was screaming in joy while he was shooting college girls. This is the guy who nearly strangled me in the woods. And he's on our side?"

"He nearly strangled you? What?"

"Did I leave that part out before?"

Jason looked pissed. "Yes. You did." He sighed. "Well, I don't know about our side, but he seems to have gone renegade, hence the name on his email account."

"What about the rest of it?" I asked. "Wanting to show you things? Bethlehem?"

"I don't know," said Jason. "He wants me to go him."

"Where is he? In Bethlehem?" I considered. "Isn't there a Bethlehem, Pennsylvania?"

"He wouldn't put the actual name of where he was in the email. It's on the Sons server. They're probably reading all of my email messages." Jason shook his head. "Bethlehem? What could he mean?"

"Are we going to him?" I asked. "Is that safe?"

"Where else would we go?" he asked. "And is anywhere safe?"

He had a point.

"Okay," he said. "So what's Bethlehem? It's the place where Jesus was born, right?"

"Right," I said. "The birthplace of the messiah." I paused. "Oh."

Jason had figured it out just as I did. "He's in Georgia. He's in the town where I was born—Shiloh," he said.

"Are we going to Georgia?" I asked.

"Got any better ideas?" he asked.

I didn't.

* * *

The first order of business was ditching the car. We drove a few exits down on the interstate to a rest area, where we stole a Volkswagen Beetle. We left them the BMW. We even moved their luggage and CDs over into the Beamer. I figured it was a fair trade.

With a less flashy car, we switched off driving as we drove down Interstate 81. I drove for hours, until we were somewhere in Virginia. Then Jason took over. While we drove, we played road games to pass the time, finding the alphabet on road signs, trying to spot license plates from all fifty states. We were bored, and there were places that we drove through where we could barely get any radio stations besides country or gospel music.

Jason drove faster than I did. I glanced at the speedometer once, and we were going nearly 90 miles an hour. We were flying past all the other cars around us.

"Jason?" I asked. "Is it wise to be driving so fast in a stolen car?"

The words weren't out of my mouth before there were immediately sirens and flashing lights behind us. A police car.

Jason glared at me. "You jinxed me," he said, speeding up.

"What are you doing?" I demanded. "You're not going to pull over?"

"Azazel, we're in stolen car, and we've got guns on us. I'm not pulling over."

"Good point," I said, gripping my seat in terror as we got even faster. "So what are you gonna do?"

"Lose him," said Jason. He jerked the car into the right lane, right between two other cars. The police car slowed down, trying to get into the same lane as we were in.

Jason took an exit, racing the car down the deceleration ramp. Unfortunately, the cop had managed to take the exit too and was right behind us.

Jason weaved in and out of traffic, but the cop kept up. We ran a stoplight, nearly causing a head on collision. Somehow, the cop made it through the intersection as well.

We'd exited into a suburban area. The landscape was dotted with restaurants and chain stores. Ahead of us loomed a huge sign for a mall. Jason slammed on the brakes and turned into the mall, fishtailing as he barely made the turn.

I was going to be sick.

The cop wasn't as lucky as us. He missed the turn, but screeched to a stop. He had to back up to make the turn.

We lurched forward, rounding a corner. For the first time, we were out of sight of the police car, even it was only for a few minutes.

Jason didn't waste any time. He drove the VW straight up to the entrance of the mall and threw open his door.

We hurried out of the car. Sprinted into the mall. Immediately lost ourselves in the crowds of shoppers just as the police car pulled up right beside the Beetle.

"Damn it," I muttered as I watched the police officer get out of his car, run into the mall, and look around frantically.

"What?" asked Jason, tugging me into Bath and Body Works and pretending to be very interested in some scented body lotion.

"We had to leave the clothes," I said.

Jason rolled his eyes.

"They were very nice clothes," I said. "They were expensive. I *liked* those clothes."

"We'll get other clothes," said Jason.

I stuck out my lower lip. "But not those. We'll never get those clothes back ever again."

* * *

We wandered around the mall for an hour before stealing another car out of the parking lot. This time we didn't have a car to leave in exchange, but I found that car theft was really not bothering my conscience nearly as much as I thought it would. After all, Jason and I were running for our lives. Well. We were running for my life anyway. If the Sons caught Jason, they weren't going to kill him. But they were going to force him to be the Rising Sun, something he didn't want to do.

Unfortunately, we stole a car that didn't have much gas in it. Jason was angry with himself, saying he should have checked the gas tank before we took it. I told him it was okay. We were both under a lot of stress. We had to pull off at an exit to buy gas.

I teased him. "You sure you don't just want to rob the convenience store?"

"Our trail of crime should probably stop with stolen cars, don't you think?" he asked.

I shrugged. While Jason pumped gas, I used the bathroom in the convenience store and bought a few snacks for the ride. We hadn't eaten since breakfast, and I was feeling peckish.

At the register, the cashier eyed me. She rang up my pretzels and soda, but she didn't stop looking at me.

I paid, thanked her, and turned away.

"Azazel?" she said.

Without thinking, I turned around.

"I knew it!" the woman exclaimed. She waved a missing persons flier at me. There was my senior picture emblazoned on the front underneath huge letters reading: MISSING. Damn it. I hadn't expected to be reported missing!

I fairly flew out of the store. "We have to go, Jason!" I said. "I'm missing!"

We had to leave before Jason was completely finished pumping gas. I was sure the woman had called some kind of authorities. It wasn't good. She'd probably be able to give them a description of the car we were driving.

For the third time that day, we switched cars. We took a Ford Aspire from another rest stop. It had a full tank of gas.

Exhausted, we drove into the evening and the night. Virginia gave way to Tennessee, and eventually, Tennessee became Georgia. When we arrived in Shiloh, it was nearly four in the morning.

Shiloh wasn't a big town. It was about the size of Bramford, actually. A few streets. Several businesses and restaurants, all closed because it was so late at night.

"Well," I said, looking around. "Here we are."

"Yeah," said Jason.

Now where were we going to go? It seemed we'd have to go outside of town to even find a hotel to stay in. I hadn't seen any as we were driving in. Jason drove up and down the streets, searching. "If Hallam is here," he said, "there's only one place he'd go."

"Where's that?" I asked.

"Sanctuary," said Jason.

"A church?" I asked.

"A Catholic church," said Jason. "Keep your eyes open. This far south, there shouldn't be too many."

"Why Catholic?"

Jason shrugged. "Their doors are usually open at odd times."

And then we spotted it. A little outside town, all by itself, was a small Catholic church—Christ is King Catholic Church, read the sign outside. It too boasted some spires and ornate architecture. It was nothing like the church we'd gone into in New York City, but it was still very beautiful. I wondered why Catholic churches always looked ... fancier than other ones. I mentioned it to Jason.

He gave me a funny look. "Did you ever pay attention to any of your father's history lectures?" he asked.

"What?" What did that have to do with anything?

"The entire Protestant Reformation had a lot to do with the fact that the Catholic church was spending money on ornate works of religious art. The Protestants thought the parishioners' tithes should go to more holy enterprises."

"Really?" I said.

Jason parked the car and got out. I followed suit.

We stared at the church. It didn't look open. But we moved forward anyway, walking up to the front doors. Jason put his hand on the door and tried the knob. It was locked.

"So now what?" I asked. "We try another church?"

Jason looked dead on his feet. "Maybe we could break in," he said.

"Seriously?"

"No," he said. He shook his head and yawned. "No, we'll sleep in the car."

"Will that be safe?"

Jason shrugged. We got back in the car. Cranked back the seats so that we were semi-reclined. There were some blankets in the backseat. We huddled under them. Jason gave me one of the guns. He showed me how to take the safety off.

"Don't shoot unless I tell you," he said.

I turned the gun over in my hands. It didn't make me feel much safer. But I clutched it in one hand and closed my eyes. Snuggling with the gun, I feel asleep.

* * *

I woke up slowly, the sound of voices close to me. I didn't move for a few moments, just listening. One voice was British, and I recognized it as Hallam's. The voices were muffled. They were coming from outside the car, but I could still understand what they were saying.

"Who is she?" asked Hallam.

"I thought you two had met," said the other voice, Jason's. "She said you tried to strangle her."

"I remember her," said Hallam. "I just meant why is she here?"

"Did you try to strangle her?"

"What is she, your girlfriend?"

"Yeah. I guess she is," said Jason. I tried not to smile when I heard that. "Did you try to strangle her?"

"She exaggerates," said Hallam. "The Sons know about her?"

"Yeah, I guess so. I killed five Brothers trying to protect her."

"Oh wonderful. I'm sure they love that. I'm sure this turn of events has them in ecstasy," said Hallam.

"I know. Killing their own."

"I meant the girl," said Hallam.

"Oh," said Jason. "Right."

"Honestly, Jason, they're not wrong about that, you know. Attachments, to women especially, tend to make one less focused."

"No," said Jason. "No, she focuses me. She gives me something to focus on."

Really? That was sweet. I loved Jason.

Hallam sighed. "I didn't know if you'd come."

"Your email got me curious," said Jason. "What do you need to show me?"

"Oh, we'll get to that," said Hallam. "We will. First, I think, we need breakfast. Wake up the girl."

"I should let her sleep," said Jason. "We haven't done a lot of sleeping lately."

"Really, Jason, I'd rather not hear details about that kind of thing," said Hallam.

"Because of danger," snapped Jason. "Not because of ..." He cleared his throat.

"Oh, so then you haven't been intimate with her? The Sons will approve."

"No," said Jason. "We have." Why was he telling Hallam this? "But then, I didn't think you wanted to know about that."

"Wake her up," Hallam growled.

Jason opened the passenger side door. I had to pretend to wake up when he shook me. I think I might have overdone the stretching, but Jason didn't seem to notice. I sat up and rubbed my eyes, pretending to notice Hallam for the first time. "Hello, Hallam," I said.

He glared at me. I didn't think Hallam liked me very much.

We ate breakfast with Father Gerald, the parish priest, in his rectory, which was attached to the church. Father Gerald, Hallam explained, had knowledge of the Sons of the Rising

Sun. Their paths had crossed in the past. At least that was how Hallam put it. He didn't elaborate. At any rate, Father Gerald had been kind enough to allow Hallam to stay there. Jason could apparently stay too, but I was a woman, so that meant it was improper for me to stay in the same place with the other three men. Jason promptly announced that we would get a hotel room. I was now totally convinced that Hallam hated me.

Father Gerald seemed nice enough. He didn't say much during breakfast, however. No one did. We ate quickly, and then Hallam took us back to the room he was staying in. It was apparently a room for visiting priests, and it was quite sparse, containing just a bed and a desk. However, Hallam did have a computer. He sat down in front of it at the desk. Jason and I sat down on the bed.

"So," Hallam said, "I know you're wondering what it was that I wanted to show you, Jason."

Jason nodded. "We came all the way from Pennsylvania."

"And you probably want to know why I'm in Shiloh," said Hallam.

"Yeah," said Jason.

"I'm guessing it's got something to do with Jason's birth," I said.

Hallam glared at me. "Well, obviously," he said.

Why was he such an ass? Maybe he just hated women. Maybe that was why he'd had no problem killing all of those sorority girls.

"So, spill," said Jason. "Why are we here?"

"Well," said Hallam, "it started right after you ran away. I got transferred back to England to a desk job at the Council. They transferred everyone who lived at our old Society house after Anton died and you ran away. I think they were afraid. They wanted to know if Anton had gotten to anyone."

"Gotten to anyone?" Jason asked.

"That's what this is about," said Hallam. "Why they killed Anton. What Anton knew."

"Really?" said Jason leaning forward, interested now. Huh. He didn't care about his birth, but he cared about Anton. "So what did he know?"

"I don't know," said Hallam.

Jason threw up his hands.

"Yet," said Hallam. "I don't know yet. I'm getting there. I could use your help actually."

"All right, all right. So what do you know?" asked Jason.

"I was getting to that," said Hallam. "So ... where was I? Right, I got transferred back to England. And I didn't like that one bit. If they'd left me where I was, I maybe wouldn't have gotten suspicious. But because they shipped me off, I began to wonder if there was something to Anton's death and your disappearance, so I started digging into records, which I now had easy access to.

"I was working in payroll, believe it or not, so, on a whim one day, I looked at the payroll records from the year you were born. And I found that the Sons had paid out a significant amount of money to a woman named Marianne Wodden. That, of course, is your last name, Jason. So, I set about trying to find this woman."

"She's dead," said Jason.

"Dead?" said Hallam. "I don't know if she ever existed."

"What do you mean?" I said. "The Sheriff in my town found death records for her. She was murdered by her husband."

"Oh, I found those death records," said Hallam. "But I couldn't find any death records for the supposed husband, what was his name ..."

"Ted," supplied Jason.

He remembered that, huh? Maybe he cared more than he let on.

"Right. This Ted Wodden. No death certificate. And he supposedly committed suicide after shooting his wife. So, I looked for a birth certificate for Ted Wodden. Nothing. Chagrined, I looked for a birth certificate for Marianne Wodden. Nothing."

"She doesn't have a birth certificate?" asked Jason.

"That's right," said Hallam. "Death certificate, no birth certificate."

"What does that mean?" asked Jason.

"Well, I always thought that name was just a little too perfect," said Hallam. "I mean almost cutesy in its rightness for the mother of the Rising Sun."

"Rightness?" I said.

Hallam shot me a withering look as if I couldn't possibly

understand. "Marianne," he said. "Mary the Mother of God."

Oh. Duh.

"And Wodden. It's so close to Woden, isn't it?"

That I understood. Determined to show Hallam up, I said, "Like the day after tomorrow."

Jason and Hallam both furrowed their brows at me.

"It's Wednesday," I said. "Woden's day. Woden is the British name for Odin, from Norse mythology."

Hallam looked grudgingly impressed. "Right," he said. "And Odin is a dying god who's resurrected, which is what the sons believe the Rising Sun is, essentially."

"So, you don't think that she was real," said Jason. "Like I have no mother?"

"Well, I'm not sure," said Hallam. "The death certificate seemed real enough. I figured in a town this size, someone would remember something like that. A battered woman being shot to death? So I came here. I asked around. No one remembered anything like that."

"But, Jason and I saw a memorial on a website," I said. "Someone said she was a sister and an aunt."

"Right," said Hallam. "And they'd listed a maiden name of Aird. I looked into an Aird family. That turned out to be a dead end. Aird is a typical Muscogee surname, apparently, and, until about the late 1700s, this land belonged to the Muscogee."

"Muscogee?" Jason asked.

"The Creek Indians," said Hallam. "Most of them were

sent away during several treaties, which eventually relegated them all to Oklahoma, but some had intermarried, and their families stayed in the area. The point is, there were too many Airds. Furthermore, there was no one in the area who had even heard of Marianne Wodden, let alone been related to her."

"And you think Anton knew this?" Jason asked.

"I think Anton knew something about your birth," said Hallam. "He said to me, before he died, that he'd found out something about your origins. He wouldn't say more. He wanted to tell you first. Then, of course, they killed him."

"What does it mean?" I asked.

"It doesn't mean anything yet," said Hallam. "But I tried one more lead. I emailed the person who runs the memorial website. Apparently, she takes information from people who email it to her, and she puts it on the website. I said that I was an old friend of Marianne's who had recently learned of her demise, and that I wanted to get in touch with her surviving family to pay my respects. I asked for the contact information of the person that posted Marianne's memorial information.

"The woman who runs the memorial website just got back to me this morning. All she gave me was an email: webmaster@thegreatgodazazel.com." Hallam looked at me pointedly. "Isn't that your name?"

"Yeah," I said. "Weird coincidence."

"I don't believe in coincidences," said Hallam.

"Jason does," I said, thinking about the vision the

Satanist woman had had about me killing him.

Jason didn't respond to me. Instead, he said to Hallam, "We've got to go to that website, then."

"Of course," said Hallam, turning to his computer.

Jason and I both got off the bed and crowded behind Hallam. Hallam typed "thegreatgodazazel.com" into his address bar on the internet. He hit enter.

A black background filled the screen. In red letters, the website proclaimed "The Great God Azazel Network." Underneath, in smaller letters, there were links: Satanism, Philosophy, Azazel in Other Cultures, Blog, and Contact Me.

"Click on the contact link," said Jason.

Hallam did. It just brought up an email message addressed to webmaster@thegreatgodazazel.com.

"Um, click on the blog," I said.

Hallam did. The last entry was dated October 31st. It was entitled, "Samhain." "Should I read it?" Hallam asked.

"Okay," said Jason.

"On this very ancient and powerful day," Hallam read, "it is important for Satanists of all walks and beliefs to take stock of their lives. This is a day to celebrate—" Hallam broke off reading aloud and began skimming to himself. He scrolled down the page. Then he hit the back button. "Nothing there," he muttered.

Hallam clicked on the "Azazel in other Cultures" link. There was a list. It read, "Prometheus, Pan, Loki, Dionysus, Rabbit (Creek, Southern North America), Coyote (Western North America) ..." The list went on, below the screen.

"Didn't you say something about the Creek Indians?" I asked.

"Yes," said Hallam, already clicking on the link.

"A Promethean and Azazelean figure, Rabbit steals fire to bring back to the people," read Hallam. "Interesting stuff, I guess. I didn't know Native Americans had myths so similar to Europeans." Hallam turned around. "This site is a dead end, though. There's nothing here."

"Except for the fact that the same person who put up a memorial website for my mother is also running a Satanist website," said Jason. "And Azazel's parents were Satanists. That's weird. There's some kind of connection, don't you think?"

"Maybe," said Hallam. "I don't think we're going to find it on this site, though."

"Just try to find a name," I said. "Who's the webmaster? Who puts up the page?"

Hallam hit the back button again. He scrolled to the bottom of the main page. "Here's a copyright," he said. "Michaela Weem," he said. He looked at Jason. "Now we know that last name, don't we?"

"Yeah," said Jason. "But that can't be connected. Right?"

"Someone clue me in here," I said.

"One of the High Council members has the last name Weem," said Jason.

"Edgar Weem," said Hallam.

"That's my middle name," said Jason. "Edgar."

"The initials match," I said. "Marianne Wodden.

Michaela Weem."

"They do," said Hallam thoughtfully.

"Maybe there's a connection," I said.

We were all quiet for several minutes.

Finally, Hallam sighed. "No," he said. "I've got nothing."

"Me either," said Jason. "I mean, it doesn't add up to anything."

"I think it does," said Hallam. "We just don't what it is it adds up to."

Jason sat back down on Hallam's bed. "It doesn't matter anyway," he said. "Even if we could figure it out, it wouldn't change anything. The Sons are still tracking me across the U.S. I have to keep running. I guess I have to keep running forever."

"No, no, Jason," said Hallam. "That's where you're wrong. I wouldn't have asked you here if I thought it was as hopeless as all that. Listen, whatever the secret was that Anton knew, it was so powerful that the Council had him killed. They didn't want anyone to know. If we can figure it out, we'll have a weapon against the Sons."

Chapter Sixteen

To: Joseph Andrews (jandre@risingsun.org)
From: Alfred Norwich (anorwic@risingsun.org)
Subject: Go with God
Joseph,

After the tragic loss of Richard Durham, it is even more imperative that you and your team are successful in recovering Jason. He is stronger and more capable than we have realized, and this dalliance of his has gone on quite long enough. Richard seemed to believe that there was evidence indicating Jason was heading south. We feel this is the best course for you to take in your search for him.

Yours in the pursuit of the Purpose,
Alfred

Jason and I checked into a hotel room a few miles outside of Shiloh, in another small town (which was still bigger than Shiloh), where we would spend the next several days. For the first time in days, we had a stretch of time in which we were not bothered, not threatened, and felt relatively safe. Jason and Hallam kept puzzling over the strange set of connections that we'd uncovered, but neither of them came up with many ideas.

Jason and I spent time with Hallam, but we also had ample time alone. We ate in restaurants. We went for walks in the woods. It was much warmer in Georgia than it had been up north, even though the residents of Shiloh seemed to think it was very cold. At night, we slept in the same bed and tried to work on perfecting our lovemaking technique. The second time, it was much less awkward, and much nicer. Still. There was something about it that was ... disappointing. It wasn't that having sex with Jason was bad. It was very nice. I really liked being close to him. And it felt ... Well, that was the problem, really. It felt good, but I had a sneaking suspicion that it felt way better for Jason than it did for me. Of course, we didn't really talk about it. I didn't know how to bring it up.

Overall, it was the most pleasant time that Jason and I had been able to spend together. I felt happy. I even felt content. If it weren't for the fact we were holding our breaths, waiting for the Sons to show up at any minute, it might have been idyllic. Might have been. But there were other things. Jason and I had baggage. Sometimes, out of nowhere, it hit me that my parents were dead. I remembered them the way they had been, before Friday night. I had thoughts sometimes, like when I saw a book in a bookstore that my father might have liked. I thought that I should pick it up for his birthday in December. Then I remembered that he was dead. I started to cry. I couldn't believe it. It just seemed so unreal.

Then I remembered the last night I'd seen my father. I remembered him backhanding Jason in Aunt Stephanie's dining room. Thinking about that was so hard. I couldn't reconcile the man I'd seen in that dark room, ready to let me be raped by Toby, with the man who I'd grown up in the same house with. How had my father hidden that side of himself from me? How had I only seen the gentle, good parts of him? Sometimes it hurt too much for me to bear.

I didn't feel like I could talk to Jason about it. Jason had been through much worse things than I had. He didn't need to listen to me talk about how much it had hurt to lose my family. Jason had never had a family to lose. Why couldn't I be thankful for what I'd had instead of bemoaning its loss?

Furthermore, I think we both knew that all of this was only temporary. We wouldn't be able to stay in Shiloh with Hallam forever. We would have to leave at some point. If Hallam didn't come up with some kind of breakthrough on the Marianne Wodden idea soon, we'd have to leave before figuring anything out, making our trip here mostly pointless.

Sometimes, lying next to Jason while he snored gently, I cried softly to myself. I didn't want him to hear. I was happy to be with him. I was lucky to have him. Even though I'd lost everything else, I at least had Jason. He was all I had left. The most important thing to me. I didn't want to live without him. And I didn't want him to think I wasn't happy with him or that I wasn't grateful that he existed.

So I cried quietly, hoping he wouldn't wake up and hear me. In the morning, when he woke me up with kisses, I never let on that there were times when I sobbed. And it went on like that for four days. Four days, we had. Four days before all hell broke loose.

It started when Hallam woke us up by pounding on our hotel room door early in the morning. Jason, who apparently always woke up completely alert, leaped out of bed, threw on his pants, and went to the door. I didn't appreciate this because I wasn't wearing any clothes, so the conversation that followed was conducted while I pulled the covers of the bed up to my chin.

Hallam swept into the room, his eyes bright. "I think I've got it," he said.

"Got what?" I said. "Can't it wait a couple of hours?" I could see that the sun was barely up. It was early. I wanted more sleep.

"Oh whatever, I'm awake," said Jason. "Tell me what's up."

"Okay," said Hallam. "I started thinking about this Michaela Weem, right? I decided she was the missing link. She was going to pull this whole thing together."

"Yeah?" said Jason, sitting down on the bed.

"So, I decided to do some research on her. Figure out who she is. Then I figured it out. It was because of something that you said, Azazel." He looked at me, huddled beneath the covers, and seemed to actually take us in. "You know, it occurs to me that I might be more comfortable having this conversation if the two of you were actually clothed."

"What?" demanded Jason. "No, tell me now. You can't just build it up like that and then stop."

"Tell you what," said Hallam. "You two get dressed and

come meet me back in Shiloh at the rectory. I'll tell you there."

"You've got to be kidding me," said Jason.

"Sounds like a good idea to me," I said.

"Good, then," said Hallam. He started towards the door, then stopped. "Look," he said, "just because I'm not insisting on anything else, and just because I'm no longer a member of the Sons doesn't mean ... I just want you both to know that I don't condone the two of you living in sin like this."

And then he left the room, closing the door after him.

I had to work hard to keep from laughing until after he was gone. Then I burst out giggling. "Living in sin?" I guffawed.

Jason wasn't laughing.

"Come on," I said. "That's funny."

"To you it is," he said.

"What?" I said. "Are you feeling guilty?" I couldn't believe that.

"Of course not," said Jason. "But the Sons are pretty ... conservative. And, you know, I was never supposed to ..." He grinned. "... know the touch of woman at all. Supposedly, it would taint me."

I crawled out from under the covers, still giggling. I straddled him. "Oh yeah? Am I tainting you now?"

He kissed me. "Definitely. I'm very, very tainted."

He ran his hands over my shoulder blades, over the curves of my hips. He groaned. "You're distracting me."

"It's all part of the tainting, baby," I joked. "What can I say?"

"I want to know what Hallam found out," he said. "Don't you want to know?"

"I don't know," I said. "Hallam is going to be there for a long time." I arched an eyebrow suggestively.

He grinned. "Come on, Azazel. We have to go."

"Fine," I said, pouting. I climbed off of him and stood next to the bed, my eyes darting over the floor in search of my clothes.

"Wow," said Jason.

I glanced at him. I realized he was staring at me.

"Stop," I said, feeling self-conscious.

"Do you have any idea how beautiful you are?" he asked.

I blushed. Trying to recover, I teased, "We have to find out what Hallam wants to tell us, remember?"

Jason stood up. "Yeah, well, we should probably shower first, so we look presentable."

"I guess."

Jason leaned close, a smile twitching at his lips. "We'll have to do it together to save time."

* * *

Hallam was waiting in the rectory with breakfast. "I don't want to know why it took you so long," he said.

Jason and I just grinned at each other. We sat down at the table. Father Gerald wasn't there, so I couldn't help teasing Hallam a little bit.

"Now, Hallam," I said, "there's no need to be grouchy just because you're not getting any."

Hallam narrowed his eyes. "This one is a very bad influence on you, Jason."

"Don't make Hallam mad," Jason said to me.

Oh right. Hallam was dangerous and violent and all that. It was hard to remember. He just seemed so tight-laced and ... British.

"I am not mad," said Hallam. "I just happen to believe that self-restraint is a virtue. Controlling one's urges isn't easy, certainly, but just because something's hard doesn't mean one should abandon it entirely."

I shrugged. "Some things are easy because you're supposed to do them," I said. "Like eating for example. It's hard not to do it and for a good reason. Otherwise, we'd all die."

"Oh," said Hallam. "Yes, and I do suppose reproduction is necessary for the advancement of the species. But then I rather imagine that's the last thing on either of your minds."

Reproduction? Right. As a public service announcement, I would like to say that Jason and I had always used condoms, even though the first time, the condom had been in Jason's wallet since probably the Crustacean Age, and I had my doubts about its total effectiveness.

"Let's not talk about this anymore," said Jason. "We came here for a reason. You were in the middle of revealing something, and I'm dying to hear what it is."

"Oh," said Hallam. "Of course. Well, as I was saying, I

started thinking about what Azazel had said about the initials of Michaela Weem and Marianne Wodden being the same. I'd done all this research on Marianne Wodden, but not on Michaela Weem. I thought Azazel had to be right. They were connected in some way, the two women."

Maybe Hallam didn't hate women after all. He was giving me credit for figuring something out, after all.

Hallam continued, "So I started researching Michaela Weem. I looked for a birth certificate. Couldn't find one."

"So it's another dead end?" asked Jason.

"No, not exactly. I started thinking about the oddness of your middle name being Edgar, and about Edgar Weem, and just on a whim, I decided to hunt for marriage certificates."

"Marriage certificates?" I said, not following.

"Yeah," said Jason. "Why?"

"Well, as we know, Council members don't get married. They've taken a vow of celibacy, just like the Brothers. And I looked through marriage certificates in England, and of course there wasn't anything for him.

"But then, I decided to look through marriage certificates in the states. In Georgia. And guess what I found?"

"A marriage certificate for Edgar Weem?" I asked.

He nodded. "And Michaela Aird." Hallam was excited. "And it all checks out. They got married in 1991. Edgar Weem was on an extended leave of absence at that time. He was in Georgia."

"So?" said Jason.

"Don't you see?" Hallam asked.

Jason shook his head. I didn't get it either.

Hallam began to gesture wildly in his excitement. "Azazel was the one who pointed out that Marianne Wodden and Michaela Weem had the same initials. That's because they're the *same person* . Jason, you did not *happen* to fulfill a number of prophecies about the Rising Sun. You were *made* . Edgar Weem *created* you. He waited until the right time—1991. He came to Shiloh, married a woman, impregnated her with you, and then the Sons paid her off—that enormous amount of money I saw in their ledgers. Edgar Weem is your father. And this Rising Sun thing is a hoax. Clearly the Sons engineered the entire thing to set up you up in a place of power. To give *them* more power."

Jason and I were both quiet.

"Well," said Hallam finally, "what do you think?"

"So ..." said Jason, "Michaela Weem assumed the identity of Marianne Wodden. And then she faked her own death?"

"I don't know about Michaela Weem," said Hallam. "That's the part of the puzzle that I don't exactly understand. But it's not important, really. She was a tool. An incubator. The Sons paid her off to take away her baby to raise him—you—the way they wanted to. She disappeared. The important thing is that we have evidence here that proves that Edgar Weem tried to *engineer* a Rising Sun."

"Evidence?" I said. "We have a marriage certificate."

"It's enough," said Hallam. "The idea that Edgar Weem

was married at all is enough to ruin him within the Sons. But the implications here, they could tear the entire establishment apart. This information, Jason, can buy us our freedom. They'll *have* to leave us alone."

"If they find out we know," said Jason, "they'll just kill us. Like they did Anton. How can we tell anyone?"

"That's where Father Gerald comes in," said Hallam. "I will compose an email message to multiple addresses, all important ones within the Sons of the Rising Sun. I will then contact Edgar Weem. I will tell him what I know. And I will tell him that unless he gives me what I want, I am prepared to tell everyone what he did. I will also tell him that if I do not check in within a certain period of time, I have someone—who will be Father Gerald, but Weem won't know that—who will send a message to everyone within the Sons."

"He might not believe you," said Jason. "He might just kill you anyway."

"Well, that's the beauty of it," said Hallam. "I will be telling the truth. So if I die, everyone in the organization will find out what happened. Then the entire organization will crumble."

"I don't get it," I said. "Why don't you just tell everyone anyway? I mean, the Sons are evil. Shouldn't their organization crumble?"

"Azazel," said Jason, "if the Sons self-destruct, they'll try to take us with them. It won't end things. It will just make things worse."

"Oh," I said, alarmed. The magnitude of what we were up against suddenly seemed overwhelming.

"So, then, it's a good plan, isn't it?" asked Hallam, looking very pleased with himself.

"No," said Jason.

"No?" said Hallam.

I didn't understand either. I thought it was an excellent plan.

"You're taking all the risk," said Jason. "I should approach Weem. They won't hurt me."

"They might, Jason," said Hallam. "If they know that you know you aren't really the Rising Sun, they might very easily silence you."

"I still can't let you be the only person putting your life on the line," said Jason.

Hallam smiled. "Well, there are two things working against you as the candidate to speak to Weem. The first is that you aren't in contact with Father Gerald. And the second is that ..." Hallam paused. His smile faded. "The second is that if you were to die, it would affect more than just you." He looked at me. "I don't think it would be right for you to do that to Azazel."

I looked at Hallam, grateful.

"But—" Jason protested.

"No," said Hallam, "and listen to me please. There is more logic to celibacy than you may ever have given thought. There's a certain responsibility a man takes on when he begins a relationship with a woman. A responsibility to live. I have always known that it would be foolhardy for me to attempt to take on such a responsibility. But the two of you. You could live, and you could be happy. And I could give you that clean slate that you asked for."

Jason was quiet for a few minutes. "Even so, Hallam. I don't like you taking risks like this for me."

"Well, it's for me too," said Hallam. "I don't like being pursued by the Sons anymore than you do."

"Eventually, they'd give up on you. They won't ever give up on me," Jason said. "You could just lay low. It would blow over."

"Maybe," said Hallam. "Maybe you're right. But maybe I owe you something. I think there was a night, the two of us together, when I watched something ... break in you."

Jason looked away.

Hallam must be referring to the night with the college girls. That night had changed Jason, I knew. It was hard for him to talk about it.

"I stole your innocence, Jason," Hallam whispered. "Let me give you your life."

Maybe Hallam really was not such a bad guy after all. Maybe I'd seriously misjudged him.

"For me," Hallam said. "Let me do it for me. I sometimes feel the need to atone for the things that I've done."

Finally, Jason nodded. He offered his hand to Hallam and Hallam grasped it.

"Okay," said Jason, and when he spoke, his voice was hoarse, "when do we do this?"

"Pretty much now," said Hallam.

* * *

It took some time to get everything set up. Jason and I hung around the rectory while Hallam arranged things. Jason was quiet, and I didn't try to draw him out of his shell. What Hallam had said to Jason must have been difficult for Jason to hear. I knew that Jason felt a sense of honor deeply. He had very clear-cut ideas about right and wrong. Jason allowing Hallam to put himself in danger was hard for Jason. Especially because Hallam was doing it for Jason's sake. And it didn't matter to Jason that Hallam had influenced him in certain negative ways.

I also knew that Jason probably understood what Hallam meant about atoning. Though we hadn't spoken about it since that night in the hotel room, I knew that Jason still felt deeply guilty about killing the men in New Jersey. Sometimes, when I was sobbing silently in bed next him, I heard him mumble in his sleep, things like, "I didn't want to kill you." Since I wasn't revealing the fact that I was crying at night, I didn't think I should confront him about his dreams. For now, at any rate, we'd have to deal with our own demons in our own ways.

Sometime that afternoon, Jason and I gathered around while Hallam made the phone call to Weem. It took him a long time to get through to him. Weem apparently didn't take calls from just anyone. Finally, after what seemed like hours, Hallam had Weem on the phone.

There were pleasantries. Hallam said hello. He asked

after Weem's health. I could tell that Hallam was enjoying this. Drawing it out. Finally, Hallam got down to business. He said he'd come across a very interesting document involving Weem, and he'd like to discuss it with Weem. It involved, Hallam said, someone named Michaela.

In a few minutes, Hallam hung up the phone. "I'm on the next plane to London," he told us, triumphant.

Hallam left within the hour.

On Hallam's advice, we weren't going to stay in the hotel room that night. If something happened to Hallam, the Sons might come directly after Jason and I. Because of the Sons arranging a plane ticket for Hallam, they knew his location. Hallam figured it would be safer if we stayed in the church, so it was going to be another uncomfortable night sleeping on church pews. Jason and I stuck around in Shiloh and went out to dinner at a local restaurant. We ordered at the counter, subs and French fries. Retiring to our table, we waited for one of the waitresses to bring us our order. Finally away from the rectory, I asked Jason how he was feeling.

"Nervous," he said.

"Me too," I said. "But I guess I meant about the other stuff. I mean, suddenly, you have a father. Who's alive."

Jason let out a breath. "I haven't even thought about that stuff," he said. He considered. "I mean, on the one hand, this guy's a jerk, right? He sort of created me, a means to an end."

"And on the other hand?"

"On the other hand, I wish I remembered more about him."

I nodded sympathetically. The waitress arrived with our drink orders, two sodas. I toyed with my straw. "Did you ever meet him?"

"Yes," said Jason. "When Anton and I were in England. A member of the Council came to visit me once or twice. I can't be sure, but I think it was Edgar Weem. I was a kid, and they were all old British men. They all looked the same to me."

"What was he like?"

"That's the weird thing," said Jason. "He was very stiff. Anton was stiff. They were all stiff. But Weem. He always brought me something. Like a piece of fruit or a chocolate or something. And then ... he would just grill me on subjects. Things like history or algebra or something. At the time, I just assumed it was all part of the battery of tests they were giving me to find out if I was really the Rising Sun. But now I wonder if it was his way of trying to get to know me."

"Maybe," I said. "If nothing else, he must have been curious about you. You're his son. He must have wondered."

"He must be a pretty arrogant guy," said Jason.

"Why?"

"The Sons of the Rising Sun are an organization that exists entirely to wait for the coming of the Rising Sun and to prepare the way for him. They've existed since like the fifteenth century. To think that his genes were good enough to create a fake Rising Sun, he must think pretty highly of himself."

I smiled. "Well, now I know where you get that from."

"Hey," said Jason. "I'm not arrogant."

"Of course not," I said. "'I've been shooting guns since I was five,'" I mimicked.

Jason threw his straw wrapper at me.

The waitress brought us our subs then. They were enormous, and it was too much of a task just to try to fit them in our mouths to do much else. We didn't really talk until we were finished eating.

While we were eating, I started to think. Everything was all tied up now. Since Jason had appeared in my life, I'd wanted to know who he was and where he came from. And now I did. I even knew who his father was and why he'd been brought into the world. I knew everything about him except for one thing. I didn't know anything about his mother. Michaela Weem. Who was she? Was Hallam right? Was she not important? Just an incubator? Somehow, I didn't think so. It was too strange that Michaela Weem ran a website dedicated to Azazel. No, there was something else there.

What had happened to Michaela Weem? Hallam had said that she and Edgar had been married in Georgia. And Jason had been born here. Hallam said he'd asked around about a Marianne Wodden, and no one had known anything about her. But he hadn't done any asking about Michaela Weem.

"Jason," I said. "Do you think Michaela Weem could still be in Shiloh?"

Jason had a fry in his hand, halfway to his mouth. He froze. Put down the fry. "Maybe," he said. "Who cares?"

It was weird that Jason was so nonchalant about his parentage. "She's your mother," I said. "Don't you care?"

"No," said Jason. He shoved the French fry into his mouth.

"Why not?" I asked.

"I don't know," said Jason. "It's not like I remember anything about her, but whenever I think about her, I just get a weird feeling. A bad feeling."

"A feeling?" I repeated.

"I guess that's stupid," said Jason. "Maybe I'm just nervous. I guess she could live in town."

"I think we should try to find her," I said.

"How?"

"Well, nothing too complicated," I said. "But we could try to look her up in the phone book."

"She probably doesn't live here anymore," he said.

"Well, it couldn't hurt."

"Fine," said Jason, but he didn't sound happy about it.

We went up to the register to pay for our food. I asked the girl behind the counter if she had a phone book we could use. She knelt behind the counter and placed one in front of us.

I handed her our ticket. She punched buttons on her cash register and then gave me our total. I gave her the credit card we were using. It was the one Marlena had gotten us. Jason had said yesterday that when left Shiloh, we were going to have to get another credit card, because it was too risky to use the same one for too long. They could be tracked too easily. Cash was safer.

While I waited for the credit card to go through, I paged through the white pages, looking for Michaela Weem's name. It wasn't there. Disappointed, I closed the phone book. "She's not in the phone book," I told Jason.

"Told she didn't live here anymore," said Jason.

"Who are you looking for?" asked the girl behind the counter.

"A woman named Michaela Weem," I said.

"Crazy Lady Weem?" she said. "I know who that is. Everyone knows Crazy Lady Weem. She lives on Spring Street in the old house that's practically falling down. I can't believe somebody actually knows her."

"We don't know her," said Jason.

"She's Jason's long lost mother," I informed the girl.

Jason glared at me, so I shut up. I guess he didn't like my telling people about his personal business.

Outside the restaurant, Jason and I debated quickly. I thought we should go see her. She was Jason's mother! Jason didn't know if he wanted to see her, especially if she was crazy. I argued that we knew where she lived and that it wasn't that late. We should just go to her house. Maybe she wouldn't even be home. We were actually in the same town with Michaela Weem. It was kismet. It was meant to be. We had to go see her. Jason eventually caved.

It didn't take long to walk to Spring Street, which was on the other side of Highway 85. And once we got there, it wasn't difficult to tell which house belonged to her. It really did look like it was falling down. It was a two-story house with a veranda-style porch. Half of the porch had collapsed. The other half was dangling precariously, looking like it might fall down at any second. The house was painted white, but the paint was cracked and peeling.

Eyeing each other, Jason and I approached the front door and tentatively knocked. At first nothing happened.

"Well," said Jason. "We tried." He turned to walk away.

Then the door opened. A tall woman stood behind the screen door. She had long, dark hair, dusky skin, and a heart-shaped face. Jesus, she *looked* like Jason.

"Yes?" she said.

"Mrs. Weem?" I asked.

She opened the screen door. It creaked on its hinges. She was wearing a full-length black velvet dress. Her nails were very long and painted with dark fingernail polish. She looked at both of us. "You've come," she said, her voice eerily solemn.

Did she know us? "You don't know us," I said.

"I know you," she said in the same even tone. "You may enter my home."

Okay. This lady was seriously creepy. Jason must have been a little freaked out too, because he grabbed my hand. We walked over the threshold into Michaela Weem's house.

Inside, all the furniture was covered in a thin layer of dust. I looked around, half expecting to see spider webs in the corners. But instead, there was just antique furniture and several black and white portraits on the walls.

"I've been waiting," said Michaela Weem. "Please have a seat in the parlor." She gestured to a doorway to our right. Jason and I entered the room she'd suggested. There were several mismatched antique settees, the kind with high, upholstered backs and long curving wooden legs. Jason and I sat down on one. Michaela Weem sat down on another.

"Azazel," said Michaela, "when your father told me that he would wait until Samhain to conduct the ritual, I knew that things would go wrong. It isn't safe for the two of you to be so close."

Okay, how did she know my name? And why was she talking about my father? And Samhain was Halloween right? Did she mean the ritual to kill Jason? How did she know about that?

"Um," I said, "we actually wanted to talk to you about Edgar Weem. Your husband?"

Michaela made a face as if she's smelled something bad. "Vile man," she said. "Vile."

Right then. "So you did know him?" I asked. "You were married to him?"

"You already know this," she said. "Why question me about things you already know?"

A black cat wandered into the parlor. It jumped up onto Michaela's lap. She stroked it absently.

Jason finally spoke up. "What should we question you about then?"

Michaela looked at him. "You," she muttered. "You. I had forgotten what an abomination you are."

Jason sat back as if he'd been stung.

Geez. That wasn't exactly the greeting you'd want from your long lost mother. Michaela Weem sure didn't know much about manners, did she?

"I'll tell you what you want to know," said Michaela. "Then, perhaps, Azazel, you will fulfill your purpose. Then, perhaps you will understand."

Okay. This was just getting gradually weirder and weirder by the second.

"I was raised in Oklahoma in the Muscogee Nation," said Michaela. "I grew up learning stories about Rabbit, the cunning trickster animal spirit of our people, whose power was more tremendous than any could possibly understand."

Great. Now we were going to have to sit here and listen to this woman's life story. I wondered if Jason and I should just bolt. But no. I had to admit, I was too curious. She'd said too many things that I didn't understand. That I wanted explained.

Michaela continued. "When I was older, my father, who was not Muscogee, sent me away to school abroad in Europe. There I studied comparative religions, and I learned that Rabbit was not confined only to our tribe. Oh no, he was present in nearly every religion, sometimes revered as was his right, sometimes denigrated and improperly categorized as evil. I became intrigued with my studies, and I stayed in Europe for quite some time, hunting down what information I could about the incarnations of Rabbit in the world.

"In my studies, and my searches, I quite accidentally became entangled with the Sons of the Rising Sun, with whom I know you are quite familiar. I did not know that the school I attended had ties to the Sons. And when I met Edgar Weem, I had no idea of the depths of his perversity.

"Since the abomination is sitting here, in front of us, you may have some idea of what he forced me to do. But whatever ideas you think you may know, you can't imagine the horrors. Edgar was obsessed with creating the Rising Sun. He believed it could be done, with the combination of the right rituals, the right herbs, the right substances. I drank blood for him. I drank cocktails of bull semen and psilocybic mushrooms. I allowed my body to be branded and cut. And when he was finally done, he'd created it. Oh, he had. I had the evil, squirming thing growing in my belly."

Michaela turned her huge dark eyes on me. They burned into my own. I shivered involuntarily.

"He set me up in America, then. It was important that the abominable spawn be brought into the world in Shiloh. He wanted it to be in Israel, but I convinced him to come to this Shiloh. I knew this was my people's ancestral home. I knew that I would have more power here. Many things were important to him. It was important that we be married. I hated him. I didn't want to marry him. But he insisted, so eventually, I gave in.

"That was when the visions started. I saw the abomination, older, more powerful. I saw that he had taken over the world, just as Edgar wanted him to. He had forced people to his will and the entire world was consumed with his darkness." Michaela paused and hissed at Jason.

Jason flattened himself against the settee. His face had gone pale.

Visions? She ran a Satanist website. Michaela Weem was the woman that Lilith had told me about. The woman who'd had the vision of Jason! Oh my God. It was Jason's mother who wanted him *dead* .

Michaela turned back to me. "I was too weak. I tried to dash its brains out when it was born. A thing conceived in all that horror could bring nothing but trouble into the world. I couldn't do it. It looked so helpless. It looked so small.

"They took it away of course. They gave me money. They told me live under that name. That name that Edgar had forced me to assume. I wouldn't. I refused. I made him make her disappear. She died. She was the representation of the woman I was before Edgar Weem used me to conduct his evil. I mourn her."

"That's why you put up the memorial website?" I asked.

"Yes," she said, smiling as if I understood.

"Why did you say you were killed by your husband? By someone named Ted?"

"Ted was Edgar's nickname. He told me to call him that. 'Teddy.'" She spit the name out like something that disgusting. "It was fitting. He all but put a gun to my head and killed me."

I guess that kind of made sense. If you were crazy. Which Michaela certainly seemed to be. She'd tried to kill her own child! "So, if you really hated Jason so much, why did you put his name on the memorial as well?" I asked.

"Because he should have died," she growled. "Because if I'd only been strong enough, he never would have breathed."

Okay. Perhaps it was better not to ask Crazy Lady Weem questions. I swallowed and tried to smile at her, to calm her. I couldn't quite manage it.

"Where was I? Oh, yes. The abomination was gone. I had failed. He was in the world. He was being raised by the Sons to do their evil work. But since I had been back in the United States, I had been getting in touch with other people who worshipped Rabbit. Oh, they didn't call him the same names. Different names. Satan. Azazel. Loki. But I had already studied this. I already they were one and the same. That was when I met your mother, Azazel. Pretty woman. So desperate for a child. Willing to do anything. And the night after I met her, I had a vision. I had a vision of you Azazel, rising up and crushing the abomination. Grinding him to dust.

"Then your mother became pregnant. And just a few months after they took away the abomination, you were born. And the visions stopped. I was relieved. Rabbit had prevailed. He had seen to it that his enemies would not enslave the human race.

"But weeks ago, weeks ago, the visions began again. And they began to change. Suddenly, you were not crushing the abomination, but copulating with it. Suddenly, Azazel, everything changed. The two of you. Together."

Michaela stood up then. The cat was disrupted. It jumped to the ground, shooting a look of reproach at Michaela. She crossed the room to me. She knelt next to me, taking both of my hands. Her voice was wheedling, pleading. "You don't understand. You have power. The power of Rabbit, filling your body. Your power feeds his. Together, the things you will do. The terrible, terrible things you will do. Do you know what he is capable of?"

Michaela paused. "Ah, I see that you do. I see that you have seen his face. His true face. Do you think it will stop, Azazel? No! It will only get worse. Soon it won't be a handful of men shot in the head. Soon it won't be his hand ripping at your undergarments, fury in his face. Soon, Azazel, soon, it will be thousands upon thousands of bodies heaped on a pyre. And you—" Her voice grew louder, rising to a fevered pitch, filling the room— "you will lie dead as he feasts on your guts!"

I pulled my hands away from hers. "We need to leave," I said, standing up. I reached for Jason. Jason looked white as a sheet. He took my hand gratefully, standing up on shaking feet.

We started towards the door.

Michaela reached for us, her hands like claws. "Mark my

words, Azazel," called Michaela after us. "The power you have together. The power! It will *strike men mad*!"

She was still on her knees, clutching at the air, her eyes wide and fiery.

I started to run, yanking Jason along behind me. We stumbled through the door and into the November twilight. Her screen door clattered closed behind us.

Jason and I looked at each other. We dropped our hold on each other's hands. Silently, we trudged back to the church. Neither of us said a word.

Chapter Seventeen

To: Joseph Andrews (jandre@risingsun.org)
From: Alfred Norwich (anorwic@risingsun.org)
Subject: Shiloh
Joseph,

Word has reached us that Hallam Wakefield has been located in Shiloh, GA. We have strong reasons to believe that Jason is with him, not least the email message which your team brought to our attention. The stage is set. We must not fail.

Yours in the pursuit of the Purpose,
Alfred

"She was crazy," I finally said.

Jason was sitting in one of the pews. He almost looked catatonic. He hadn't spoken. He'd barely moved. I was pacing in front of the altar, glancing over at him every once and a while to see if there was any change. We were alone in the church. When I wasn't looking at Jason, I was glancing around, my eyes resting on the statue of the Virgin Mary at the front of the church, the ornate stained glass windows, the polished dark wood of the pews.

I didn't know what Jason was thinking. He just looked blank. I wanted him to say something, do something, anything. He was starting to freak me out.

"She was just crazy," I repeated. "All that stuff she said.

The visions and stuff. She admitted that the Sons forced her to take drugs. After a while, too much of that stuff can just unhinge someone's brain."

But Jason wasn't talking. He was staring blankly into space, his eyes glassy. He was really freaking me out.

"Jason!" I said.

"She knew things," Jason said quietly. "How did she know those things?"

I stopped pacing. Shook my head violently. "She didn't know anything. Not really. She said things, but we attached significance to them. It's the way TV psychics work. They say something and wait for someone to acknowledge what they've said. We just read into it."

Jason stared straight ahead. "No," he said. "It was specific. She knew I'd shot people in the head. And she knew about the ... the time in the hotel room. She *knew* . How did she know that?"

"She didn't. She knew that the Sons raised you. She assumed you'd shot people. She saw us hold hands when we walked in. She knew we were a couple. She assumed that there could have been an incident. It's nothing." And I turned away from him, because I was trying to convince myself as much as I was trying to convince him.

There were other things that Michaela Weem had said. Things I couldn't explain. How had my mother, who'd been told by doctors she'd never have a child, gotten pregnant? And why had it happened just after Michaela had a vision of me? And if there wasn't a connection between Jason and I, why had he run out of the woods into my life? Why that moment, that spot, just in time for me to see him? Toby and I had been ready to leave. A moment or two later, and he would have missed me. Were Jason and I connected in some unexplainable way? And if we were, was there something sinister about that connection?

"Do you really think that?" Jason asked.

I turned back to him. "Yes," I said. "I really do." I didn't know what to believe. I didn't want to think that what Michaela Weem had said was true, but she had frightened me with her strange accuracy and with her disturbing images. I didn't think there was anything dark or evil in Jason. I really didn't. I loved Jason.

But there was the nonchalance with which I'd seen him shoot people. Certainly, he felt deeply guilty for the men he killed, but what about the men in Bramford who he'd shot, but not killed? He'd never seemed to feel a shred of remorse over that. In some ways, Jason was casually violent.

And I still remembered the urgency in his hands the night in the hotel room. No restraint. No concern for me.

No. Jason was perfect. Jason was wonderful. Jason didn't want to hurt me. Jason didn't want to hurt anybody. I refused to let that awful, bitter woman poison me against him. Jason was the most important part of my life. No one could say anything that would make me turn against him. No one.

"Maybe you're right," said Jason.

Good. If I'd convinced Jason, half the battle was won. I

just needed to convince myself.

"The rest of it, though," said Jason. "I didn't need to know that. I wouldn't have minded never finding out about my parents."

"I'm sorry," I said. It was my fault. I'd pushed us to go there.

"That's where I come from? My father was insane? He forced my mother to do horrible things? I come from rituals and rape and drugs?" Jason covered his eyes with his hand.

"Hey," I said. "My parents conceived me in order to kill you. Neither of us have exactly stellar parents."

He didn't uncover his eyes.

I went to him. I sat down beside him on the pew. I rubbed his back. I kissed his neck. I laid my head on his shoulder.

He didn't look at me.

"Jason," I said. "Look at me."

He didn't at first, but finally he swung his eyes up to meet mine.

"My parents were total whack-jobs," I said. "But they didn't always act like whack-jobs. And they taught me that my life isn't controlled by anyone except me. They taught me that my choices make my life. My life is made up of the consequences of those choices. So I'm going to make a choice right now. I'm going to chose not to listen to anything of the awful things that awful woman said to us. I'm going to chose to trust what I know about you, what I know about us. You are the best thing that ever happened to me. You're strong and moral and kind and wonderful. And nothing that some crazy woman said could ever diminish what you mean to me."

Jason pulled me into his lap. Kissed me. He whispered to me, "This is why I need you," he said. "You can always do that for me. Put things in perspective. Make me see the world the right way. Without you, I'd just wallow and drive myself crazy. You make me see things clearly. You make me better."

I cupped his beautiful face in my palms. Stared into his big, deep eyes. And I knew at that moment that I'd meant everything I'd just said. All the questions I'd just asked myself faded into the background, seeped out the stained glass windows into the evening air, and there was nothing but Jason. Jason was my reality. I trusted Jason more than anything else. Together we could do anything.

That was when the doors to the church burst open, and twelve members of the Sons of the Rising Sun stalked in.

Chapter Eighteen

International Text Message Transcript:

to 011-44-020-5555-7032 (6:20 p.m. EST): located jason
in sanctuary.

to 00-1-617-555-4236 (6:24 p.m. EST): override
sanctuary request is being made.

to 011-44-020-5555-7032 (6:26 p.m. EST): standing by.

Jason and I stood up, startled. Jason pushed me behind
him, facing the men, who were wearing all black, and had
guns in their hands. Their guns swung at their sides. They
weren't aiming at us, but with their solemn expressions and
squared shoulders, they were still quite threatening.

"I thought this was sanctuary," I whispered to Jason.

The man who led the Sons inside heard me. "Sanctuary
means no violence on the grounds. It doesn't prevent us
from entering."

"I'm not coming with you," said Jason. "Has Hallam
Wakefield been able to conduct his negotiations?"

The man sneered. "Hallam Wakefield is probably dead
by now. What would he have to negotiate with anyway?"

"That's a no," Jason muttered to me.

"So what do we do?" I asked Jason, peering over his
shoulder at the men. They were spread out in a line at the
opening of the church, standing in what looked like a
military at-ease stance. They looked so formal.

"Nothing," said Jason, loud so they'd be sure to hear. "We're in sanctuary. We'll just wait them out. Either Hallam will get what he wants or his messages will go out."

The leader held up a cell phone. "I don't think so. I'm waiting on the response to a request to override sanctuary. Considering how important you are, I'm sure it'll go through."

"Can they do that?" I asked Jason.

"I don't know," said Jason. "I've never heard of such a thing." He went tense in front of me. I could tell he was thinking. Weighing our options, pondering escape routes. "How about a deal?" Jason asked.

A deal? Jason didn't make deals. What was he doing?

"I'll come with you," he said.

"No," I said.

"But you leave the girl alone. The girl walks, you understand?"

"Jason—" I said.

"Shut up, Azazel," he snapped at me.

The leader only chuckled. "I don't think you understand the situation, Jason. We were close to the Brothers you killed. Richard Durham was my mentor. Now, we know we can't kill you, but as long as we get you back alive, we don't think anyone will mind too much if you're a little ... damaged." The leader smiled cruelly. "We'd all kind of like to damage you a little bit."

Oh, this wasn't good. This was very, very bad.

Jason reached back for my hand. I wondered what he

was planning.

The leader's cell phone vibrated. He raised it to look at it. Almost simultaneously, Jason twisted, grabbing me by the waist and throwing us behind the statue of the Virgin Mary in the front of the church. At nearly the same moment, the Sons opened fire on us.

The statue exploded, blowing bits of colored cement all over the floor of the church. They skittered under pews. They soared through the air, breaking chunks in the stained glass windows.

Jason covered my body with his own as the plaster rained down on us.

On our bellies, we crawled along the floor to the altar, bullets blasting through the pews.

We sat with our backs against the altar, only the wooden box between the Sons' guns and us. A bullet splintered through the wood, right between our faces. I yelped.

Jason was pulling a gun out of his jeans. I hadn't realized he was carrying it. I didn't have a gun. He leaned around the altar, squeezed out several shots.

I wanted look to see if he'd hit anything, but I didn't dare. The sound of gunfire was ringing in my ears.

Jason leaned back against the altar, his eyes alert.

Now, I couldn't help but steal a look around the altar.

None of the Sons were down. They were approaching the altar, closing in on us, firing all the way.

Jason ducked back out to shoot again.

More bullets riddled the altar. One skidded past right

next to my cheek. Too close for comfort.

Was this it? After everything we'd been through, after all the running, all the fighting, after discovering everything we'd discovered, was it going to end here? Just when Jason and I had realized exactly how much we meant to each other?

It didn't seem fair.

Jason's head thudded back against the altar. He turned to me desperately.

"There's no chance, is there?" I asked.

"I love you," he said.

"I love you," I said.

Our lips met hungrily behind the ruined altar. Behind us, the staccato beats of gunfire underscored our final moments together. They were going to kill me. They were going to take Jason. We kissed like it was the end of the world, because we knew that, for us, it was.

As our lips parted, I waited to see the Sons swarming around the altar, thrusting their guns in our faces.

They didn't come.

Actually, it was quiet.

Jason's eyes caught mine. We listened.

Nothing. Silence.

At once, we jerked our necks around, staring around the altar.

The Sons were still there. They were standing in the aisle of the church, looking bewildered. A few were staring at their guns, scratching their heads.

What was going on?

The leader's brow was furrowed. He glared out over the others. "The bathtub is full!" he announced to them determinedly.

One of the Sons started crying. Another dropped to a crouch, his hands raised in protection against an unseen attacker. One of the men ran screaming out of the church, yelling something about bees.

Jason and I slowly looked at each other. He looked just as confused and astonished as I felt.

Carefully, we moved out from behind the altar, stepping over the debris left from the gunfight. There were shards of stained glass littering the floor like shiny pieces of hard candy. All of the statues had huge holes in them. Jesus was missing an arm. Mary was gone from the waist up. The pews were covered in bullet holes.

We stepped in front of the Sons. They didn't seem to see us.

We took their guns from their hands. They didn't protest. One of them said to me, "Is it time for Cheerios yet?"

What was going on here? What had just happened?

I approached the leader last. I took his gun.

As if he were trying to be helpful, he handed me his cell phone. I took it. It was black and cold in my hands. Suddenly, it vibrated. I opened it. There was a text message. In all caps, it read: "RESCIND OVERRIDE. THIS IS FROM THE TOP. ABORT MISSION. REPEAT. ABORT. WEEM'S

ORDERS."

I handed the cell phone to Jason. "I think Hallam got through to Weem," I said.

We stared at the now seemingly harmless members of the Sons of the Rising Sun, all of whom seemed to have gone crazy at the exact same moment. They milled about the church, gazing at the damage they'd caused. They seemed confused. Disoriented. Blank. What had happened?

Jason took my hand. I searched his deep, dark eyes for answers. His eyes were so similar to the eyes of the Michaela Weem. And I shivered as her words echoed back to me from earlier that evening.

The power. It will strike men mad.

Epilogue

I shifted position on my beach chair, flipping the page of the Robert Anton Wilson novel I was reading. The Florida sun beat down on me. I luxuriated in it, feeling its warm rays caress my skin. It might be winter in the rest of the world, but here it was in the mid seventies and sunny. A shadow fell over me.

I looked up. A dripping Jason was standing at my feet. He bent down over me, nuzzling my neck. I shoved him out of the way, giggling. "Jason!" I protested, "you're getting my book wet."

Jason flopped onto a towel that was lying next to me. "Stop reading," he said. "Come in the water with me."

I shot him a disbelieving look. "It's too cold to get in the water."

"You're starting to sound like one of the natives," Jason muttered.

"Well," I said. "I'm planning on living here for a very, very long time. Might as well start acting like we're from here."

It had been a little over a month since we'd officially moved to Florida. It was exactly what Jason and I had imagined when we'd talked about our perfect place to live. Our house was a ten-minute drive from the ocean, and it was warm. We took walks on the powder-white sand in the evenings, watching the sun set over the blue, blue water.

"I'm bored," said Jason.

"Too bad," said Hallam, who was seated in his own beach chair on the other side of Jason's towel. "I had too much trouble finding a parking space. We're not going anywhere for quite some time." Hallam was our legal guardian these days. He'd been successful in making the deal with Weem. In exchange for Hallam keeping his mouth shut about Jason's origins, the Sons would leave both Jason and Hallam alone. After the deal had been made, we hadn't exactly known what to do with ourselves. Jason and I were both still minors, but neither of us had parents. Hallam had agreed to take responsibility for us, considering he was oh-so-much older than us. Twenty-two.

Mostly, Hallam was cool. He had his conditions, however. Jason and I were forbidden to share a room. By extension, Hallam meant that we weren't supposed to have sex either. "Not under my roof," he had thundered. Considering Jason and I both had part-time jobs to help out with rent and bills, it really wasn't just Hallam's roof anyway. Besides, what Hallam didn't know wouldn't hurt him.

"It's crowded because it's Saturday," I told Hallam. "We wouldn't have a problem if we came on a weekday."

"On weekdays," said Hallam sharply, "you and Jason are at school."

That was another of Hallam's conditions. He wanted us to finish high school. This didn't really bother me, because I didn't feel prepared to step out into the real world without an education. But I figured Jason already knew enough worthless knowledge to skip to his second year of college. Jason seemed to like the idea of going to school, however. I liked it too. We held hands as we walked together to classes. We complained about the amount of homework we had. Overall, going to school wasn't so bad. It beat stealing cars and running from the Sons.

"The water is not that cold," Jason said, lying back on his towel and throwing his arm over his face.

"I'm fine on the beach," I told him.

I gazed at him, water glistening against the hard muscles of his body. As usual, his beauty left me breathless. I gazed at him, marveling that just the sight of him could turn my insides to jello, even now. Jason was amazing.

My cell phone rang from inside my beach bag. Now that I had my own cash flow, I was happy to have joined the twenty-first century and finally own one. I reached into the bag and got it out. It was Chance!

"Hey!" I said into the phone. "How's my little brother?"

Poor Chance. He really had no idea what had been going on in Bramford. No one knew about the coven until they were initiated when they were eighteen. He'd only known that I'd run away and that my parents had gone to look for me. He'd been nearly destroyed when he found out they were dead.

My parents' other foster children had been farmed out to other families. I hadn't been able to get in touch with any of them. I hoped they were okay.

"I'm fine," said Chance. "How are you?"

"I'm on the beach!" I gloated. "In a bathing suit!"

"You suck," Chance said. "It's snowing here."

I laughed. Chance was living with Grandma Hoyt in New Jersey. Though she'd offered to take me in as well, she'd seemed relieved when I'd told her Hallam had already started proceedings to take over my guardianship. According to Chance, Grandma was never around, and he had the run of an enormous house. I didn't feel too sorry for him, snow notwithstanding.

"Well, you've got to come visit," I said. "Soon!"

"Oh believe me, I'm planning on it. Maybe Christmas break," he said.

I hadn't seen Chance since our parents' funeral, which had been a pretty awful event. Grandma Hoyt had flown both Jason and I up to New Jersey. My parents' bodies had been cremated right after their death. That was the way they wanted things. Still, my grandmother insisted on having a memorial service for the family. At the request of my grandmother, no one from Bramford had been invited. That was just fine with me. I didn't have any desire to see any of them again, not even Lilith. Grandma, Chance, Jason, and I had huddled in the church as the pastor read my parents' eulogy. I'd listened, waiting to be wracked with sobs or even for a few tears to leak out of my eyes. I hadn't cried. Chance had cried. I'd given him a huge hug, but Chance was taller than me, and it was hard for him to cry on my shoulder.

I didn't know why I couldn't cry. I ached for my parents'

loss. But I was angry with them and disgusted by their actions. They'd always be my parents. I missed them. But maybe I'd done all the crying I could in that hotel room in Georgia those four nights. Maybe there just wasn't anything left for them.

No one had heard from my older brothers Noah and Gordon. The last I'd seen them was when they'd unexpectedly shown up at the ritual on Halloween. After that, they seemed to have disappeared. They hadn't come to the funeral.

"Let me talk to Chance," said Jason. I handed the phone to him.

I listened as Jason quizzed Chance about the level he was on in *Grand Theft Auto* . I chuckled to myself, thinking that Jason and I had been involved in the real thing. And Jason had been right. The Sons had covered up all of our criminal activities.

Gazing out at the horizon, at the aqua water glittering like turquoise in the sunlight, I couldn't help but feel like my life was nearly perfect.

I didn't think about the things Michaela Weem had said to me. I didn't think about her threats that Jason was violent or that he and I shared a terrible power. Or. At least, I didn't think about it much. After all, I'd made my choice. I had rejected ancient destinies and visions. I'd decided to make my own future. And my future was Jason.

Breathless for more?
Trembling, Jason and Azazel, Book Two
Keep reading for a sneak peak at the first Chapter.

Want freebies, information on new releases,
discounts, and more?
Visit my website to join my email list.
vjchambers.com

Trembling, Chapter One

michaela666 (01:34:22): Is it done?

aird92 (01:35:01): yep. success. it's all good.

michaela666 (1:35:24): And it went well? No snags? No interference from Jason?

aird92 (01:36:12): dude's damned clueless, r u kidding? went perfect.

michaela666 (01:36:54): You're sure? They shouldn't be underestimated, you know. The two of them together are quite powerful.

aird92 (01:37:17): i know this, ok? stop worrying. everything's fine.

My brain felt like it had exploded while I was sleeping and the pieces of brain matter were straining against my temples, trying to get out. My head hurt.

I squeezed my eyes shut against the bright Florida sun that was streaming through the window. Damn it, but my head hurt. Really, really bad.

Tentatively, I opened one eye. The room was blazingly bright. I closed my eye again. Maybe it was better to keep my eyes closed.

Wait.

I opened my eyes again.

Where was I?

Jason's room? Jason's bed? Why was I in Jason's bed?

How had I gotten here?

Damn it. I didn't remember going to sleep. I must have been really drunk when I went to sleep. Blackout drunk. I didn't think I'd ever been blackout drunk before. What *did* I remember from the night before?

A loud voice sliced into my temple. "I don't how many times I've told you that you two are not supposed to sleep in the same bed!"

That was why I had woken up. Hallam was yelling at Jason. Ugh. I pulled a pillow over my head, but I could still hear them.

"Jesus, Hallam, I carried her to her own bed, but she crawled in here with me," Jason was saying. "I couldn't get her to go back. Nothing happened. She was way too drunk."

I was? I didn't remember any of that at all.

Jason was my boyfriend. He and I lived with Hallam, who was our legal guardian. Hallam was pretty cool most of the time. He didn't have any problem with my going out and getting wasted or coming home at four in the morning. But he was insistent that Jason and I did not sleep in the same bed. He said he didn't want us to conceive our firstborn on his watch. But that was silly, because when Jason and I actually did get to have sex (which was rarely), we were careful. Really, Hallam was just a prude, and that was all there was to it.

"I don't want to hear excuses, Jason," Hallam said. "You two know the rules. You both agreed to them."

It was amazing how, in just a few short months, Hallam

had begun to sound remarkably like a parent. He was only twenty-two, just five years older than Jason and me. But he sounded fifty.

"You're blatantly disobeying," Hallam went on.

"What was I supposed to do?" Jason said. "She could barely stand, she was so wasted."

Really? That wasn't good. Okay, okay. What had I done last night?

Um, I'd gone to a party on the beach with Jude and some of the other guys from work. I worked at a movie theater here in Bradenton, Florida. I remembered that I'd been drinking a lot of shots. I'd been talking to some guys around a bonfire. For a long time. And then ... I'd lost Jude. I couldn't find him anywhere. And I was so drunk... So I called Jason, because I couldn't find Jude, and I was freaked out. Being alone like that. And drunk. And then ...

And then, *nothing* .

God.

That was terrifying.

"She's been drunk a lot lately, hasn't she?" asked Hallam.

"She's seventeen," Jason said. "It's what young people do."

Jason was seventeen too, but when he said that, it sounded like he was so much older than me. In some ways, maybe Jason was. He'd been through a lot in his young life. Jason had spent his childhood on the run from men with guns, who were trying to kill him. He'd held his mentor Anton in his arms while Anton bled to death. Jason had shot five men in the head point blank to save me from getting killed. It made sense that Jason would seem older than me.

But.

"You're seventeen too," Hallam pointed out. "You're not getting fall-down drunk."

Why was Jason so much more responsible than I was? After all, while it was true that Jason had been through a lot, the last six months of my life had been no picnic either. I'd found out that my entire town was controlled by a Satanist coven who wanted me to kill Jason. Then I'd seen my parents and my aunt all shot dead in front of me. Yeah. Things weren't easy for me either. Most days, I felt older than seventeen.

"Well, someone's got to stay sober," Jason muttered.

Great. He didn't sound happy. But I guess I couldn't blame him. It didn't sound like I'd been much fun last night. I really shouldn't have gotten so drunk.

"Just keep her out of your bed," said Hallam. "I don't care how drunk she is."

I heard the door to Jason's bedroom slam as Hallam stormed out.

Sheepishly, I pulled the pillow off my head and looked at Jason. "Hey," I said.

"Good morning," said Jason, but he didn't sound at all happy about it.

Jason was probably one of the most beautiful human beings I'd ever seen. He had dusky skin, perfect and unmarred, huge dark eyes, and a shock of dark hair that tended to fall into his eyes. Looking at him, no matter where I was or what I was doing, nearly always took my breath away, made me tremble inside.

"I'm sorry?" I said. I hoped he wasn't going to be too mad.

Jason sighed. He sat down on the edge of the bed, next to me. "What are you sorry about?"

"Sorry I got so drunk," I said.

Jason shook his head. "It's not your fault," he said. He reached for me. Stroked my cheek with the back of his hand. "It's Jude's fault."

"Jude?" I asked. For some reason, Jason did not like Jude very much.

"He got you all messed up and then he just abandoned you," said Jason.

It was true that Jude had disappeared last night. But I wanted Jason to like Jude. Jude was probably my best friend. "We were at a party," I said. "I'm sure he just got distracted."

"Don't defend him," said Jason.

"He's my friend." I had to defend him. If I didn't, Jason would never start liking him. Ever.

Jason rolled his eyes. "I don't know why you spend so much time with that jerk, anyway."

"He's fun!" I said.

"Right," said Jason. He looked down at his hands. "Unlike me, right?"

"Jason!" I rolled over in bed, frustrated. My head pounded angrily at the sudden movement. "There is no reason to compare the two of you. You're Jason. He's Jude. You're both fun, just in different ways."

"I just feel like I never see you anymore. You're always hanging out with him. You're never hanging out with me."

"You sound jealous."

Jason shrugged.

"Jesus, he's gay!" I exclaimed. "He's like a girl."

"Except he's not a girl," said Jason.

"Oh my God," I muttered. I sat up in bed, carefully this time, so as not to upset my throbbing head. I crawled over to Jason. Hugged him from behind. "Don't be jealous of Jude," I murmured, kissing Jason's neck. "You shouldn't be jealous of anyone, ever. No one could ever be to me what you are. You're ... Jason."

Jason turned his head and his lips met mine. "I know that," he whispered in a husky voice. It always made me swoon. It was the voice meant only for *me* . He didn't talk to anyone else in that voice.

I caressed his face. Ran my finger over the line of his jaw. He winced.

I leaned forward. "Are you hurt?"

"It's nothing," Jason said, standing up.

I flopped back on the bed. "What did you do? Did you get in another fight?"

"I ..."

"Jason!"

"I'm sorry," he said. "But you should have heard this guy. He had it coming. That bastard."

"What happened?" I asked.

"I couldn't find you when I got to the party. But I found that jerk, Jude, and he said he put you in a tent. And you were fine." Jason glowered into space.

"A tent?" I had no memory of being in a tent.

"Yeah," said Jason. "That dickwad just dumped you there and ran off."

"At least he put me in a tent," I said. Wow. How drunk had I been? A thought suddenly occurred to me. "Oh God. You didn't beat up Jude, did you?"

Jason shook his head. "No."

"Good," I said. Because if my boyfriend had beaten up my best friend, it probably would have meant I didn't have a best friend anymore. And the thought of Jason punching skinny, prissy Jude was almost too much to handle. He would have *destroyed* Jude.

"Jude never could have gotten a punch on me," said Jason.

Of course not. I snorted.

"So I found the tent, and this guy was standing outside. I looked inside. You were in there, passed out. And you were only wearing your bikini."

"What?!" I demanded. I had gone to that party *clothed* , damn it. "Where were my clothes?"

"In the tent," said Jason.

So how did they get off? I didn't ask that question out loud. Concerned, I wiggled my pelvis. It felt ... fine. "What happened?" I repeated.

Jason didn't look at me. "The guy outside the tent said that he wouldn't say anything if I ..." Jason whipped his head around and looked straight in my eyes. "He said to save him seconds."

I covered my mouth with my hand. "Oh my God."

"Yeah," said Jason. "And Jude just left you there. With people like that around."

"So you beat up the guy outside the tent?"

"I did. I wasn't going to, because it wasn't like he did anything. I just told him to shut up, because you were my girlfriend. And he said, 'Your girlfriend looks like a drunken slut.' That's when I beat him up."

"Oh," I said. I was quiet. "How bad?"

Jason shrugged. "I don't know."

"Did they have to call an ambulance again?" I asked.

"I don't know. I took you and left."

I didn't say anything.

"He was bleeding a lot, I guess," said Jason. "Maybe I broke his nose. I don't know."

"Oh God, you shouldn't have done that."

"Can you blame me? He was clearly a total bastard."

"I just don't think it's a good idea for you to do things that might attract attention to us," I said.

Jason sat back down on the bed. "Azazel, we're safe."

"I know," I said. "But I don't trust the Sons. And I just feel like every time you do something like that, it sends out a beacon to them screaming, 'Here we are!'"

"They probably know where we are, anyway," said

Jason. "They're a huge, powerful organization. I'm sure they haven't just forgotten about me."

"Maybe they did," I said. "Maybe they did." I wished I could believe that. I wished I wasn't worried nearly every second of every day that the Sons of the Rising Sun were going to burst into our house, guns blazing, kill me, and take Jason. We were blackmailing them with information we had, and so far it seemed to be working. But every day, I worried that it wouldn't work anymore. They'd find some way around our deal. They'd come for us.

Jason lay down next me on the bed. He gathered me in his arms. I buried my head in his chest.

"We're safe," he whispered into my hair. "I swear we're safe. I swear I'll keep you safe."

And I wanted to believe him. I did.

"All I want to do is keep you safe," he said. "You know that, right?"

I lifted my head to look at him. He was so heartbreakingly beautiful. "I know."

"That's why I hit that guy," said Jason. "When it comes to you, Azazel, I just ... I can't think straight. If anyone ever hurt you, I'd go absolutely insane. You're so important to me."

I kissed him. "I love you," I said.

"I love you," he said.

We kissed again, Jason's hands stroking my back. I moaned softly.

And Hallam stormed into the bedroom. "Out!" he

thundered. "Azazel, get out of this bed!"

I got out of the bed, folding my arms over my chest and glaring at Hallam. "We were just kissing," I said.

"Sure," said Hallam. "It's all just kissing until someone gets pregnant."

I rolled my eyes. But I went to my own room anyway. I needed to find some ibuprofen.

* * *

It was nearly eleven-thirty, and I had to be at work at noon. I worked at the Regal Cinemas on Cortez, a ten-minute drive from our apartment if the traffic wasn't bad. Which it always was. Jude said that in the summer, there was no traffic in Bradenton at all. Once all the "snowbirds" left, no one was left in Florida except the people who lived there full time. Snowbirds were rich, old people who came to Florida during the winter to escape the snow up north. Since Jason, Hallam, and I had only lived in Bradenton since November, I had never witnessed a summer in Bradenton.

Bradenton was a very, very big town compared to Bramford, West Virginia, where I grew up. However, according to most people, it was a relatively small place. It was located about forty-five minutes south of Tampa and twenty minutes north of Sarasota, on the west coast of Florida. The rent there was a little cheaper than what you'd pay in Sarasota, which was why we'd decided to live in Bradenton. At the time, I wasn't in touch with my grandmother, who was insanely rich and lived in New Jersey, so we didn't think we'd have enough money to live in

Sarasota.

When we first moved to Florida, we didn't really have much money. Hallam had a little bit of cash which he'd squirreled away. Jason and I had a fraudulent credit card. We were barely able to get enough money to move into a three-bedroom apartment. We got jobs as quickly as we could. Hallam insisted that both Jason and I finish high school, so we had to get jobs that wouldn't interfere with our studies. I started working at the movie theater, and Jason got a job waiting tables. Hallam, who was highly educated and British, somehow managed to swindle himself into a job as a professor at New College, the honors college of Sarasota. Both Hallam and I still had our original jobs. Jason, however, had been fired four times. He kept getting in fights. Currently, he had a job working at another restaurant, but he was in the kitchen, so he didn't have to deal with the public.

We had a very hard time at first, because we didn't have a car, so we had to rely on buses and on favors from co-workers. Sometimes it worked out, sometimes it didn't. Finally, Jason suggested that I should get in touch with my grandmother. She was my only living relative, besides my three adopted brothers.

I didn't want to contact Grandma Hoyt at first. I was worried that the Sons could use her to get to me, or that she might be in danger. After all, it was the Sons who had shot my parents. They didn't seem to have qualms about killing whoever got in their way. Jason and Hallam were sure that the Sons were out of the picture, so eventually I did.

Grandma Hoyt bought me a car, and started sending me a pretty decent allowance every month. It helped make our situation more comfortable, but I still worked, because I liked having the extra cash. Besides, with Jason working as well, if I stayed home, I'd be alone most of the time. I really didn't like being alone anymore. I got really freaked out when I was by myself in our apartment. I didn't know if I was really worried about the Sons busting in and shooting me or not. But I did know that I got very, very frightened, and I couldn't handle it.

So I worked. That afternoon, I was so hung over and miserable that I really wished that I didn't. But I dragged myself into the shower, got dressed, ate something, and went to work. The night before, I'd left directly from work and gone to the party, and I'd accidentally left my uniform in the staff workroom. When I arrived, Jude was waiting for me, holding my uniform.

"Girl!" he exclaimed. "I cannot believe you are standing!"

"Oh my God, Jude! How drunk did I get last night?"

Jude shook his head in awe. "You were wasted," he said. He handed me my uniform. "Better get changed. We've got to start slinging popcorn in two minutes."

"Ugh," I muttered, taking the uniform from him.

Jude was tall and very skinny. He was a quarter Cherokee, so he had dusky skin and dark eyes. (Like Jason, in fact, who was also a quarter Native American, but Muscogee.) Jude liked to wear heavy eyeliner, but at work, it was against the dress code, so Jude only wore a little bit. He also had three holes in each of his ears, plus a nose piercing. He had to take out all his piercings for work too. The theater couldn't do much about his hair, however, which he dyed various unnatural shades. Currently, his hair was electric blue. Last week, however, it had been bright orange. I'd seen it green, purple, and fire-engine red. Jude also made it a point to paint his nails. At the moment, they were purple and sparkly.

"Come into the bathroom with me while I change," I said. "I want to know everything about what happened last night."

"While you change?" Jude said.

"Yeah," I said. I took him by the arm and pulled him into the staff bathroom with me.

The staff bathroom didn't have stalls. It just had one toilet and a sink. It was for either men or women. Once inside, I locked the door, and pulled my shirt over my head.

"So where did you go?" I asked, folding my shirt and searching for my uniform polo.

Jude wasn't looking at me. He was staring at the floor, like he was embarrassed.

"I'm sorry," I said. "Does it make you uncomfortable that I'm taking off my clothes? I just thought ..."

Jude looked at me, grinning. "No, girl, you're fine," he said.

"Okay," I said.

Jude took a deep breath. "I wouldn't have left you if I

thought you were so drunk," he said.

"I didn't mean to get that drunk," I said.

"You weren't when I left," he said.

"Left?"

"I didn't leave the party," Jude said. "I just started chasing this yummy boy with long blonde hair."

I unbuttoned my jeans and wriggled out of them. "And?"

"Oh, he turned out to be straight."

"Sorry."

Jude shrugged. "Whatev." He glanced at me and then looked away. I *was* making him uncomfortable. I needed to try to remember that being gay did not make Jude a girl. Maybe I was being rude. "So, what do you remember?"

"Not much. I remember looking for you, not being able to find you, and calling Jason."

"Oh yeah," said Jude, "your boyfriend's intense, isn't he?"

Intense? That was one way to put it. "How do you mean?"

"He hospitalized that guy. I've never seen anyone fight like that. He was like a machine."

Damn it. Why was Jason always getting in fights? "He had to go to hospital, huh?"

"Yeah. Broken ribs."

Ribs? "Damn it," I said, shaking my head. I thrust my leg into my uniform khakis. Jason had to stop this.

"You remember the fight?" Jude asked.

"No. Jason told me about it."

Jude nodded. "You don't remember anything, then?"

I shook my head. "Not really."

"Is that weird?" he asked. "I've never blacked out before."

"Neither have I," I said. I remembered drinking, but I really didn't think I'd had *that* much to drink. The whole thing was weird. I buttoned my khakis thoughtfully. "Jason said something about that guy outside the tent. Like he said something about me."

Jude raised his eyebrows. "What did he say?"

I was probably being paranoid. "Jude, you don't think I was like roofied or something, do you?"

Now that I was fully dressed, Jude was looking right at me. "Why would you think that?"

"Jason said that when he found me I was only wearing my bikini. And the guy told him to save him seconds."

Jude made a horrified face. "Eew."

"Yeah."

"Well, are you okay? I mean, do you think ...?"

"Oh, no. I'm fine. I mean, I don't think *that* happened. But maybe someone was trying?"

Jude crossed to me and hugged me tightly. "Omigod," he said. "I am so sorry. I will never leave you alone at a party again."

Work would have been torturous without Jude. He kept me laughing, whispering jokes about what the customers were wearing or saying when no one was looking. I really liked Jude. He was one of my favorite things about living in Florida. I'd always wanted to live someplace like this. Someplace warm. Near a beach. And being able to be close

364

to Jason was a definite plus. Jason was my soul mate. Nothing could be too bad whenever he was around. But in all honesty, my life was far from perfect anymore.

Six months ago, my biggest problem had been that I thought I was the oldest virgin on earth. I wasn't a virgin anymore, but sometimes, I almost wished I could go back to my life before. Then, my parents were alive, and I loved them. I lived in a busy, crowded home full of teenage foster boys, but I didn't realize how great it was to feel loved like that. I didn't realize how great it was to trust people implicitly. Now, I didn't trust anyone. I had nightmares a lot. I dreamed about my parents getting shot. I'd see it over and over again, in slow motion. The surprised look on their faces. The blood. The way their bodies had crumpled. In the worst dreams, the ones that always made me sit up straight in bed, screaming, I'd see Jason's face when he was shooting the members of the Sons who'd killed my parents. He looked determined and dangerous. Frenzied. Angry.

After that nightmare, Jason would rush into my room, and he'd be so sweet and comforting that I'd wonder how I could ever feel frightened of him. He was perfect. He was wonderful. He was mine. He wasn't scary.

But other times, when the dream didn't go that far, I wouldn't wake up without screaming, just seeing the image of my dead parents engraved on the back of my eyelids. And I'd think about other things. I'd think about Michaela Weem, Jason's crazy mother, who had screamed at me that together Jason and I would destroy things. She had told me that Jason was destined for violence on a grand scale. She had wanted me to kill Jason. Michaela Weem had believed that Jason was too dangerous to live. And she'd been able to convince a lot of people that she was right. I tried to tell myself she wasn't. I loved Jason more than life. I would die for him. I would kill for him. He was all that I had.

But Michaela had been right about one thing. Once. She'd told us that together Jason and I would "drive men mad." And we had. When we kissed, a whole group of the Sons had stopped shooting and completely lost their minds. If she'd been right about that, maybe she was right about ... But no. No. Jason was not going to enslave the world. I didn't think that. I *refused* to think that.

Between freaking out about the Sons trying to kill me, reliving the trauma of my murdered parents, and worrying that my boyfriend was actually the anti-christ (instead of the messiah, which was what the Sons thought), my life was not exactly a cakewalk. I longed for the days when I worried about my history exam or whether girls at school were gossiping about me. All of that just seemed ridiculous and childish now. Sometimes, I felt very old. Jude was right. Jason was intense. Ever since he'd appeared in my life, everything had been intense.

That was why I liked Jude so much. He made me feel normal, like a regular teenage girl again. One who thought about parties and boys and make-up. I used to think that kind of stuff was shallow, but now I wished like hell it was all I thought about. I missed it. I felt like my innocence had been stolen or something.

Thanks to Jude, the six hours of my shift went by pretty quickly. Afterwards, we sat outside of the theater, drinking huge sodas (one of the perks of working at movie theater). I was waiting for Jason to pick me up. We only had one car, and I hadn't wanted to monopolize it. Jude was just hanging out with me.

"You wanna go to that party at Rachel Kline's next weekend?" he asked.

"God," I said. "I'm not sure if I ever want to drink again."

Jude laughed. "I've heard that before."

"Hey!" I said. "I don't drink that much."

"You can hold your own, girl," said Jude, with a touch of admiration.

I rolled my eyes. "I just like to have fun. Is that so wrong?"

"You are fun," said Jude. "That's why I like you so much."

I'd always been such a goody-goody back in West Virginia. Now that I was free, I was able to make my own decisions. Hallam thought I was a teenage alcoholic, but then, Hallam didn't have a very high opinion of me. I was over-sexed. I drank too much. I didn't study enough. He was like the father I never wanted. Sometimes, I thought about packing up and moving to New Jersey to live with my grandmother. She had custody of my younger brother, Chance. But I didn't really think that Jason would be welcome, and there was no way I'd go anywhere without Jason. So I put up with Hallam, because I had to.

"Well, Jude," I said, "you're kind of fun, yourself."

"Kind of?" he said. "I am a blast, and you love it."

I laughed. Jude *was* a blast.

"So, party, then?" he asked.

"Maybe," I said. "I'll ask Jason if he wants to come. He might have to work, though."

Jude raised his eyebrows.

"Jason can come, right?"

"Keep him on a leash. He can't beat anybody else up."

I sighed. "I can't believe he did that."

"He was protecting you," said Jude. "It's sweet and all, and I understand, but didn't he get in a fight at school last week?"

"Yeah," I said, inwardly groaning. Jason had anger issues. "Speaking of Jason, where the hell is he?" He was at least ten minutes late.

"Call him," said Jude.

"I'll give him another minute or two," I said. "You don't have to wait if you don't want."

"Are you kidding? Of course I'm going to wait with you. I wouldn't let you sit outside the theater by yourself."

"Thanks," I said. But I remembered that earlier that day Jason had called Jude a jerk, and I wondered if it was a good idea for Jude to be there when Jason pulled up.

I scolded myself. It wasn't like Jason just started punching people for no reason. He had to be provoked. The guy he'd beat up last week at school, for instance, had been threatening some poor freshman girl and being really vulgar. To Jason's credit, he hadn't started the fight. He'd asked the guy to cut it out. The guy had started swinging. It was just really stupid to try to fight Jason. Jason was too good at beating people up.

"Maybe I will call him," I said to Jude. I got my phone out of my purse and selected Jason's name out of my recently dialed log. Holding the phone up to my ear, I waited while it rang.

Jason picked up. "Azazel."

"Hey," I said. "Are you coming to pick me up?"

"Crap," he said. "What time is it?"

I told him.

"I'm sorry," he said. "We've got a little situation here."

My heart started to race. A situation? It was the Sons, wasn't it? What had happened? "What?" I said, serious now.

"It's Lilith," he said.